CO-AUG-569

the marble forest

The Marble Forest

by
eaton k. goldthwaite

Doubleday & Company, Inc.
Garden City, New York

For George Harmon Coxe, Frederic Dannay, Davis Dresser,
Dorothy B. Hughes and Rex Stout and to the memory of
Anthony Boucher, Erle Stanley Gardner and Dashiell Hammett

All of the characters in this book
are fictitious, and any resemblance
to actual persons, living or dead,
is purely coincidental.

Copyright © 1971 by Eaton K. Goldthwaite
All Rights Reserved
Printed in the United States of America

part one

one

Vince Maggione made it up the steep iron steps and through the heavy sliding door into the car. About a quarter of the way down the car to his right, on the station side of the train, there were several vacant two-seaters and, as he followed the procession along the narrow aisle, he hoped all of them wouldn't be taken. He chose a seat, shifted his full weight to his left leg and, stretching precariously, put his Pan Am carryall bag on the luggage rack. Then, by grabbing the seat backs and shifting his weight again, he managed to seat himself next to the cracked window without an upset.

He was doing a lot better than he had been; it was too bad Frances hadn't been there to see him. In a few more weeks he would be able to manage the transition from an automobile to a railroad car with no trouble at all. Not that he intended to do much riding on the railroad, even if Frances did work for it. Whether he went back to St. John's, which was what Frances wanted him to do, or went through with this deal that his sister, Gloria, and her husband, Al, were trying to get him to, he would have no particular reason for riding the train.

He pulled himself up beside the window, gathering his legs— the right one still needed the aid of his hands—and fixed a smile for his brother-in-law, Al, who had walked in his own halting fashion along the ground-level platform, following him.

Al was in his early fifties and arthritis had made curving talons of his hands and would long since have locked his knees if he had been less stubborn. When Vince had questioned Gloria about the wisdom of letting Al drive a car, Gloria had said, "He drives better than I do, and a lot better than you ever did . . . But you can see why he has to sell the business."

Al was standing out there, beside the dinky, dingy railroad station. He was drawn up tall, which must have hurt him. He had an imbecile smile on his thin, twisted face and he was moving his curved talon hands up and down in motion supposed to suggest flying.

"The geese—"

Although Vince couldn't hear the words, he could read them on Al's lips and see the meaning written all over Al's face. Vince nodded, moving his right hand in a vague forward direction and mirroring Al's idiotic smile as he mouthed in repetition, *the geese.*

The train began to move and for a few valiant crablike steps, Al followed Vince's window. Then, mercifully, the train gained momentum, leaving the station, the down crossing gates with their flashing red lights, the line of automobiles waiting in the street, buildings, parked cars, houses.

Vince leaned back in the seat, closed his eyes and said, "Christ!"

Watch for the geese, both Gloria and Al had told him. And on the ride to the station, Al had dropped his sales talk to speak about the geese. They're Canadian honkers, Al had said as if he was proud. They come twice a year, Al had said; this visit, they were the harbingers of spring. The reason they came, Al said, was because they liked the gleanings in these particular fields; he'd learned that from the farmer to whom he'd sold a complete installation of storms and screens and jalousie-type doors. Al had a good business, all right. But he had to sell it. Were the geese part of the sales pitch? Both Al and Gloria had talked about the geese, recalling how they had fascinated Vince's only brother, Mario, the one who was killed on Guadalcanal in World War II.

Vince had been much too small then to remember much about Mario now. It was hard to accept the fact of a brother, let alone giving him a name and trying to fit him with a face. Last night, sitting in Gloria's and Al's comfortable living room while listening to Gloria talk about his dead brother and their three other sisters,

8

all of them had seemed like strangers. He remembered the sisters, well enough; they were still living on Long Island, at a safe distance from East New York. But, Mario. He remembered the picture enshrined on the bureau in his mother's bedroom. He remembered another picture, too, the one alongside Mario that they said was his father . . .

Suddenly, Vince saw the geese. He'd been only half watching, seeing little more than mud-flaked brown grass in long gulleys with patches of red-brown earth showing between. And then, there they were. Fifty or more of them, moving around like a disorganized platoon seeking cover.

Geese, Vince said to himself, trying to imagine that he was his brother Mario, looking through Mario's hunter's eyes. As the train passed by, he aimed with his forefinger, cocked his thumb like the hammer of a pistol and said, *"Bang!"*

The goose he'd aimed at flapped his wings and hopped maybe four feet in the air. Then he glided back to earth to settle down with the rest.

Startled, Vince laughed. He'd have to remember this, to tell Frances. He was still chuckling about the goose when the train began to slow with a grating whine of steel against steel. On the left side of the train the sun was rising fast and its strengthening rays, reflected from a great gray building on the right, brought violet edges to the silver streak of the long, irregular crack in the car's dirty window.

Vince recoiled and for an instant shut his eyes, remembering the chopper and looking down at the river crawling across the land below; remembering how silvery the river had looked when first seen from the chopper, and how muddy brown it had been in actuality.

When he opened his eyes, the train had stopped for a station and the first thing he saw was a spare, hawk-faced, impeccably dressed man who was standing on the platform. Flanking him, a little apart and a step to the rear, were two others. They were both less tall and less impressive than the hawk-faced man, but they were equally menacing as their quick, bold eyes joined his in searching the windows of the train.

Vince sought to hide, to withdraw, to escape, to get away from there if he could only organize his legs. But he was too late. One of the lesser ones saw him and, with a deference not unmixed with insolence, touched the tall man's arm.

It was funny, in a way. In all the world, he could think of only two people—no, three—he never wanted to see again. One was the miserable bastard who had left him and another near death in a stinking hole in Nam and was probably now dead himself. Another was his mother, who should have been dead but she wasn't—and it wasn't likely she would be for quite some time.

The third was his mother's brother, Uncle Vincent Spotafore, who would be very dead if a great and growing number of people could have figured out some way to arrange it without becoming dead themselves. And here, incredibly, on this bright, cold March morning was Uncle Vincent accompanying his nephew and namesake on the return trip of the first train ride Vince Maggione had taken since Christ only knew when.

"Thank you, Vincent, for saving me a seat," Uncle Vincent said in his resonant voice as his thin, strong hand gripped Vince's shoulder.

"I was expecting you, of course," Vince said, recovering from his shock and beginning to think black thoughts about sister Gloria, who had been awfully damned privately busy with the telephone that morning and the night before.

"Of course." Uncle Vincent settled himself as if he was in his own Lincoln Continental. In a moment the train started, and as if it had been last month instead of four or five years ago Uncle Vincent said, "I suppose you have seen your mother—my sister. How is she?"

"You know damned well how she is," Vince said angrily. "You've seen her since I have." He didn't feel like reminding Uncle Vincent that the last time he had seen *my* mother, *your* sister, was more than two years ago when she had thrown a whole pot of *pasta* sauce at him as he stood in his new uniform in her kitchen, all the while she was screaming at him, *"Blood, blood—your brother's blood—"* while the rich, red sauce ran down over him and puddled around his carefully polished shoes.

Uncle Vincent's deep set, bold eyes challenged him. "Of

10

course," he said. "I had forgotten. Your first time home was for your wife— You have been home, what, a couple of months? It must be difficult, the adjustment, after what you have been through. But you are looking well, better than I expected to find you."

"I wasn't aware you had expected to find me. And now that you have, I can't say I'm happy about it."

"I suppose not— You never have been happy at any mention of your mother. Perhaps this is not so surprising. It must remind you of what you cost her. A woman, forty-seven years old, having a baby. A ten-pound baby— You!"

"Too bad you didn't mention it to my old man."

"What makes you think I didn't?"

"But my father died before—" Vince paused in mid-sentence to stare at the aging man beside him. With the sun behind him, his lean head and long, dark face with its hawk-beak nose and hooded eyes gave him the appearance of a loathsome predatory bird. Despite his obviously expensive, properly aged hat, his carefully selected topcoat, his sober tie and exactly right business suit, he still looked like the bandit he had been born in a Sicilian hovel. It was not new, this suspicion that started like a sickness in Vince's stomach. *You killed my father— You either killed him or had it done—*

It wasn't new, and he was older and should have been able to handle it better, but he couldn't. He couldn't even face down his Uncle Vincent's mocking, insolent eyes, or close his ears to the too perfectly enunciated voice now blending so soothingly with the clicking of the wheels on the rails.

". . . your mother was not my only sister. There were two others—" For an instant, Uncle Vincent's voice lost its impersonal detachment. "One of them died so early I hardly remember her— There was no harvest that year, no one had anything worth stealing, and all of us starved. My other sister grew up and married a farmer, a landowner. I have not seen her in forty years. She still writes me for money which she does not need, and sometimes I send her a few dollars . . .

"Your mother was different. Even as a child she was so beautiful people would turn their heads to stare at her as she passed by. And the older she grew, the more beautiful she became— You remember her, Vincent, not as she was before child-bearing and drudgery had drained her. However, she still had some of her beauty when her first son Mario, your only brother, was killed at the same kind of business that nearly killed you.

"After that, you know—you saw—what happened to her.

"I did not approve her marriage to your father. What was he? A *nothing*. And she worshiped the ground he walked on—"

Uncle Vincent blew a puff of air through his thin lips. "I will say this for him, he was faithful to her. If he had not been, I can assure you he would not have lived to be your father—I suppose that old fool, your father's brother, Joseph Maggione—and your sisters, Rose and Maria and Angela—I suppose they have had plenty to say to you about *me*. They would not let me help them. And they turned your mother, my sister, against me— All of them but Gloria. Only Gloria had the courage and loyalty to stand up to them— Let me finish, Vincent. I do not have much more to say—"

He sighed. "I know what you think of me. To you, I am an evil old man, engaged in a dirty business— You are young, Vincent, and foolish. Have you ever thought of me as loyal? I am. Have you ever thought of me as kind? I can be. You and your sisters together have been contributing a hundred dollars a month to keep your mother where she is— Do you know how much your hundred dollars pays for? Three days!"

"She was all right at home, where she was," Vince said, angrily defensive. "With her widow's pension and the money we sent her, she was all right. And it helped Mrs. Molinari, too. Mrs. Molinari treated her like a sister— It was your idea to put her in a nursing home, not ours!"

"Mrs. Molinari isn't a nurse. What does she know? What could she have done if something happened? All right, it was my idea. And I'm paying for it. Have I asked you for more money?"

"So, what do you want from me, a letter of recommendation?"

"Don't get smart, Vincent. What I want from you is loyalty and respect, nothing more. I am a rich man. I have no children of my own; at seventy years of age, there is little likelihood that I ever will have. You are my namesake, the son of my favorite sister— Does this mean nothing to you?"

"If you want the truth," Vince said, "it makes me sick to my stomach."

The train had stopped again, and now passengers were standing in the front end of the car and scattered down the aisle. At the trainman's request for his ticket, Uncle Vincent took out a thin, gold-cornered wallet and said sourly, "New York, one way."

The trainman, a stocky man with a round, pleasant face said, "You got on at Huntington? That'll be two sixty-five. If you'd bought your ticket at the station, you could've saved a quarter."

Uncle Vincent appeared unmoved by this intelligence. He handed over a crisp, new ten-dollar bill and suffered the train-man's careful scrutiny of it, and of him. Then he waited sourly while the trainman made a flourishing ritual of punching out a ticket and making change.

It wasn't until the trainman sold two more one-way tickets to New York that Vince realized his uncle's two companions of the station platform had followed him into the car and were sitting just two seats behind them.

After some minutes of stony silence, Uncle Vincent turned abruptly. "So you don't like me," he said. "Very well, then. For-get that I am your mother's brother; forget even that you know me. I am a businessman. I will make you a business proposition. You can take it or leave it. Fair enough?"

"If you want to lend me money, I'm not interested."

"Not for any purpose?"

"Look, I know Gloria was talking to you on the telephone, last night and this morning, two or three times. That's why you left your mansion and came down to meet this grubby train— You wanted to see me because Gloria wanted you to see me, because Al has to sell his business. Isn't that it?"

"What? If you think I would lend you money to buy a nickel-and-dime business from Gloria's husband, you're crazy! If he was still in the junk business, like he started, maybe yes. But, putting up window screens? What kind of a business is that?"

"Al does okay," Vince said, angrily defensive again. He'd been so sure of what Gloria had been up to. "I saw his books and his income tax returns. He has a damned good business!"

"Not for you. I wouldn't give you a nickel for it."

"What, then?"

"The money to complete your education."

"*What?* I don't need *that*. I'll have my GI money!"

"Sure. You'll have your GI— You and a million others. Your wife will keep on working and you'll live on hot dogs. And then you'll have a kid, or get sick, or something will happen. Whatever it is, you won't have enough. And you won't be able to go far enough. You need two more years of college. *And* a year of law school. You have any idea of how much that will cost? At least twenty thousand— You got twenty thousand GI coming? Like hell you have!" In his intensity, Uncle Vincent pounded his knees with his fists. "I will lend you, in monthly installments, six thousand the first year and seven thousand for each of the next two years, twenty thousand dollars total. A year after graduation you begin to pay back and take ten years for the balance. All right? And we will go to whatever lawyer you say to make a contract. Fair enough?"

Vince sat stunned.

Uncle Vincent rubbed his thin hands together impatiently. "Well, what do you say?"

"Christ Almighty— Wait a minute! What kind of interest?"

"Six percent a year. Try and get *that* in a bank!"

"What else do I have to do besides pay back the loan?"

"You have to study," Uncle Vincent answered promptly. "You have to pass. You have to graduate. You have to become admitted to the bar. And then, you have to practice law."

Vince smiled. "I see. And I suppose you'll help me pay off the loan by supplying me with clients?"

"I am a businessman. I have many connections. Even without these connections, I can give you the names of several highly respected lawyers who will tell you that I am a valuable client of my-

14

self. If you are in doubt about me, or how I meet my obligations, I can give you plenty of references."

"No."

"No, what?"

"No to the loan. No to your proposition. *No!*"

"Vincent— You are young. And you are foolish. And with it you have the stubbornness of the Spotafores. I know a hundred young men in your position who would give an arm for a chance like this. I suggest that you think about it. Your wife seems like a sensible girl. Talk it over with her. Explain it exactly as I have put it to you. If it will make you feel any better, the money need not come directly from me. It can be advanced to you from any one of a dozen different corporations. And no one has to know about it."

"No."

"Vincent, listen—" Beads of sweat had begun to appear on Uncle Vincent's upper lip. "What do you think you will do? What price do you think heroes bring these days? You were in a war nobody understands. And nobody cares. You think you're popular because you are a veteran of this war? You'll be lucky if they don't picket the place that hires you! The war your brother Mario died in, that was different. It meant something— Okay. You think I'm bad? The interest I charge on the money I lend is less than the finance companies are legally permitted to charge. What do you think of that? I charge my agents *two* per cent a month. The finance companies charge, legally, *three* per cent a month— What do you think of that?"

"Maybe so," Vince said, "But if a man can't pay *them, they* don't break his fingers."

The train had stopped again, and Vince glanced idly through the window at the people who were struggling to get aboard the already crowded train. His talk with his uncle had ended badly, with Uncle Vincent becoming angry and abusive. If the train had been less crowded, Uncle Vincent would most likely have moved to some other part of the car; now, any movement was impossible. Yet, there on the platform at least a dozen people were trying with the force of their own weight to compress those ahead of them to make room for themselves. And then, from the straining faces above the struggling, pushing bodies, came a face remembered. Out of context, and time, and in the wrong place and the wrong setting, but a face and body that carried Vince Maggione back more than a year and caused him, involuntarily, to wince with pain while holding his shattered right leg together with both hands:

"Charley! Charley Bennett— Over here—"

The owner of the face heard the scream and the face turned to peer in the cracked, dirty car window. Then the line began to move and the remembered face moved with it beyond Vince's sight. He turned clear around, gripping the back of the seat, watching the people in the aisle surge forward from the pressure in the rear. So many of them were packed there now it was impossible to distinguish one from another.

Vince turned to face his uncle's scowl.

"What was that all about?"

"That fellow on the platform, Charley Bennett— He's in this car. Or the one behind."

"Charley Bennett— So what?"

"He's the one who saved my life!"

"So?" Uncle Vincent scowled. "Why?"

16

two

The platform at Jamaica station was a discouraging place to try to single out one face from all the others. The New York train was waiting and beside it, at a different platform, was the Brooklyn train. As if Vince no longer existed, his uncle and the two "agents" followed the crowd to the New York train; whether they had business in Manhattan was less important than the fact they had paid for tickets and wanted their money's worth. At Vince's back loomed the building where Frances was at work. Today she would be on the third floor, filling in for someone in the Pass Bureau who was on vacation. Vince had been there, at the very desk, three years ago—they'd been married nearly a year, then—and he knew the place well enough. It probably hadn't changed much in three years. But he didn't want to go there now, not even to see Frances.

There weren't many people on the platform now. He was standing at the head of one staircase and could see the other just by turning his head. He didn't see Charley Bennett. Charley, being one of the last aboard, would have been one of the first off. He could now be on the New York train, waiting for it to pull out. Or he might have gone down the stairs, or crossed through the New York train to the Brooklyn train. Or, if he worked in Jamaica, he might have gone down the stairs and out on to Sutphin Boulevard.

And there was another possibility: he might have gotten off

when the train had made one more stop, at Mineola, before reaching Jamaica.

Vince wasn't sure when, or how, he'd first met Charley Bennett. Even during the long weeks of lying in hospital, with all the time in the world to sort things out, Charley had eluded him. He couldn't remember whether Eddie Durfee had introduced Charley to him or he had introduced Charley to Eddie. *That* much was understandable since Vince had never liked Eddie despite his being from Brooklyn and having attended Bishop Loughlin High at about the same time Vince had gone there. Not that Vince had remembered Eddie. Eddie wasn't the kind of person you could remember from one day to the next—his quality of nothingness was such that the first sergeant of Alpha Company could go down a line of men looking for Eddie and pass right by him without spotting him. Eddie had hit it off with Charley Bennett because he'd had some wild tales to tell, a city boy's stories of intrigue and beating the system, that seemed to hold a peculiar fascination for this unsophisticated product of a small upstate village. Eddie had been two years ahead of Vince at Bishop Loughlin; he'd been in Jack Keegan's class and most of the things he'd said about Jack checked with what Vince knew about his wife's sister's husband. Eddie had dropped out of Bishop Loughlin to take a job as freight handler at JFK International Airport while it was still being called Idlewild. Most of Eddie's yarns had to do with thefts of air freight, consummated with great skill by well-organized gangs right under the noses of airline officials and police alike. Vince caught him telling the same story about jewels, only belonging to a different Big Name and being stolen from a different airline, and so promptly marked him down as a liar. But Charley Bennett, who was less fussy about details, had been visibly impressed.

Another reason why Vince had so much trouble in pinning down the exact beginnings of his friendship with Charley could have been because of Charley's close relationship with Noble S. Wright. Noble was one of the Negroes in Alpha Company, and not withstanding the equalizing force of military service and the uniform, Vince had never quite overcome the prejudice nurtured in him by the Negro invasion of his once solidly white Italian-

18

American neighborhood. When he thought about it, which was often enough, he told himself that they, too, were God's children and his blood brothers. It was when he didn't think about it that the prejudice was there, deep down, forming little blocks to trip him. Like not being able to remember everything about Charley Bennett because of Charley's friendship for Noble S. Wright. Charley was from an all-white community south and west of Utica and *his* only prejudices were against Jews and Catholics. He was fond of saying that his prejudices were all he had inherited from his parents. Although this was what he said, he was different from Vince in that he apparently never thought about his prejudices and they didn't seem to bother him. He hadn't hesitated to risk his own life to save a Catholic when he could just as easily have saved the Methodist who had been lying in the same hole and in about the same condition as Vince.

Charley's liking for Eddie Durfee, an Irish Catholic, was because Eddie could tell him stories that let him escape, however momentarily, from the grim business they were all engaged in. His liking for Noble probably came from the delight they obviously shared in taking things apart and putting them back together again. They were both happiest when working on somebody's ailing watch or one of the Hong Kong-made Swiss cuckoo clocks or transistor radios the boys were always getting stuck with in Saigon. Noble had graduated from vocational high school and was a wizard at electronics. Noble's liking for Charley, however, was deeper than a mutual sharing of hobbies. Vince had once overheard Noble tell another Negro: "Charley Bennett? Maybe he is a square. But he's A-okay. He's never patronized me. Have you got one white friend who hasn't patronized you?"

There was a time, in the early stages, to sort out friends and form attachments before these became necessities of the moment. Vince hadn't made friends easily. He was an Italian with a Brooklyn accent and so had himself been subject to a fairly strong level of prejudice. He was married to Frances and deeply in love with her and so, by refusing to share with others in the readily available pleasures, was marked as queer. He also had a tendency to withdraw, to prefer a book to company; this, together with his

19

constant refusal to join in gambling games, left him pretty much to himself.

It must have been Charley Bennett who had made the advances; why, Vince didn't know. And just where, he couldn't remember. However, somehow it happened, and by the time Alpha Company had been firmed up, he and Charley were friends.

"So, you live on Long Island, huh, Vince?" Charley Bennett said. They were sitting in the shelter of a pile of supplies and about a mile away The Hill, shrouded in mist, was waiting for them. They could see The Hill if they wanted to by standing up and peering over the top of the pile. They'd spent some time in looking silently at it, as had most everyone else in Alpha Company.

The area was strangely quiet and Charley's voice sounded unnaturally loud.

"Well, geographically," Vince replied. "But not exactly." How could you explain to someone who didn't know that Long Island was really a state of mind, separated from Queens and Brooklyn by a non-existent wall? It was difficult to tell at what point you actually crossed the wall. But it was nonetheless there. "I live in East New York. It's a suburb of Brooklyn," Vince said.

Noble S. Wright looked up from the letter he'd been trying to write, off and on, for a couple of weeks. "East New York," he said. "I've got an old aunty living there. On Linden Boulevard."

"I thought your folks lived in Harlem," Charley Bennett said.

"Not all of 'em. Just *most* of 'em— Man, I've got a lot of folks!" Noble S. Wright laughed, showing all his teeth.

Charley Bennett said, "Long Island. They used to get *The New York Times* at the *Citizen,* where I worked as a Linotype operator, and Old Man Potter would save the Sunday real estate section for me. Boy, those houses on Long Island—and the easy terms! Hank Strickland, he was the foreman at the *Citizen* when I first went to work there, Saturdays and during summers when I was in high school. Then Hank quit the *Citizen* for a job on a big tabloid daily on Long Island. And he wrote and told me he could get me a job any time I wanted."

Noble glanced up, interested. "You got a union card?"

"Hank said that'd be no problem, with my experience and

20

speed. And my proofs were clean, too. He'd stop by the shop every time he was home on vacation, after I graduated from high school and was working full time. And he'd always ask me, 'You ready yet?'"

"Why didn't you go?" Vince asked.

"Uh, well—I'd met this girl, from New York City. She was there on vacation, and she really liked that place. It's a real pretty town, only kind of slow. She was staying with her grandfather—he had a farm on the edge of town and the state took a big piece of it for the Throughway. But that was later. We'd started getting serious, and she wanted to stay in Winfield."

"She the one you married?" Noble asked.

"Yes. Blanche," Charley said. "And wouldn't you know, when her grandfather died and they sold the rest of the farm, which was after I was drafted, after we were married, which was before they sent me to this damn place, she moved back to New York."

"Not to Harlem, I'll bet," Noble said, laughing.

"Hell, no. On West 84th Street, in a lousy two-room apartment. She's a beautician, went to school for it and graduated. So, soon's my time is up and I can get back there, we're going to move to Long Island— Vince, do you know anybody who lives out there?"

"Some. Like my four sisters. And an uncle."

"Yeah? Where on Long Island do they live?"

"Two of my sisters live on the North Shore. And two live on the South Shore. And they've all got the kind of houses you used to read about in those real estate ads. But my uncle— The last I heard, he had a little pad of twenty rooms on four acres with his own beach on Long Island Sound."

"The hell you say!" Charley Bennett said.

Noble glanced up from his writing. "Your uncle— He's an Italian?"

"Uhuh."

"Same name as you, Maggione?"

"No. His name is Spotafore."

"*Vincent* Spotafore?" Noble said. "*He's* your uncle?"

Vince started to reply, but Charley Bennett, angry at Noble for interrupting his dream, said, "What the hell do you know about anything?"

21

"I know something about *him*," Noble said. And then, without changing his expression, he asked, "How do you spell 'Dak To'?"

It was their last chance to be together, except in the larger sense of being members of Alpha Company and sharing the Communist mortar and ground attack which met the 2nd Battalion's initial assault at the base of The Hill. Of the 285 Americans who died in the twelve-day battle of Dak To, three miles from the Cambodian border, 105 were from the 2nd Battalion, 503rd Parachute Regiment, 173rd Airborne Brigade, and of their fallen comrades the survivors spoke most frequently about a Catholic chaplain from Jersey City and a Puerto Rican boy from the Bronx.

After a three-day pounding by artillery and air strikes, Hill 875 was finally taken at fifteen minutes before noon on Thanksgiving Day.

Vince Maggione wasn't there to see the victory. In fact, it was more than a month later that he was told about it. Eddie Durfee, he later heard, was killed in action. He never did find out what happened to Charley Bennett, or if Noble S. Wright ever finished writing his letter.

three

The house was the third from the corner. It had once been the fifth, but when Vince was eight years old the first and second houses had been torn down and a gas station had been built on the corner. The station had passed through a succession of owners until Uncle Joe Maggione bought it, and Vince had worked there weekends and vacations from the time he was fourteen until he was drafted. Uncle Joe still owned the property along with the house next to it, although he had leased the business to a nephew on his wife's side.

The Maggione house had been built of frame, narrow and high, on a 30-foot lot which it shared with a driveway that ran beside it to a one-car garage in the rear. Zoning had been unheard of when the house started life with a uniformity of design shared by every other house in that particular area. The passage of time and changes in the fortunes of the individual owners, however, had brought variations. The Maggiones had held out against imitation brick, simulated stone, interlocking asphalt shingles, sun porches, pseudo marble columns and other "improvements" until Gloria's husband had gone into the aluminum storm window, screen and siding business.

In fairness to Al, he had done a workmanlike job, and at cost.

The odor of coffee met Vince as he let himself into the house. He crossed through the hall between the neat, dark living room and the open, straight staircase and entered the kitchen where he dropped his Pan Am bag on the table. Gloria had given him a good breakfast of ham and eggs, but with all her years of marriage she still didn't know how to make a decent cup of coffee. Frances had left the pot on the stove, with the burner on simmer. And she'd left a note, tacked to the door of the dish cupboard with a square of Scotch tape:

I'll be home by 5:30. Dinner's in the oven, you don't have to do anything about it. If you need to call me for any reason, I'll be at Ext. 940. Hope everything went well with Gloria and Al. Love, Fran.

Frances had had to attend a union meeting the night before. She was a member of the Clerks and she had enough seniority to be guaranteed a job five days a week. She was a very serious and dedicated union member and last night's meeting was important.

Vince poured himself a cup of good, strong coffee, pulled out a chair and, shoving the blue plastic bag aside, sat down at the table. Did he want to buy Al's business? He hadn't been very keen about it until Uncle Vincent had put in his two cents' worth. He ought to buy it just to show the old man. He and Frances had better than $5000 in a joint savings account, more than enough to meet the down payment Al was asking. He also had some income in the form of a disability pension. It wasn't much, but it would help meet the payments on a nice new ranch, one at least as good as Gloria and Al's, out on the Island. And, since Frances had made it plain she intended to keep her job, they should get along all right.

But, did he really want to go into business for himself? Damn Uncle Vincent, anyway. He supposed this was what the psychiatrist at the VA Hospital called "reacting," warning that it could be an expensive pastime . . .

If they could just sell this house. There was nothing wrong with the house; it was the neighborhood— Vince pulled himself up, poured another cup of coffee and sat back down again. The slightest of frowns furrowed the smooth skin on his forehead. The real reason Frances wanted to keep her job was to help him go back to St. John's. In two years—less, if he really worked at it—he could get a degree. And with a degree, he could get a *good*

24

job— A lot of Frances' work was in Personnel, and she knew what they were offering college graduates . . .

Vince thought about Frances, and how he had almost let her slip by. Frances was Irish; her father was a fireman, a lieutenant in the East New York station, and she'd been around ever since he could remember. He'd never given her a second thought, which was partly because of his sisters who had wanted him to marry an Italian girl. There had been a niece of Uncle Vincent Spotafore, the daughter of one of his wife's brothers. This girl, Louise, was a very striking-looking girl. She was tall, with the creamy skin that some Italian girls possess; she had fine raven black hair and wide-set gray eyes in an oval face that could be reserved and animated according to her interest. Vince had liked Louise very much and would have liked her more if it hadn't been for his sisters always scheming to throw them together. He did *not* like Louise's brother, Frank, who was an obnoxious punk. It had been bad enough before Frank had been picked up by Uncle Vincent. After that, when Frank deigned to visit East New York in his tailor-made suits and fancy sports cars, he was impossible.

Vince might have gone for marriage to Louise except for something that happened between them one time when they were alone, by accident rather than design. It wasn't supposed to happen between a man and a woman, a boy and a girl, unless they were married. Vince knew it happened often enough, even though it had never before happened to him. Although he was twenty years old at the time, a high school graduate and a student at St. John's, he had never had a woman. Until Louise. Perhaps he had been too clumsy or she had been too urgent; whatever the cause, the experience had not been completely satisfactory and there had been only that once. After that, he called her any number of times and she would talk to him, pleasantly enough. But she would not go out with him again.

The whole matter of Louise might have remained in limbo indefinitely if she hadn't announced her engagement, at Christmastime, to a man at least a dozen years her senior. He was a bachelor; he handled some of Uncle Vincent's enterprises and, despite the difference in age and height—he was a full head shorter than Louise—the match had the blessing of her parents, Uncle Vincent, and her brother, Frank.

Vince's sisters had been so upset by the announcement they refused, on principle, to attend the wedding at Eastertime. Vince went, however, and it was there he at last discovered Frances. She was one of the bridesmaids and with her auburn hair and in her green chiffon dress she caused almost as much of a sensation as the bride.

Frances didn't catch the bride's bouquet but, within a year, she and Vince were married in the same church.

Sitting now in the kitchen of this old house that had been his father's before him, Vince Maggione hadn't intended to drag up up the memory of Louise. She no longer meant anything to him —after Frances, there had been no one else. He could blame the churning of his mind on the session with Gloria and Al, or the unexpected, highly disturbing meeting with Uncle Vincent . . .

Or the one-in-millions chance of seeing Charley Bennett on the station platform at Hicksville.

Vince made himself a ham sandwich for his lunch and put it, unwrapped, in the refrigerator. He washed and dried his coffee cup and saucer and put them away. He did what he did slowly, consciously delaying his climb of the stairs to take the "horizontal, relaxed rest" he was supposed to get for a minimum of two hours each day. Exercise and rest, the doctor had said. He wasn't due back at the VA Hospital until the middle of next week, which would be the last of the weekly visits before going on a monthly basis. He was coming along fine, the doctor had told him. He wasn't to worry about anything. Outside of his leg, he was all right physically. His problems with Frances—and equally, hers with him —were all in his mind. The more he tried to force it, the longer it would take, the doctor said.

He started to read the printed forms Al had thought Vince should familiarize himself with. A business card, *Suffolk Metals, Inc.;* Al had carried the name over from his junk business, and a four-page section from *Newsday* with the two-column, four-inch ad Al used to bring in business.

The section from *Newsday* had been pulled out of the paper to save his carrying a lot of bulk. The first of the two left-hand pages was a news page and the first of the two right-hand ones was a home improvement page. An article near the middle of the news page caught Vince's eye. Two men, wearing Halloween masks and rubber gloves, had held up a branch bank on Jericho Turnpike and escaped with $3500 in cash in a shopping bag. Both men were of medium height, believed to be twenty–thirty years old, and the masks, gloves and method of operation were identical to those used by two similarly described men who had similarly help up another branch bank in Melville on February 15, that time getting $6225. An alert teller, name withheld, had seen a one-inch section of brown wrist and was postitive that at least one of the robbers was a Negro. Detectives of the 2nd Squad, Suffolk County Police, were working on the case . . .

The telephone rang.

Frances, Vince told himself. Probably she'd just found out that she'd have to work overtime . . .

He hobbled to the telephone in the hall. "Hello?"

"Vince?" A man's voice, hesitant and vaguely familiar.

"Yes."

"Are you the Vince Maggione who was in Alpha Company—"

"Charley Bennett— For Christ's sake! I *thought* I saw you— Where the hell are you?"

"And I was pretty sure I saw you, too, on the train—" Suddenly, Charley Bennett's voice sounded old and tired. "I'm in Mineola. I live here now— How are you, Vince?"

"Me? Oh, I'm just the same— Christ, Charley, it's been a long time— So, you finally made it to Long Island!"

"Yeah—" A pause. Something indistinguishable. Then, "—not exactly like I planned it. But— Will you be home tomorrow?"

"Sure! Tomorrow, today, now, any time! Can you come over?"

"Not today. I'm working on a morning paper, in Deer Park. Last night was a bitch, with all the market ads to set. But I'll be rested up tomorrow. And I'd sure like to see you, if you don't mind—" He sounded unsure of himself.

"I'd be mad as hell if you didn't. After all, I do owe you a little something!"

"You didn't have to bring *that* up. But, since you have, I'll settle for a beer— Better make that a couple of beers. Big ones." For a minute, he sounded like the old Charley.

"A couple? I'll lay in a whole damned refrigerator full! What time can you come?"

"Oh, say about this time, if that's all right. And I may have a surprise for you, if that's all right, too— Your address the same as the one in the phone book?"

"It sure is— Christ, Charley, it'll be good to see you!"

"Same here. See you tomorrow, Vince."

"Right, Charley!"

He replaced the telephone and stared for a long time at the diamond-shaped mirror of the old-fashioned golden oak clothes rack in the hall. The face that looked back at him was Vince Maggione. Same face, same dark fine thick hair, same hazel eyes, same short, straight nose, same lips—more like a girl's than a man's—out of place in the dark shadow of his cheeks, but fitting the dimpled chin that could already use another shave. The face was the one he'd carried with him to Vietnam and back; it hadn't changed a hair. And all five-ten, 160 pounds of the rest of him was the same, too; he'd gained back, to the ounce, what he'd lost those first months in the hospital. The same; he looked neither older nor younger than he had when Charley Bennett and the others in Alpha Company had known him.

He was just the same, except for his leg. And something deep in his mind.

four

Vince was thinking seriously about climbing the stairs when his Uncle Joe Maggione stopped in. Uncle Joe had been born in Calabria two years after the birth of Vince's father, which meant he was now about sixty-eight years old. He had a thick shock of white hair and the blue eyes of the Maggiones in a furiously sculptured, unfinished face. His sturdy peasant's body was long, as were his arms, and his hands were thick and rough.

"I thought you went to Al and Gloria," Uncle Joe said as he rocked on bowed legs into the kitchen and poured himself a cup of coffee. "I didn't think you were here—I came by and tried the front door. That was maybe nine o'clock." He smiled as he sat down in the straight chair at the end of the kitchen, beside the back door.

Vince glanced at him and away. *Sure you did,* he said to himself. *Just like every day after my father died, they told me, you visited this house to do chores for your sister-in-law—even long after she'd stopped recognizing you— Just like you did, morning and night, while I was in Nam, and later in the hospital, to look after Frances and her sister Margaret who had moved in here with her kids while Jack was over there somewhere with the Marines— And Uncle Vincent calls you "an old fool"—*

"You know how it is," Vince said, replenishing his own cup and choosing to stand for the moment. "They wanted me to stay with them so I could go out with Al on a job this afternoon. But

I told them last night I wouldn't— I don't think Al believed me. But Gloria did; she knows me."

"Gloria," Uncle Joe said. He smiled. "I don't see them, maybe six months. How are they?"

"Gloria's fine; she's getting fat. But Al—" Graphically, Vince doubled his hands until his fingertips touched his wrists.

Uncle Joe nodded. "A bad thing he has. Never get better— He wants to sell you his business?"

"Yes."

"You want to buy?"

"I don't know."

Uncle Joe nodded again. "Better you wait," he said. He finished his coffee, got up and with great care put the cup in the sink. Then he returned to sit down again, with his hands on his knees.

"You saw your Uncle Vincent," he said. It was a statement, not a question.

"Uh—Gloria told him what train I was on. He rode with me from Huntington to Jamaica."

"I thought he might come to their house. You know he wants you."

"He wants to lend me some money."

"So, that's his plan. A loan— The money means nothing to him. It's you he wants, Vincent."

"Why? He knows damned well I can't stand him!"

"He doesn't care what *you* can stand. He wants you. He will try every way to get you. You will see."

"But, why? What the hell does he want with me?"

"Vincent, before you went away you didn't swear. I'm sorry. It's the war— He wants you because you are honest. You are young. You are family. He wants you because he needs you."

"Why me? He has Frank Mastretta. Frank's still young. I don't know how honest he is. I'd sure like to know how the—how he's avoided the draft. But he's strong enough. And he's family."

"Yes, but not blood. Your Uncle Vincent is an old man, older than me. He knows he will die, maybe sooner, maybe later. He wants everything settled first."

"He isn't planning on dying for several years," Vince said. His leg was bothering him now and he pulled out the other chair and sat, facing the old man. Then he recited the conversation on the train, ending with his refusal to accept a loan and his Uncle Vincent's subsequent resort to abuse. "He's through with me," Vince said.

Uncle Joe shook his head. "Oh, no he isn't."

"But I want nothing to do with him. He's evil. He disgusts me. He makes me sick, and he knows it."

"He knows only that he is rich and powerful, and he gets what he wants. The less you want *him,* the more he wants *you.* If he can't get you one way, he'll try another. Believe me, he is *not* through with you. He has offered you a choice which you have refused. He may offer you other choices. If you refuse him again, he will use other ways—ways in which the choice will not be yours."

"What? This isn't Sicily! This is the United States!"

"Sure," Uncle Joe said, unsmiling.

"All right. What can he do to me?"

"He can trap you. You think he can't?"

"I don't know. I haven't thought about it. I suppose he could, although I don't know why he would want to. I'll admit I don't understand him—" A sudden thought struck him and for a moment he experienced the familiar sickness starting in his stomach. Keeping his voice as casual as he could, he said, "My father died three months before I was born— What do you know about his death?"

The old man's head came up straight. His blue eyes mirrored swift panic. "Why do you ask this?"

"Because I'd like to know. I never could get anyone to talk about it. My mother—well, she wouldn't talk straight about anything. But, Gloria— I asked her, a long time ago, and I'll never forget how frightened she looked. She told me I should *never* mention it again, not to anyone— Why?"

Uncle Joe sat very still, his eyes clouded as if he was looking into the past. Very carefully, as if some blame might fall to him if he remembered wrongly, he said, "I was not here, I was in Florida at the time. I had driven a car down there with another in tow—they were Cadillacs, used but very clean—and I had a crazy idea I could sell them for much more money than here—

31

I sold them okay, but it took me longer than I thought and I ran into trouble besides— And I lost money, too— When I came back here it was a month later, and your father was dead—" He shook his head. "I went to his grave. My wife told me, every-one told me, he was killed on the railroad."

Vince said, "Gloria once told me that your family didn't want your brother—my father—to marry my mother. I used to think it was because they were Calabrians and the Spotafores were Sicilians and a lot of them were in the *mafiosi*. Then when I grew older, I realized Uncle Vincent was dead set against *his* sister marrying *your* brother— He reminded me of it again today. It was bad enough in his book that they were married and had five children. But when his sister became pregnant again—at forty-six years of age—it isn't hard to imagine that he had some pretty harsh words for my father."

"So?" Uncle Joe shrugged. "What business of his?"

"The point is, he might have made it his business. We both agree that he is an evil man. He violates the law and seems to get away with it— Suppose my father's death wasn't an accident? What if Uncle Vincent arranged it?"

Uncle Joe stood up. "I have no knowledge of this," he said, looking down at his hands. "I know only of my dead brother. And of him, Vincent Spotafore; I know him. Evil he is, Vincent, but not a killer. This is a reputation he does not have. But, if I find out he killed my brother, I would break him like a stick."

At five-thirty, Vince was seated at the kitchen table, concen-trating on an article in the *New York Post* about husbands and wives in business, when Frances came in. From where he was seated, he couldn't immediately see her although he did hear her cheery "Hi, darling!" as she closed the door. And he heard her stamping her feet on the mat while she cried, "Do you know, it's *snowing?* Huge flakes— But it won't last. It's melting as fast as it hits!"

Then he could see her when she put her hat and coat on the rack, pausing for a quick glance at the mirror while she tucked in a stray wisp of hair. She'd let her hair grow long to form a knot at the nape of her neck because Vince liked it that way. Vince also liked her to wear her hemlines lower and her necklines higher than the prevailing fashion and she did. Not that he minded other men looking at her, he just didn't want them getting wrong ideas.

Frances finished her inspection and came into the kitchen, moving quickly as she always did when she had things to do. She was smiling and her eyes were sparkling, which meant that she'd had a good day at work and was happy to be at home now with Vince. She stopped behind his chair, put her hands on his shoulders and leaned down until her cheek touched his.

"Hello, Mr. Maggione," she said.

"Hello, Mrs. Maggione— What's the chance of a man stealin' a wee kiss, my pretty Irish lass?"

"Good, I'd say—" She pressed her hands against his cheeks, turned his head and kissed him full on the lips. It was a provocative kind of kiss, one she did not often give him; a kiss calculated to bring an eager response. It had been the same kind of a kiss— how long ago?—that had started them to undress each other, right in this same kitchen, and had ended upstairs in bed.

It wasn't happening now. His response was tender but there was no urgency in it and in a moment she turned away.

"Are you all right, darling?" she asked.

"Sure. Just a little tired. I've had a big day— What's for supper?"

"I thought you'd like lasagna. And a good, green salad. We can eat here in the kitchen, if you'd rather— Don't get up. I can manage, if you'll just move the paper— How were Gloria and Al?"

Already she was away from him, moving swiftly, gracefully, with an economy of motion as if, during the train ride from Jamaica and on the bus from the station, she had planned exactly what she was now doing.

"Gloria's fine," he said as he gathered and folded the newspaper. He was glad Frances had turned her face from him; he didn't want to see her eyes, not after his cold-fish response to her kiss. "But Al—I don't know how he keeps going. This was the first time I'd seen him—in two years? I remember your telling me about him. But— Well, I was shocked."

"He's always been so active. It must be dreadful for him." She made fresh coffee and gathered plates and silver from the cabinet.

She put two place mats on the table, folded paper napkins and arranged the settings. Now her face was exposed to Vince and he saw that her blue eyes were filled with concern. "Did he talk about the business?" she asked. The question didn't sound as casual as she had hoped it would.

"Oh, yes. He talked about it a lot."

"Uh—what do you think?"

"It's a good business, all right. But I didn't commit myself to anything—" He slid a little way down the table to give her room. "And guess who I saw on the train this morning—Uncle Vincent."

Her head came up. "Yours or mine?" she asked. She had an uncle, Vincent O'Brien, who was retired from the New York City Police Department and living in Kew Gardens. *Her* Uncle Vincent was always talking about getting out of the rat race and moving to a farm in Vermont. Although he'd never farmed a day in his life and had visited Vermont only once, he regularly received farm agency catalogues and went through frequent emotional crises, particularly when he'd had too much to drink.

"Mine," Vince said.

"Oh my gosh— You saw *him?*"

"He rode in the same seat with me from Huntington to Jamaica."

"Wh-what did he want?"

"To lend me money."

"So you can buy Al's business?" She sounded dismayed.

"No."

"Oh. I suppose, because I'm still working, he thinks we're hard up or something. Thank the Lord we're not! And thank the Lord we don't have to borrow from him— What in the *world?*"

She'd opened the refrigerator door to see the stacks of beer cans.

"Oh, that."

"Vince, are we planning a party?"

"*I* am." And he told her about seeing Charley Bennett through the train window, and about Charley following it up with the phone call. "So, he's coming here tomorrow—"

She was just standing there, by the refrigerator door, looking at him.

34

"Charley Bennett," he said, misunderstanding the look in her eyes. "You remember, the guy who saved my life. I wrote you about him often enough."

"I remember."

"Well, for God's sake— He's coming here tomorrow. It seems to me it calls for *something!*"

"Vince—" She hesitated, moving a little nearer him. "This is the first time you've seen him since—since he—"

"Since he saved me, yes. I thought I'd written you. The *last* time I saw him was when he bent over me and picked me up—"

"But he never wrote to you?"

"Charley? All the time I knew him, I never knew him to write anybody. I wrote *him,* a letter of thanks, and it must have been delivered because I didn't get it back— What the hell difference does it make?"

"I just don't want you to get hurt," Frances said.

"What? You mean Charley wouldn't be glad to see me? You should've heard him on the phone!"

"I mean that times change and so do people. It's true, you and Charley were friends in the service, and he did save your life. But you haven't seen him in such a long time— I know how much it means to you. That's why I hope you won't be let down."

"How do you like that? I lay in a few beers so I can spend maybe an hour talking over old times with the guy who saved my life, and listen to you! I'm not inviting him to move in with us. After tomorrow, I'll probably never see him again— What in hell is the matter with you?"

"Nothing." She had been looking small and vulnerable. Now she looked calm, and tough. "Do you feel better?"

"Huh?"

"For some reason or other, you've been wanting to give me hell ever since you got home. Well, you've done it. Now do you feel better?"

"Uh—some."

"Good. Would you like your supper now?"

The idea came to him while they were lying in bed with only the sheet blanket pulled up over them. He was wearing his shorts

—he hadn't been able to sleep in pajamas since he'd left the hospital—and she had on the diaphanous pastel green shorty gown he'd bought for her when he came home. They had done the dishes together, and once more she had forgiven him. Her forgiving, however, was something else. She was soft as jelly on the outside, but underneath was a layer of flint and her manner plainly told him that if he wanted to fight, she was ready. There hadn't been enough time for her to go to sleep, so he put his idea into words.

"Fran?"

"Well?"

"My father was killed twenty-seven years ago this coming June. Do you suppose the railroad would still have a record of his death?"

She had been lying, facing away from him. Now she turned and gave him a quick, wide-awake glance. "Is it important?"

"It's important to *me!*"

"Why?"

"*Why?* Look—"

"*You* look. I don't want to start a fight. But what seems important to me is that we face forward instead of backward. You never even saw your father. Why, after so many years have passed, does it suddenly become important to dig up the past? How can that possibly help you—us?"

"When you have a lot of time on your hands," Vince said slowly, "like in a hospital, you think about a lot of things. One of the things I thought about was my father, whom I had never seen, and how he died. And the more I thought about it, the more it bothered me that nobody in the family would ever talk about his death—it was almost as if he had never existed."

He sighed. "Today, I learned something significant—at least, I thought it was significant. My father died while Uncle Joe Maggione was in Florida, on a business trip."

"What's significant about that?" she asked.

"You remember how you used to write me that Uncle Joe was here, every day, morning and night, to see if he could do anything for you and your sister, and the twins, all the time I was away? He was the same after my father died—I can remember him while I

36

was growing up—coming here day after day to look after the family, although my mother didn't speak to him in the early days, and didn't recognize him in the later years— The point is, he was devoted to my father. If anyone meant harm to my father they would have waited until Uncle Joe was out of the way—"

"Vince! Do you think that what happened to your father wasn't an accident?"

"I don't know what happened to my father. All that I know is he died as a result. For some reason, Gloria and the rest of them hushed it up. They didn't want to talk about it, even to me. It's no secret that Uncle Vincent Spotafore hated my father. And *I* think —although Uncle Joe doesn't agree—Uncle Vincent is fully capable of killing anyone—"

"Vince! You can't believe this!"

"Cut it out, Fran. You've told me your opinion of Vincent Spotafore enough times—I don't believe, or not believe. I'd like to see the official railroad records. There should be some names, possibly witnesses. People who worked with him. Something. If there is anything, I have a right to know."

"Is this your idea, or Uncle Joe's?"

"Mine."

She gave him a worried glance. "Vince, I wish you wouldn't push this."

"Why not?"

"Because I don't see any future in it. Suppose you *did* discover, somehow, that there was something suspicious about what happened to your father—twenty-seven years ago—and that in some way your Uncle Vincent *was* involved— What would you do?"

"I'd be more interested in knowing what *he* would do—Uncle Joe is convinced that he has started a campaign to get me into his 'family.' Whether Uncle Joe is right or not, we'll know soon enough. I don't want to fight Uncle Vincent, and I certainly don't want to join him. I *would* like to have a weapon against him, one that might save me from him. Or make his gorillas keep their filthy hands off *you.*"

"Oh, Vince, what you've been through—" She rolled to him, pressing her face against his chest.

37

"Hey, cut that out! Remember, we agreed, no sympathy and no emotional crises!"

"I can't help it—I love you so much—"

"Yeah. *Now* I suppose you're going to tell me you were true to me all the time I was away."

She sat up, glaring at him through her tears. "That isn't funny!"

"Well, I guess it isn't. I guess you were."

"You *guess!* Don't you *know?*"

"Fran—"

"Does it matter to you if I was or not?"

"You know damn well it does!"

"All right, you dumb Guinea! Will you tell me how, even if I'd had ideas, I could possibly have done anything with all the sisters, cousins and coompaddies you have around here—not to mention Uncle Joe? If I'd so much as looked at a man, my throat would have been cut, and you know it!"

Vince grinned. "I guess there are some advantages to being a Guinea at that," he said.

five

Charley Bennett's "surprise" turned out to be Noble S. Wright, who had taken the day off from his job in a Port Washington electronics plant to join the reunion. Now that Noble was out of uniform, Vince could hardly recognize him. Although he was still thinned down fine, as he had been in the service, and he still wore his hair cut close on the sides and no more than a regulation half-inch-long on top, there were differences. His eyes were clearer than Vince remembered, and a lot more direct; he seemed to be altogether more alert. He was wearing a business suit which fitted him as if it had been tailor made; his white shirt with gray pencil striping, white collar and charcoal gray tie, held with a narrow gold bar, were smarter than anything Vince owned. The tie bar and an expensive-looking wristwatch were the only items of jewelry Noble wore. His shoes, alligator loafers, also looked expensive.

The real surprise, however, was Charley Bennett himself. Charley had aged visibly. His remembered unruly sandy hair had thinned and now held streaks of gray. The trim, hard-muscled litheness that had marked him as a combat soldier was now blurred by fat; his shoulders sagged and he was developing a paunch. The transition from military to civilian garb in which Noble had bloomed had caused Charley to go to seed. And, most noticeable change of all, his eyes were lackluster with deeply etched lines around them.

The impressions flashed swiftly in Vince's mind, to be instantly erased. It was one thing to be defensive to Frances about his friends; he had no intention of being defensive about them to himself.

Both Charley and Noble seemed happy to see him and, after the first strangeness of their meeting had worn off, when they arranged themselves around the kitchen table and were getting started on the beer, their real reunion began. They talked with vanishing shyness and growing excitement until, at moments, all of them would be talking at once. Events were given substance by names recalled and actions remembered; each name and action had a different shade of meaning for each of them. Whenever a name came up, one of them—usually Charley—was able to supply information; as often as not, it was that the man had died. For a while each of them was again a member of Alpha Company and the method of a man's dying was as important as the fact of his death. And a hell of a lot of them had died— A grenade. A mortar shell. A rifle bullet. A Claymore mine . . .

One man all of them knew had been killed in a brawl in a Saigon bar, and for a moment each of them marveled at what he had survived to come to such an end.

When they talked about their war, the interchange was brisk and on an equal footing, and tiredness and age slipped from Charley Bennett as he had once been able to shake off sleep. Not all of their talk was morbid; some of it was funny, such as Noble's contribution about the time the captain had stepped out of a jeep into a puddle that proved to an armpit-deep hole. But when Vince tried to bring the conversation into the present he ran into resistance from Charley and in-depth resistance, accompanied by warning eye signals, from Noble.

Vince was at the refrigerator for another round of beer when he noticed the cigarette in his hand. He looked so startled, Noble, who was watching him, burst into laughter.

"What's funny?" Charley asked, blinking owlishly.

"Vince," Noble said. "We're leadin' him astray. He's smokin'!"

"What? Well, I'll be damned—I don't remember you smoking, Vince," Charley said. "When did you start?"

"Beats me," Vince said. "I used to smoke when I was at St. John's, but I gave it up when I went in the Army. Then I started

40

again in the hospital, but I hadn't smoked since I came home, until now— Who did I bum this from?"

Noble grinned. "Help yourself, any time," he said, pushing the pack across the table.

Vince brought three beer cans, bunched together, and put them down. "This stuff must be getting to me," he said.

"It sure is getting to *me,*" Charley said. "Where's your john?"

"Top of the stairs, first door to your right."

"Okay. No more stories 'til I get back."

When Charley had climbed the stairs and the sound of the bathroom door's closing echoed down, Vince said in a low voice, "Noble, he looks terrible! What's happened to him?"

Noble's eyes flashed in a quick ceilingward glance. "Workin' a little too hard," he said. "He worked all night, you know."

"He should be home, getting his sleep. I didn't realize—"

"He wanted to see you. Besides, it's a lot when he gets four, five hours sleep. That goes for Saturdays and Sundays, too."

"Why can't he sleep?"

"He works night *and* day. He's got two, three jobs."

"Christ! Why?"

"Money."

"What does he need that much money for? Isn't his wife working?"

"Not the last I heard."

"He—he *is* still married?"

"He's married."

"Kids?"

"No."

Vince said, "I don't understand it. Printers make good money; why does he need so much more? How can he hold down so many jobs? What keeps him going?"

"Speed," said Noble.

"Speed? You mean goofballs?"

"Yes."

"What the hell— Has he got troubles?"

"Well, some."

"What are they?"

Noble said, "That's not for me to say, is it? I mean, if *he* wants to tell you, that's *his* business—"

The sound of the toilet being flushed caused Noble to glance upward again. Then, with the squeak of the bathroom door, he flashed a warning with his eyes. "I didn't tell you anythin' about him, you hear?"

"I— Damn it, okay."

Noble nodded. Then he said loudly, "This is a nice pad you got here, Vince. You own or rent?"

"This house is really my mother's," said Vince. "She's in a— She hasn't lived here since I went in the Army. My sisters signed their shares over to me because I pay the taxes and keep the place up. You get problems like that when your father dies without making a will—"

Charley came back to resume his place at the table. His eyes were brighter than they had been and his shoulders were straighter. His right hand was holding a sheet of paper, one of Al's business forms; Vince remembered having left it in the bathroom.

"I hope I didn't interrupt anything," Charley said.

"No. I was just telling Noble about this house. My father bought it, years ago, and my sisters and I all grew up here— What's that?"

"I was about to ask *you*," said Charley. "It's an order form for Suffolk Metals, Inc." He pronounced it like the word *ink*. "That the business you're thinking of buying?"

"I'm considering it, yes."

"How much can you make with a business like that?"

"My brother-in-law has been clearing three hundred a week. He says I should be able to make four hundred easy."

"Why should you be able to make more than he does?"

"He's crippled with arthritis and can't do much."

"Three, four hundred a week," said Charley in a different tone. "How much would it cost you to buy it, that is, how much down and what kind of payments?"

"He wants twenty thousand, with the truck and equipment and including eight thousand or more in inventory. He'll sell it to me for twenty-five hundred down and two hundred a month on the balance."

42

Noble looked interested. "He'll sell it to you for that. How much would he want from anybody else?"

"I didn't ask him. I suppose it would depend— It isn't that he wants to sell; on account of the arthritis he has to."

"It sounds like a damned good buy to me," said Charley. "Any business that throws off that kind of money— Mind if I borrow this form?"

"Be my guest— What the hell do you want it for?"

"Saturdays and Sundays I work for a crazy Swede job printer, in Huntington. He lets me use his equipment any time as long as I'm not in competition with him, or the U. S. Government. When I get a chance I'll shoot this form, make a plate and knock out five hundred copies or so. It'll be good practice for me and it might help your brother-in-law. Or you, if you buy the business."

"Uh— How much would it cost?"

"Nothing. Hell, I was planning on doing it as a favor."

"Charley, you don't owe me any favors. Christ knows what I owe *you!*"

Charley scowled. "I wish you wouldn't keep bringing *that* up."

Noble said softly, "Hell, Charley. No cause for you to get sore. Vince just wants to show his gratitude to you for savin' his life. He feels obligated— That's it, isn't it, Vince?"

"Of course I feel obligated," said Vince.

Charley shrugged. "I guess if the shoe was on the other foot, I'd feel the same. Okay. If you want to do *me* a favor, tell me something."

"Sure. What?"

"One time, when we were in Nam, you told us you had an uncle on Long Island rich enough to live in a twenty-room house— That was just a story, wasn't it?"

"Oh, no!"

"You weren't just pulling our legs?"

"No."

"I told you," Noble said. There was a faint shine of perspiration on his face, as if the beer was starting to work out of him. "But you wouldn't believe *me*— Where does this uncle of yours live, Vince?"

"In Huntington Bay."

"He lives in a *bay?*" Noble looked startled and succeeded in knocking his pack of cigarettes to the floor. While he was retrieving them, Charley said, "Shut up, Noble. I happen to know that's a very exclusive area— You been to his house, Vince?"

"A couple of times."

Charley took a long swallow of beer and settled back. The dream was on him; it showed in his eyes. "I don't suppose—" He hesitated. Then he shook his head. "No. That would be too much."

"What would be too much?" asked Vince.

"Well, I was thinking he's your uncle and all, and one time— just *one* time—in my life it would be nice to set foot in a house like that. But—"

"We're not on the best of terms," said Vince in a blunt voice. "I'm afraid that's out."

Noble said, "You could tell us about the house. You never did finish that time."

"Yeah, because you kept interrupting him!" said Charley.

"See what I've had to live with on my mind?" muttered Noble.

"Well—" Vince frowned. "The last time I was there it was because something had to be done about my mother. I'd been drafted and had just a month to get things settled. Frances was working five days a week in Jamaica and she wanted to stay here. But I didn't want her to, not with my mother the way she was—" Vince shot a hard glance, first at Charley and then at Noble. "You see, my mother is crazy. Crazy insane. She's been that way ever since I was born. Only, the last few years it's been worse."

Noble shook his head. "That's tough."

Charley said, "I'm sorry, Vince. I didn't know." But he sounded faintly annoyed. This wasn't part of the dream.

"Even with Mrs. Molinari in the middle bedroom," Vince continued, his frown deepening, "I didn't want Frances staying on here with my mother when I wasn't here— My mother thought my wife, Frances, was my sister Rose; she was all mixed up. But it hadn't been too bad for Frances and me; we had our nights together, and most of Sundays. We would only see my mother at suppertime, then she and Mrs. Molinari would go upstairs—"

Vince drew a deep breath. "I know this isn't what you want to hear. You'll see, in a minute, why I'm telling it, because it explains

44

why I was in my uncle's house— He sent for me. He said that with me in the Army he didn't want his sister staying on in this house, even with Mrs. Molinari, not even if Frances stayed too. He said we'd have to move my mother to a nursing home and that he'd make up the difference between what my sisters and I had been paying— That solved the problem of my mother. And the problem of Frances was solved when her married sister, Margaret—*her* husband was in Vietnam with the Marines—moved in here with her. All the time I was in the outfit and then in hospitals, Frances and Margaret and Margaret's two kids lived in this house. And every day my Uncle Joe Maggione stopped by to make sure they were all right—"

Vince shook his head. "Whoo-ee— This beer is getting to me. I'm not used to drinking this much. I think I am getting *drunk—*" He pushed himself to his feet. "Anyhow, my bladder's about to bust. I gotta go— How about you, Noble?"

Noble grinned. "I'm good for two, three more cans. I inherited my old man's kidneys along with his good looks."

"Vince—" Charley's glance was as apprehensive as a child's. "You're going to tell us about the house?"

"As soon as I get back— Help yourselves to the beer."

They looked as if they hadn't moved. And, the way they were sitting, they hadn't talked to each other. How often, Vince wondered, did they see each other now that they no longer had the common bond and interest of their war?

Vince sat down, facing them. He had begun to shake and to cover it he lifted his can of beer and didn't put it down until he had drained it. The beer was still reasonably cold and he wished he could pour a whole, fresh, cold can of it down over his aching right leg. He'd made it up and down the stairs just a little too fast.

He'd drunk the beer a little too fast, too, and his voice was gassy: "You . . . thought I was . . . kidding you? Oh, no . . . Vincent Spotafore, the big *mafiosi,* is my uncle . . . my mother's brother. When you saw me . . . on the train . . . yesterday morning . . . man in the seat next to me . . . that was *him—*"

Vince emitted a lengthy belch, bringing a hoot of laughter from Noble. But Charley didn't laugh. Charley's mouth was open and his eyes, fixed on the dream, were dark circles of attentiveness.

The belch cleared Vince's voice. "The house is on Juniper Lane," he said. "The street is actually a private road, about half a mile long, that winds around and dead-ends a hundred yards from the bay. My uncle's house is the only one on the east side of Juniper, and there are so many trees and bushes you can't see the house from the road.

"As I remember it—" Vince paused. The beer really *was* getting to him and he tried to keep above it by shaking his head. "I seem to remember the entrance, two brick pillars with an iron gate, is about halfway to the end of the road. There's a gatekeeper's lodge and if you want in a guy comes up behind the gate, listens to you and looks at you, and then goes back to the lodge to call the house. Once through the gates you drive up a gravel road that curves through the trees, then you see open lawn with the water down to your left and the house ahead of you sitting on a knoll . . .

"The last time I was there, a pair of big German shepherd dogs ran alongside the car all the way from the gate to the house. I was afraid to get out of the car, but a guy came out of the house and said something to the dogs, and they ran off someplace—"

Vince glanced disinterestedly at the cigarette he was smoking, another one he had bummed from Noble, and ground it out in the dish they were all using for an ashtray. He got up, went to the refrigerator and came back with three fresh, cold cans. Pushing two of the cans toward Noble and Charley, he opened the third by pulling the ring from it. He drank a short draft and when he resumed his voice was a bit slower: "All around the grounds, along the road and up to the gate, everywhere except along the beach there's a high, thick rose thorn hedge. I don't know about this myself, but I heard Glo—my sister—tell Frances one time there are fine wires all through that hedge and if anybody tried to cut his way in he'd set off an alarm in the house . . .

"They have some kind of alarms on the beach side, too, and men patrolling down there. If this gives you an idea my uncle doesn't want company, you're damned right. There's a cupola on top of the house with a guard in it, day and night—I remember my uncle bragging about that. Oh, he is some-body, all-right—"

Vince suppressed a hiccup, shaking his head. "It's a big, square

46

house, two stories high. It must have twenty rooms—just what my uncle and his wife need, since they haven't any kids. Some of the upstairs is occupied by the guards: they work three shifts, with eight hours to go to town, eight hours standby on the premises, and eight hours on the job— Uncle Vincent's and Aunt Sophie's apartment is upstairs, too, separated from the rest of the place by a gallery and a staircase that comes down from both sides to join at a landing with stairs down to the entrance hall—" He paused uncertainly.

"What's the matter?" asked Noble. "You gonna be sick?"

"No, I'm alright, I just didn't know how much more you guys want-ed to hear— Okay. Down-stairs is some-thing else. The entrance hall is full of art, like sculp-ture and paint-ings. There's a dining room can seat thir-ty people"—Vince drew a deep breath, let it out and took a small swallow of beer—"and a breakfast room, big kitchen, a den with a fireplace—and one room they really use, the side parlor. It's at the end of the entrance hall and has a bay window that looks down over the lawn to the water. Aunt Sophie sits in there at night and does needlework while Uncle Vincent watches television. He watches all the crime programs and he likes Westerns. Glo—my sister says he hasn't missed an episode of *Gunsmoke* since it started— He has color TV, of course."

Vince could think of nothing more to say, so he stopped. His throat had begun to ache with the unaccustomed talking and smoking, but he was afraid to drink any more beer.

Charley Bennett sat absolutely still, enthralled. His mouth was open and his eyes were wide, staring at the dream. Beside him, Noble was leaning forward, his face and eyes shining.

"Jee-sus Christ," Noble said. "What a pad!"

47

six

A little more than two years ago, before he had entered military service, Vince Maggione hadn't known of the existence of Charley Bennett and Noble S. Wright. They had lived their separate lives, coming by whatever paths to the place where they found themselves. For a few months they had known each other and shared with each other the little reality and sanity there was in a life which for the most part had been unreal and insane. And then they had gone their separate ways until now, in this quiet kitchen, they were fleshed-out ghosts, the living dead from a near yet distant past.

The beer finally got to Noble and he left in search of the bathroom, moving quietly so as not to disturb Charley. The dream was still on Charley; he sat enthralled, picturing in his mind the sumptuous estate and luxurious mansion. Vince, dizzy from so much beer and edgy from nausea, decided it was the cigarettes that were getting to him and, having decided to smoke no more, began to feel a little better. He had half expected Charley or Noble to ask him questions about his Uncle Vincent's house, but he wasn't disappointed that they hadn't. In fact, he would have been rather hard put to furnish more detail.

His recital had certainly filled the bill for Charley and Noble, to whom Vincent Spotafore was only a name printed in the newspapers; Uncle Vincent, and the house he lived in, were objects of disgust for Vince, a disgust he took no pains to conceal. He would have been just as happy to have described Al's modest ranch house in Greenlawn, but that, of course, wouldn't have supplied the morphia Charley needed to turn on his dream.

"Charley!"

Charley's mind came back to the kitchen and a brief look, akin to pain, crossed his face. "What?"

"Please don't get upset. But I do thank you for saving my life."

"What the hell— They gave me a bronze star for that."

"So I was told, at Long Binh hospital."

"Okay. Seeing you alive is thanks enough."

"I don't think so. What kind of trouble have you got?"

Charley's glance hardened. "What's Noble been telling you?"

"He wouldn't tell me anything. He said it was up to you if you wanted to tell me."

"That crazy bastard— What do you want to know for? Seems to me you've got your own troubles."

"I wouldn't have troubles or anything else if it wasn't for you. I have an obligation to you—don't shake your head—whether you realize it or not, I'm in your debt. If you don't let me at least try to help you, it would be a terrible thing— Can't you understand that?"

"I don't get it," said Charley. "And, anyhow, I don't see how you could help me."

"I could try— Do you need money?"

Charley hesitated fractionally. Then he said, "No."

"If you don't need money, why are you working yourself to death?"

"I guess Noble told you that!"

"He didn't have to; I can see. Don't you trust me?"

"Damn it—" For a moment, Charley looked defiant. And then, suddenly, the bluster washed out of him and he was tired, and scared. "I haven't told anybody but Noble," he said in a low, tired voice. "I *had* to tell him. Because there was one day I had nowhere else to turn—"

Charley sighed. "It goes back to maybe a month after The Hill. You were in the hospital, in Long Binh, and last we heard you were starting to get better. We were occupying one of those villages in the Mekong Delta, making friends with the Viets and keeping our eyes open for the Cong— The last letter I'd had from

Blanche, she was going to a little town in Virginia to visit a cousin of hers. This cousin was married to a guy who was making it pretty big with a textile company and Blanche had been to visit them the year before.

"Well, I got a letter from the cousin: while her husband went to his bowling league, she and Blanche had gone to the movies; when they got home, he was already home and in bed. The cousin and Blanche sat downstairs for a while, talking about the movie. Then the cousin went up to bed, and Blanche got into her night-gown and robe and stretched out on the living-room sofa to read a newspaper—and smoke a cigarette.

"The next thing the cousin knew, she heard Blanche screaming her head off— It woke her husband up and both of them ran down the stairs. Blanche was all on fire— The husband grabbed a rug and started beating the flames while the cousin got on the phone to the fire department and the ambulance—"

Charley breathed in and out raggedly. "When they got Blanche to the hospital, they found she had second degree burns over the whole front of her body. She was in so much pain, they had to give her two shots of morphine to knock her out— The letter had been written the next day, and the way I read it they didn't expect Blanche to live.

"I went to the chaplain, the CO, the Red Cross, anybody who could swing enough weight to get me home— I must've made a nuisance of myself because I was sent on five different patrols before I got smart enough to write to my congressman back home.

"In the meantime, the letters were sounding a little better. Blanche was beginning to respond to treatment. Of course, they still had to give her something for pain— A month from the day I wrote my congressman, four months after I got the letter and started making requests, I finally got my orders to go home."

Charley sighed and shook his head. "I lost some time by going straight to the town where Blanche was in the hospital. It was a hell of a place to get to—the nearest airport was fifty miles away— and when I did get there, Blanche had already been discharged and had gone back to New York.

"I realize now I should have telephoned her cousin as soon as I hit San Francisco. But when a man gets in a crack like that he doesn't always think straight. All I knew was I wanted to see her—"

Noble came back into the kitchen and sat down quietly, without Charley taking any notice of him.

"—so I went straight to where I thought she was. The people at the hospital and Blanche's cousin and her husband were very nice to me. I asked at the hospital about the bill and they told me it had been paid. I asked Blanche's cousin's husband about it and he admitted he'd advanced the money—over three thousand dollars. I had about five hundred on me, but he wouldn't take any of it. He said he would be satisfied with my note and I could pay it off whenever I was able. All the interest he asked was what he had been getting on the money in a savings account—"

Charley shook his head again. "I suppose you think, paying off that note is why I've been working my ass off. The truth is, I haven't even been able to pay the interest. When I got to New York, Blanche wasn't at the apartment; people in the building hadn't seen her since she'd left to go to Virginia. So I went looking for her and I finally found her—never mind where. And through my congressman friend I got an emergency discharge plus some other help. But it was too late. It had started in that damned hospital in Virginia. Blanche was hooked. On dope. She couldn't get morphine without a prescription. But she could get heroin, on any street corner in New York City. And she got it."

Charley sat, dry and exhausted, looking at his hands.

"Christ Jesus," said Vince.

Noble didn't say anything. He seemed curiously detached, almost embarrassed. He glanced quickly from Charley to Vince and then looked away.

Vince said, "Charley, I have some money in savings. Half of it belongs to Frances, but the other half is mine. I don't know how much it would cost, but there are hospitals where Blanche could be cured— Certainly it's worth trying. You can't go on like this."

Charley looked up scornfully. "You think I haven't tried? She's been in hospitals. The first one dried her out and she was back on the stuff within a week. The next one put her on Methadone; she was back on heroin the day she got home— She's even been to Synanon; she ran away from there. A psychiatrist at the VA

52

Hospital said it was probably hopeless, that Blanche would probably go along until she died or snapped out of it. He said confirmed addicts just go along, for months or years, until they get hepatitis or infection from a dirty needle. Or get an overdose, or die of malnutrition or heart failure. Or pneumonia. Or, they just stop taking dope. Nobody knows why *that* happens. But it sometimes does, although not very often."

Noble stirred. "She's got a real jones, Vince," he said in a soft, sad voice. "She's up to six bags a day. That's thirty bucks every day in the week. That means Charley has to get up 210 bucks every week, and that comes ahead of rent or food or anything else—210 bucks—" He paused. "Of course, that's at the *retail* price. But, *wholesale—*"

Noble's eyes became steady and his glance was hard, direct. "You got any idea how much profit there is in junk? A nickel bag —that's five bucks—costs the pusher from two to three. But the distributor *he* gets it from pays like fifty cents for it. This means users like Blanche are paying thirty bucks a day for something they could get—with the right connections—for three lousy dollars— You get the drift of what I'm saying, Vince?"

"I understand your arithmetic," said Vince. "But I don't get the point."

"I'll put it another way, then. If Charley only had to lay out three bucks a day, he could handle it easy. He wouldn't have to kill himself, working three, four jobs. He could wait it out 'til either the stuff got her or she snapped out of it— If he can't get the money up, she'll get the stuff somehow. She'll steal for it, whore for it, anything. But she'll get it. And she will, too, if you don't help Charley. Now, while there's still time."

Vince spun angrily around and glared at Noble. "What do you mean, if *I* don't help him? How in hell can I help him that way? I don't know anything about the heroin racket, or anybody in it!"

"No? I thought you said your uncle was Vincent Spotafore."

Mention of the name brought sudden quiet to the room, as if someone had pulled a plug or cut a switch to disconnect a record. And then, with sickening clarity, Vince realized how he had been trapped by his own insistence, and what price he would have to pay to discharge his obligation to Charley Bennett.

At half-past five, Frances came home with supper—stuffed green peppers, a cucumber salad and a bottle of Barberone—in a bag in her arms. The minute she opened the front door she said *"Whew!"* and dashed to the kitchen to open the back door and let in some crisp, cold, fresh air. Then she deposited the bag in an uncluttered place on the sink and returned to the hall to take off her hat and coat. She didn't have to look for Vince; she could hear him, snoring mightily, on the couch in the living room. After she'd surveyed the disaster in the kitchen, she tiptoed through the dining room and stood by the couch for a moment to gaze fondly at him.

His head was propped up by pillows on the arm at one end of the couch and his right leg, supported by more pillows, was stretched out with his foot extending over the opposite arm while his left foot rested on the floor. His right trouser leg was darker than the left; it was damp from crotch to cuff, and he smelled like a brewery.

Frances blushed and hurriedly tiptoed out to attack the mess in the kitchen.

"I thought I'd have to wake you up. But then, you woke up by yourself. And went upstairs. Without even saying hello."

"Okay— Hello! I thought it might be a good idea if I washed up and changed my pants."

"You must've had *some* party. You and your friend drank twenty-two cans of beer— It's a wonder you can stand on your feet. I'm not surprised that you did what you did."

"My *friends* and I drank *twenty-one* cans of beer— What did I do that doesn't surprise you?"

"Your friends? I thought just Charley Bennett—"

"Charley brought Noble S. Wright. You remember, I wrote you about him."

"Noble— Oh! Oh, yes, I remember!"

"Noble's working in an electronics plant. In Port Washington. He looks prosperous— What did I do?"

"Didn't you have an . . . accident?"

"What? Oh!" Vince laughed. "My pants— After they'd gone, it was about one o'clock, my leg was hurting so bad I went out and stood on the back steps and poured a whole can of cold beer

54

—the *twenty-second* can—over my leg, pants and all. It felt damned good, too. I'm going to start carrying beer around with me in one of those portable ice chests. And whenever my leg starts hurting, no matter where I am—even if I'm in church—I'm going to pour a whole cold can of beer on it. Right then and there!"

"Oh, Vince—" She thought about what kind of reaction *that* would bring in St. Rita's, and she giggled. "You're impossible! Did anyone see you? On the back steps, I mean?"

"Sure. Everybody saw me. All the neighbors. CBS sent a TV camera crew to take my picture. I'll be on the news, so we better have supper— What *is* for supper?"

"Vince Maggione, you're drunk! We have stuffed green peppers. And cucumber salad. I was planning on wine. But—"

"We'll have wine," Vince said. "I'm not *that* drunk."

During supper and after, while they were doing the dishes, Vince told her about the reunion. Up to a point, it was easy to tell and he covered in detail those items he thought would interest her. He emphasized the funny things and played down the casualties in Alpha Company. He told about the accident to Charley's wife, but he omitted the tragic end result. He said Charley was working too hard at too many jobs, letting Frances think hospital bills, medical care and the inevitable debt they caused were the reason. He made it a point that both Charley and Noble had thought Al's offer to sell him the business was a good opportunity. He was becoming enthusiastic when he noticed a definite resistance in her, so he reluctantly dropped the subject.

He could not bring himself to tell her what he had agreed to do for Charley. He would tell her, eventually. But not right now.

She cast a swift, appraising glance at the clean kitchen and was apparently satisfied. Then she said, "Vince, before we go upstairs, do you think you could stand another glass of that wine?"

"Okay."

She'd put the wine and two glasses in the refrigerator. She got them out now and brought them to the table.

"Would you mind pouring? You know how I am with a half-gallon jug."

"Delighted!" He grabbed a dish towel and draped it over his

arm. "Zis is ze wine modom ordered, yes? I trust ze table is satisfactory? Ze floor show starts in three minutes!"

Ordinarily she would have responded to his mood. Now she did not; she seemed distant, preoccupied. She sat down, tiredly, and when he had filled her glass she cupped it in her fingers and stared at it.

"I tried, Vince," she said. "I really did."

"What?"

"What you asked me to do. I've been at it, off and on, whenever I could steal the time, all day. But, I'm discouraged."

"What are you talking about?"

"Trying to find the facts about your father's death."

"Oh–" He had forgotten. "What did you find out?"

"How the Claims Department works, the system. *And* the Compensation Laws. *And* how cases are handled— Roughly, there are two classifications of claims. There are those arising from accidents on or allegedly caused by the railroad involving people who are not employees. And then there are those concerning people who are employed by the railroad—or were at the time of the accident."

"My father was an employee. He'd been one for twenty-five years— What's the problem?"

She waved her hand in a tired gesture. "It isn't that simple. Fifty years ago, which would be when your father was first employed by the railroad, if an employee was injured or killed on the job, or received injuries on the job resulting in his later death, the claim was filed with the Workmen's Compensation Board, a state agency. A detailed record of the extent of the injury, causes, time and place, a complete copy of the accident report, amount of the claim, when and how paid and to whom paid— All this was entered in a file and permanently recorded in a ledger.

"But that was fifty years ago. Some time before your father's accident, this method was changed, the system was changed, a lot of changes were made both in the method of handling and recording claims. In place of the detailed record, a card file was substituted. Only the employee's name and the date of the claim were entered on the card. The rest of the information—the nature of the accident, place it occurred, treatment and hospitalization, if any, and final disposition—all this was relegated to the files of the insurance companies issuing the policies required by the State Workmen's Compensation Department. This has been the practice for more than twenty-five years."

Vince nodded. "Okay. What we now have to do is get the date from the card file. How long do they keep those cards?"

"In the case of employees, thirty or more years. With non-employee claims, they're kept only a couple of years."

"You keep saying *non-employees*. Believe me, my father was an employee of the railroad. He never worked for anyone else, not in this country anyhow. It's easy to figure when he died—three months before I was born—that's about twenty-seven years ago. If they keep those cards—alphabetical order?—thirty years, we can get the date. Then, we tackle either the insurance companies or the state—Right?"

She picked up her glass and drank a little wine. Then she put the glass down and, not looking at him, said, "Vince, there isn't any card for your father."

"*What?*"

"There isn't any card. If there ever was one, it has been removed. As soon as I can, I'll go into Personnel. They have the records of retired or deceased employees on microfilm. There are two regular girls handling the records, and both of them are friends of mine. I'm counting on their help because this is an area of absolutely no experience for me. I don't know how long it will take. Or what, if anything, I'll learn. I do know there's no card, no record, nothing in the Claims Department to show that your father was killed on the railroad. Or even that he was an employee."

seven

Vince and Frances had been married in the church in which both of them had been christened and confirmed—the church where Frances' sister, Margaret, had been married two years before—on Saturday morning of the week Vince finished his finals and closed out his first year at St. John's. They didn't have a big wedding, with bridesmaids and flower girls, like Margaret's; Frank McNulty, an honest fireman who lived on his lieutenant's pay, was happy to grant his second daughter's request for a simple church ceremony, announcements instead of invitations, a reception for only the immediate families, and a modest check.

Frances had graduated in the top ten of her class in the one-year secretarial course and it had been an understanding of their courtship that, for the first year anyway, both of them would work. The final assignment in the secretarial course had been the drafting of a job application, with résumé and references. Frances had sent hers to three prospective employers in order of preference: a bank, an insurance broker and a wholesale distributor of appliances. Her application to the railroad had been an afterthought inspired by an accidental meeting with a friend who was employed there. When she and Vince returned from their honeymoon in Asbury Park, New Jersey—a rather difficult week, and not just because it rained practically all the time—the only reply she had was from the railroad. She was asked to come in for an interview Monday morning at ten; when she returned home late that afternoon she was able to tell her husband that she was a *working* wife.

Adjustment to the job, to marriage and to the house turned out to be easier than she had expected. As an extra clerk on the railroad she was never quite sure where she would be working next. Usually her bosses were men who had risen through the ranks to become supervisors; most of them were friendly, and all of them treated her with respect.

The house, which should have been the most complex of all the adjustments, turned out to be the simplest. At times, Mother Maggione thought Frances was her daughter, Rose, and these were the worst times; at other times, neither Frances nor Vince existed. Frances saw her mother-in-law only during the brief interval of supper, after which Mrs. Molinari would gently but firmly guide the fragile old woman up the stairs to the back bedroom; for the next hour, the creak of rockers would be heard, along with subdued voices.

Vince was now working full time in Bennie's service station. He and Frances would have breakfast by themselves. Then she would pack his lunch pail and, leaving the dishes for Mrs. Molinari, walk with him to the corner where she boarded the bus to the railroad station on Atlantic Avenue in time to make the 8:27 train to Jamaica. Returning at night, she would join Vince at the corner for the walk home. After supper, they had an hour of togetherness in the kitchen while they did the dishes and tidied things up; Saturdays, while Vince was working, Frances did the marketing. Saturday nights they went to the movies, often driving long distances out on the Island to see a picture they had discussed and planned for during the week. Sundays, they went to church and, in the afternoon, either drove around in Vince's aging car or else took walks. They saw few friends; unable, for obvious reasons, to entertain at home, they did not want to incur obligations by accepting invitations.

The summer passed pleasantly enough. Frances had made Vince agree that he would return to St. John's in the fall, and not just because they were both concerned about his draft status: she wanted him to make something of himself.

Thus, when the blow fell it was all the more cruel.

60

"I can't understand it," Vince said, reading the notice again. "There must be some mistake."

"Here, let me see that," Frances said.

He handed her the letter. "I've kept them informed," said Vince. "They know I'm a student. And, not only am I married, I'm maintaining a home for my mother!"

"*Student, St. John's University; Marital status, married,*" Frances read. "It's all on here."

"But they can't do that! With all the single guys around who haven't been called— Look at Bennie!"

"Bennie? He couldn't pass a physical if the doctor was drunk."

"All right. Frank Mastretta. He isn't married. He isn't a student. He isn't providing a home for his mother. And he's as healthy as a goat!"

"I don't know about Frank Mastretta. But, Jack Keegan. He's married to my sister. And he has two little children!"

"But he was in the organized reserve, the Marines. He was really asking for it—"

Vince took the notice from her and read it again.

All of a sudden, the meaning of it struck her and she began to weep. "Vince— Oh, my God! What are we going to do?"

"I'm going to the damned draft board. This is crazy! Some stupid clerk has made a mistake— I'll straighten them out!"

Vince went to the draft board and *he* was the one who was straightened out. He went through basic training at Fort Dix, New Jersey, near enough to keep in touch with Frances by telephone, and for a time it seemed that the arrangement at home might work out. However, during his first leave, the drama of Maggione House came to a crashing close in a shower of hot *pasta* sauce. The next day Vince, in a uniform whose camphor smell had been replaced by the odor of fresh drycleaning, stood, cap in hand, in front of his Uncle Vincent Spotafore. And three days later, Mother Maggione and Mrs. Molinari moved out and Margaret Keegan and the twins moved in.

Vince was wakened by the insistent ringing of the telephone, and his first impulse was to let it ring. Opening his eyes, he discovered, was a painful experience: there was entirely too much light. Closing his eyes shut out the light, but it didn't help his head and it didn't stop the telephone's ringing. He opened his eyes again and lifted his head a painful inch from the pillow; when the alarm clock settled in focus he saw the hour was nearly noon.

What was wrong with him, he decided, was probably the biggest hangover he had ever had in his entire life. It took three steady, impersonal, evenly spaced rings of the telephone for him to get his feet on the floor and himself upright. The impartial, unfeeling and obdurate ringing continued as he made it dizzily around the bed, through the door, across the hall and—after a wild, swaying moment in which he nearly fell headlong—down the stairs.

The ringing stopped just as his hand was reaching out for the telephone; when he raised the electronic tormentor to his ear, he heard only the whine of the dial tone.

"Son of a bitch," Vince said.

He dragged himself into the kitchen, to the sink. He turned the cold faucet on full and stuck his head under it. The shock of water brought a gasp from his dry throat, but in a moment it drove the ache from his skull and the fire from his lungs, leaving only the jumpy emptiness in his stomach. He dried his head with two damp dishtowels. Then he filled a glass with cold water and gulped it down.

"Son of a bitch," Vince said again.

In the merciless March sunlight he saw Frances had made her customary preparations for his breakfast. And she'd left a note in the usual place:

Boy, can you snore!

He scowled at the note, rubbed his fingers through the stubble on his chin, and set about the business of breakfast.

He was on his second cup of coffee when a corner of his brain opened up and he remembered what he had promised Charley and Noble he would do.

"Hello?"

He didn't recognize the voice. He said, "I would like to speak to Mr. Spotafore."

"Who?"

"Mr. Vincent Spotafore— This is his residence, isn't it?"

62

"Who are you?"

"I'm his nephew, Vince Maggione."

"I dunno— Wait a minute."

The man at the other end must have covered the mouthpiece with his hand because Vince couldn't hear anything. Maybe a minute went by. Then a new voice came on.

"Vince? This is Frank— Frank Mastretta. How are you?"

"Not bad. Yourself?"

"Okay. I heard you were back. I was talking to Louise—Monday? Anyhow, she'd heard— You out now? All discharged? Everything?"

"Everything. Is Uncle Vincent there?"

"He was just finishing his lunch. Teddy went to get him— You, uh, know how Uncle Vincent is about lunch. He ought to be— Oh, here he is—" Frank must have lowered the telephone or turned his head away because Vince heard his voice saying, distantly, "It's Vince Maggione."

A click. Then, "What do you want?"

"I want to see you."

"*You* want to see *me?*"

"Yes."

"You didn't act like it, day before yesterday. What do you want?"

"I can't discuss it over the telephone."

"Huh— So, you want to see me. When?"

"As soon as possible. This afternoon."

"What? What the hell is so damned important you couldn't tell me day before yesterday? All right, *all right*— You have a car?"

"No."

"You don't have a car, you can't come here— Forget this afternoon, and I can't see anybody tonight, tomorrow or Sunday— Maybe I can work out something for Monday."

"Tell me where, and what time, and I'll be there."

"Where I'm going to be, and when, is something *I* don't discuss over the telephone. You'll hear from me—I'm not so hot about seeing you, not after the day before yesterday. So whatever you want to see me about, it had better be important. And I will see just you. None of your friends or relatives. You understand?"

"Yes."

Vince replaced the telephone and for a long moment looked at himself in the diamond-shaped mirror. Then, a lot faster than he wanted to, he climbed the stairs. By the time he had reached the bathroom, his breakfast had become acid in his mouth, held back only by his lips and the fingers he was using to keep them closed.

eight

When Vince had said good-by to Charley Bennett and Noble S. Wright, he had been dizzy from beer and the increasing pain in his leg, and he had been frightened by the promise he had given them. It had been left that he would put the question to his Uncle Vincent in a businesslike manner, and that within a week Charley would call Vince to find out whether or not they had a deal. Noble, who had grown up in the center of the illicit narcotics trade in Harlem, had said that heroin in its pure form could be purchased wholesale at $600 per ounce. Even as little as an ounce, when cut with milk sugar or quinine and diluted to the form in which it was sold on the streets, would provide a supply sufficient to carry Blanche Bennett's "jones" for more than half a year.

Charley had said, with a solemn handshake, that as soon as the price was established and a contact could be arranged, he would take over. "You'll be out of it, then," Charley had said. "In that price range, there'll be no problem about the money. And either Noble or I will make the contact to pick up the stuff and pay the money, so you'll be clean."

With that, they had left. Vince didn't watch them go—before they had reached the sidewalk, he had been sitting on the bottom step of the stairs with his leg stretched out and his jaw rigid from pain. The pain was an immediate problem; what he had promised them was a problem that could be deferred to a more convenient time.

He had guessed that they saw little of each other, now that they were in civilian life; if he had watched them leave his house, he would have been sure that his guess was correct. Like once but no longer intimate friends departing a funeral, Charley and Noble had paused only briefly in the street before leaving in opposite directions.

Vince would have been sure about them because he would have accepted their actions, as he did them, at face value. It would not possibly have occurred to him that much of what had transpired in the past three hours had been anticipated by them and their part in it had been carefully rehearsed.

Even their leaving his house to go separate ways had been staged, although not altogether for his benefit. His failure to witness this touch of their artistry in no way lessened the calculated effect they produced.

Under the circumstances, it was just as well that Vince did not have this, too, to later remember.

Charley Bennett's direction took him to the corner where Bennie's gas station was. A half-dozen blocks to his right was Atlantic Avenue and a block beyond it, on Fulton, was the elevated structure of the rapid transit system which would take him to Jamaica and a train for Mineola. At the corner itself he could have taken a bus to speed his passage elsewhere. However, he neither turned right nor remained; without hesitation, he crossed the street to his left, heading south, and began to walk with the steady, ground-covering gait he had learned as a boy in upstate New York and later employed as an infantryman in Asia.

He walked erectly, with shoulders back and arms swinging in cadence with the motion of his feet. And as he walked he seemed to take no notice of the people who were sharing the sidewalk with him, or of the traffic in the avenue, the parked cars, the jammed together buildings, the litter. He did not act like a man walking in a strange place. His actions were those of one who knew where he was, and where he was going.

When he had walked for perhaps ten minutes and had reached the wide thoroughfare of Linden Boulevard, he turned west, toward the city. The sidewalk was uncertain here, broken in places and narrowing in others between patches of high, dead weeds. After several blocks of this he came to a mixed area of industrial buildings, narrow houses—some occupied and some boarded up— in a region where the old was slowly yielding to the new. His eyes quickened as he saw, in the block ahead, a small gray van parked at the curb.

At this point, Linden Boulevard curved to the south and the van stood at the edge of a triangle formed by two streets which intersected on a bias and had been left in an unfinished state. Evidently it was a place where countless wrecked cars had been done to death; the surrounding bits of pavement and stretches of ground were black with their blood and mounds of their unsaleable entrails were scattered in ignominy.

The van was one of the box-like models favored by owners and operators of service businesses, such as dry cleaners, and used in quantity by utility companies, particularly the New York Telephone Company. The van's gray paint was apparently an undercoating, for the legally required weight information was crudely scrawled in chalk on the door to the driver's seat.

Across the blackened intervening space of a dozen yards, in the point of land between the intersecting streets, stood a concrete block building which at first glance appeared to be abandoned. At its narrow end it was one story in height, with broken, rag-stuffed casement windows above eye level; in the wider portion a rusted, segmented steel garage door was rolled down with No PARKING printed on it in amateurish foot-high letters. Joined to the side of the low, garage-like structure was a two-story building thrown together from a mixture of concrete blocks, tile and brick; at some time in the past it had been covered with stucco which had since come off in huge, irregular areas. The two-story part was, or once had been, a residence; in the wall on either side of the door its windows were solidly boarded up. In the upper floor, however, the windows on the street side were revealed intact albeit shade-drawn; in the side visible above the garage roof, a window was open and brightly colored curtains stirred in the breeze.

Charley Bennett walked past the gray van, giving it a casual glance. The driver's seat, the only visible portion of the interior, was empty and the windows were rolled up. When he was abreast of the sagging steps of the structure, which made him think of a giant pointed-toe shoe, he stopped and glanced quickly around. Forty yards away, on Linden Boulevard, traffic was moving in a steady stream; on the intersecting streets, nothing stirred. Casually he turned, retracing his steps until he had again passed the van. Then he crossed behind it and came up to the driver's door on the street side.

He rapped on the door twice, counted silently to five, and rapped two more times.

From the van's dark interior, a hand reached out over the seat back and released the door latch.

Charley cast a casual glance up and down the street. Then he climbed in behind the van's steering wheel and closed the door. From the floor in back of the seat he was greeted by a plaintive voice: "Where the hell have you been? You've been gone more than three hours!"

"You know where I've been. And I told you how long it would take— We had to be sociable. We couldn't just get what we went for and then leave. We had to drink his beer."

"The way you smell, you must've had your share of beer!" The man on the floor changed from a squatting to a sitting position. "I don't suppose you brought *me* any!"

"Now, that would've been smart," said Charley. "I guess I should've said to him, *You don't mind if I just take a couple of these cold ones to an old friend of yours? He wanted to come with us to join the reunion. But we weren't sure how strong your heart is, not after all you've been through—*"

"Oh, why don't you shut up! Where the hell is Noble?"

"He'll be here soon enough, he took a cab. He's probably in the house, or maybe the garage. What's bugging you?"

"I'm hungry, damn it! And just try lying on your ass in this truck for three hours and see how *you* like it!"

"You're not on the floor. You've got an air mattress— Here he is now."

Noble came out of the door between the boarded-up windows and moved lightly down the sagging steps. In his right hand he carried a dispatch case and as he stepped along he glanced at the watch on his wrist. He looked like a salesman who had completed a call and was now contemplating lunch. Then, as if noticing the van for the first time, he came diagonally toward it.

Noble slid into the seat beside Charley and said, "Okay, let's go. Back on Linden to Pennsylvania Avenue, then right. We'll stop at the place a few minutes before we head back to Jamaica."

"For Christ's sake," the man on the air mattress objected, "we're not going back there *again?* When do I get something to eat?"

"As soon as we reach Jamaica, you'll eat," Noble said.

"Yeah," said Charley. "You'd better not be seen in this neighborhood, even with your new color hair, your store teeth and dark glasses. There's too much chance of somebody being around to recognize you."

"That's right," Noble said.

The man in the back of the van said something under his breath. Then he laughed. "Hell! One of these days I'm going to walk in on a couple of people I could mention. And will *they* ever drop their teeth!"

"You do," said Noble, "and you'll wind up wishing you were as dead as you're supposed to be right now."

nine

"The place" was a wide, windswept waste of land that lay within sight of the world's most imposing skyline and within sound of the world's busiest airport. Its surface was etched with vacant streets and defiled by sagging structures, rotting trailers, wrecked and abandoned cars, cast-off household goods. An area of daytime decay and nighttime violence, it was bisected by Pennsylvania Avenue, the artery connecting Shore Parkway to the south with the cemeteries—the cities of the dead—to the north. Here the alpha and omega of Pennsylvania Avenue's uncertain paving swayed and buckled over the heaps of garbage it had been built on to form an undulating memorial to political perfidies. A curbed, concrete center strip with a row of drunken lamp posts divided the highway and served to prevent the drivers of opposing automobiles from crashing head-on into each other.

Charley Bennett slowed the van at a break in the divider strip, turned left into the opening and waited until two cars had gone bouncing by in the northbound lane. Then he let in the clutch and gunned the accelerator and the little van shot across into the mouth of what had been intended for a street but was now a weed-grown, rutted path. A hundred yards in, behind a stripped car and a rusting pile of bedsprings, cans and gutted refrigerators, he pulled over the crumbling curb to stop in back of a pair of overturned and unwheeled truck trailers.

"Okay," said Charley. He shut off the ignition.

71

Eddie Durfee pushed open the right half of the rear door and crouched a moment, stretching and scratching his stomach. Then he stepped out and moved around gingerly, flexing his leg muscles. He had been wearing dark-tinted glasses in the van's interior and now, in the sunlight, he was squinting. He was a little taller than Charley Bennett, nearly as tall as Noble S. Wright. He was as slim as Noble, with a flat stomach, although his bones were larger than Noble's. His hair, naturally an undistinguished sandy color, had been dyed to an even less distinguished mouse brown. He was very careful about not letting the natural color of his hair show at the roots and so washed it two or three times a week with a special soap which contained the dye Noble had chosen for him. When he smiled, his teeth were perfect except for the two gold crowns covering his canine teeth. The California dentist who had made his dentures had added this touch and Eddie had finally come around to thinking the gold crowns made the teeth look like they were his own. He had another upper plate without crowns and this, with a different hair color, also helped alter his appearance. When he was working on a "project" he kept his dentures in a box in his pocket and the result added a good fifteen years to his face, which was a pretty good way to confuse possible witnesses.

Now Eddie lighted a cigarette and, taking a deep inhale, walked around to where Noble had rolled down the window. Shifting his weight from one foot to the other and scratching his middle, he exhaled a stream of smoke and asked:

"What did you find out?"

Noble took a flat, oblong, black plastic case from his inside breast pocket.

"Any time you're ready," said Noble.

"Yeah. Last time you used that thing, all we could hear was noise, or nothing."

"That time was different. I was experimenting with it in my pocket. This time, Vince made it easy. While he was upstairs in the bathroom, I stuck it on the underside of the kitchen table, right next to where he was sitting— Ready?"

Charley wrapped his arms around the steering wheel and leaned forward as Noble propped the recorder on the dash. Then Noble pushed a lever and, after some seconds of scraping and clanking sounds, the gassy voice of Vince Maggione filled the van:

"You . . . thought I was . . . kidding you? Oh, no . . . Vincent Spotafore, the big mafiosi, is my uncle . . ."

"It doesn't sound right," Eddie objected loudly. "It's too slow!"

"Shut up," Noble said. "Wait 'til he belches— There!"

The recorded voice of Vince Maggione gathered smoothness and volume and purpose as it described the feudal castle of Uncle Vincent and the lengths to which Uncle Vincent had gone to protect his privacy. The three listened with varying attitudes. Eddie looked impressed. Charley sat frozen: a different dream was on him now.

Noble listened as much to the tonal quality of the recording as to the words Vince was speaking.

When the voice came to an end, Noble shut off the machine. "Well?"

"Christ, Noble, that's good!" said Charley.

"Yes. Well, what do you think?"

Eddie said, "You heard him mention the beach? Both times when I was out in the boat, there was a guy. He kept crossing from one side to the other along the beach."

Noble nodded. "Okay. What else?"

"The house *is* square, with a cupola on top. I *thought* I spotted somebody up there— Remember? I told you about it— I don't think *he* spotted *me*. I was making out like I was fishing. It was a fairly warm day and there were a couple of other boats out there, too."

"That could be important," said Noble. "If the hedge is wired, like Vince says, there's probably a whole alarm system and the control center could be up in the cupola— Anything else?"

Eddie thought for a minute. Finally he said, "I didn't see any dogs."

"You wouldn't see 'em," said Charley. "They're on the road, between the gate and the house. You wouldn't be able to see the road from a boat out on the water— What?"

"I don't like the idea of those dogs," Eddie said.

"I think I know how to handle them," said Noble. He turned to look at Charley. "When you saw Vince on the train at Hicksville, was Spotafore with him like he said?"

73

"He sure was. He was sitting on the aisle; Vince was next to the window. I don't think I would've recognized Vince; I recognized *him* from the pictures in that paper we have."

"Did he see you?"

"I'm sure he didn't. He wasn't looking my way. When Vince yelled, I was in a crowd pushing toward the door. I heard my name, and I knew who he was, all right. I was some surprised. I didn't know he was out of the hospital. Remember, I'd been trying to figure out how we could go see him without him getting suspicious— Well, there was Vince looking at me and yelling, and Spotafore looking at him like he was crazy. Before the old man had a chance to see what Vince was yelling at, I was past the window. I kept going, too, and squeezed into the next car."

"Good," said Noble. "Okay, we'll put this together with the rest we've got and tomorrow or Sunday, I'll draw a map. When does the van get painted?"

"Seven A.M. tomorrow," Eddie answered. There was an odd, dancing light in his eyes. "That place in Hollis. I'm going to get there at five-thirty and finish my sleep then so I'll be first in line."

"You've got the color?" Charley demanded.

"Yeah. Noble checked their sample chips against a real N. Y. Telephone truck. I've got the sample in my pocket."

"How about the other stuff?"

"All set," said Noble. "Aunt Rachel told me you'd left the side panel covers in the garage. Before we put the lettering on them, are you sure they'll work?"

Charley grinned. "Like a charm. They're vinyl, and you can roll 'em up. When they're on, you can't tell they aren't paint on the body itself. And the pressure-sensitive tape holds 'em on so tight you need a plumber's helper to get 'em off."

Noble nodded, turning it over in his mind. Then he said, "Sounds like Project Two is shaping up. Anything new on Project One?"

"I'm still keeping contact with my friend, the miserable son of a bitch," Eddie said. "I told you, he wants twenty-five per cent."

"And *we* told *you* he gets ten or nothing," Noble said. "He doesn't have to lift a finger and he gets ten to twenty grand— Okay, we'll head back now."

74

Eddie shrugged, then he turned, walked back and climbed into the van. Charley started the engine, listened to it for a moment and nodded his head in approval. Then he backed into the rutted path and drove out to Pennsylvania Avenue. Scattered traffic was moving in both lanes, the cars bucking and swaying on the uneven pavement. In the northbound lane there was a police car. The uniformed cop who was driving it wasn't chasing anyone; his roof flasher was off and he was taking his time.

The cop spotted the little gray van in the side road and scowled at it as he drove past.

"That's right, you bastard," Charley said. "Take a good, long look. Tomorrow this baby will be Bell Telephone green!"

Charley Bennett let himself into the gloom of the shade-drawn apartment and quietly closed the door.

"Hon?" he called softly.

There was no answer; as his eyes adjusted to the semidarkness, he could see her stretched out on the sofa-bed. She was still in her nightgown and robe and it looked as if she hadn't moved since he'd left her, lying there, at nine in the morning. He knew, though, that she'd moved. She would have gotten up, two or three times, to go to the bathroom which had become the center of her life. Keeping her implements, including matches, in the bathroom, and eating a minimum of two meals a day were the only requirements on which Charley was insistent.

He didn't want her to set fire to the place. And he did not want her to die of starvation.

Distantly, a dog howled and Charley turned a scowling face to the shade-drawn window. The dog persisted in his plaint and, close by, another dog answered. Suddenly, down in the street directly beneath the window, a car started up with a shattering roar of exhaust and screeching, rubber-shedding whine of tires.

"That hot-rod bastard!" Charley fumed. "One of these days I'm going to kill him!"

Her arm moved, her head rolled and her eyes opened. Her eyes, opaque and liquid and shining yellowly, fixed on him.

"Oh," she said. "I was having the most beautiful dream—"

75

"That's my sweet baby," said Charley. Awkwardly he moved to her side and with clumsy tenderness patted her hair.

"Mmmmm—"

Her eyes closed and she slipped back into the dream.

Charley turned away from her and stood for a moment. His fists were clenched and his mouth was working. Then he quietly crossed the room and sat in his easy chair. Bending down with an effort he loosened the laces and kicked off his shoes. Straightening, he hooked his finger in the knot of his tie and pulled it down. Then, unbuttoning his collar, he leaned back and closed his eyes.

ten

It was after six o'clock when Frances got home. She was obviously tired and edgy. Without preamble, she said:

"I called you this afternoon, twice. Where were you?"

Vince put the evening paper aside. "I was down at the corner, talking to Bennie. And Uncle Joe. I was there most of the afternoon— Did you call me around noon?"

"No."

"Somebody called me. It woke me up. By the time I got down to the phone, they'd hung up."

"It wasn't me. I worked in the Passenger Department all day long. And a half-hour overtime. There's a fare increase coming up, they must've decided on it in a hurry and there was a lot of stuff to get out. I missed my morning coffee break and didn't have lunch until two o'clock. Which practically shot the afternoon. He *did* send upstairs for coffee at four. But I didn't see any of the girls in Personnel. And I didn't get a chance to call them— Do you mind if we go out to supper? I didn't buy anything to cook, I just didn't feel up to it."

"Of course I don't mind— I guess my snoring kept you from going to sleep."

"Not from *going* to sleep. You woke me up about five times."

"Why didn't you punch me?"

"I did."

Frances had to go up to the bathroom. When she came down

she brought Vince a necktie and the tweed jacket she'd bought for him while he was still in the hospital. He put them on, along with his reversible topcoat and his only hat, and they walked to Angelo's. It was a small, family-type restaurant that, as far as Vince knew, had been in East New York forever. The proprietor was the grandson of the founder and Vince knew him through servicing his car, a Cadillac.

Tony Angelo himself seated them at a corner table and took their order for minestrone, steak sandwiches and a bottle of Chianti. The place was almost full, the atmosphere was bright with the hum of conversation and laughter, and one of Frances' favorite numbers, *Tangerine,* was coming softly from the Muzak system.

"We ought to do this more often," said Vince as he spread a white napkin across his lap.

Frances nodded her head in time to the music. "I was thinking the same thing. I wish we could afford it."

"Once I'm back on my feet, there's no reason why we can't."

"There's an awful lot to be done first, though— Who do you suppose it was that called you this noon?"

"I don't know—Charley Bennett, maybe."

"Why would he call you?"

"I'm not sure it was Charley. I don't know who it was."

"But you thought it was Charley Bennett."

"Why not? He was at the house yesterday, he and Noble, for three hours. We drank a lot of beer. He works nights, so if he was going to call me it would be some time around noon— The other time he called me, it was after ten."

"Yes. But that doesn't explain *why* he would call you."

"Well, damn it, I don't know. He might call me to thank me for the beer. Or say it was good seeing me again, or tell me he had a hangover, or anything— What's bugging you?"

A waiter brought the minestrone, a napkin-covered basket of rolls and a plate of antipasto. Frances sat quietly until he had served them. Then she said:

"Nothing's bugging me. I just hope you and Charley aren't planning to go into business together."

"Oh— No."

"But you did discuss it with him. You told me you did."

78

"Frances, for heaven's sake!"

"Vince, I know you. You're keeping something back from me— I don't mind your going into business, if that's what you really want to do. You know I would rather you finished college. Even if you felt it necessary to make some arrangement with your uncle to finance it— Of course, I'd much rather you didn't get obligated to *him,* I'm sure we could manage without his help. But, if you want to go into business, if that's what you really want to do—"

"Will you please eat your soup before it gets cold?"

"I *am* eating it— Vince, I know how you are about obligations, you won't rest until they're paid. That's why I don't like to think of you becoming obligated to your uncle. Because you'd keep *your* end of the bargain no matter what *he* did. And that is why I don't want you to get any further obligated to Charley Bennett, by going into partnership with him. You *already* feel obligated to him. And if you went into a deal with him he would have an unfair advantage over you."

"Frances, what the hell do you know about Charley Bennett? You've never even seen him! And, believe you me, I *am* obligated to him. If it wasn't for Charley, I would not be here right now."

"I don't see why you feel so obligated to him. I thought that was what men did in war, saved each other, helped each other—"

"Sure, that's what they do. Only in my case it was different. Charley had a choice. There were two of us there, and Charley chose me— Let's get something straight. I am *not* planning on going into business with Charley Bennett! And now, if you don't mind, I'd like to finish my dinner without hearing any more about going into business. Or Charley Bennett!"

Saturday morning they slept late; Frances had shut off the alarm and there were no telephone calls. They had both been very tired on going to bed and only by the narrowest of margins had avoided a real battle. In the morning Vince, the first to awake, lay still for a long time, trying to reconstruct the events leading up to last night. She had been obviously overtired, which made her cross and aggressive. And he had painted himself into a corner: how could he tell her now what kind of "business" he was really going into with Charley Bennett? Possession of narcotics was a felony. Frances knew this; everybody knew it. It was because of the "Family's" trade in narcotics that Frances held his Uncle Vincent in contempt. The money-lending she could ignore on the grounds that people knew what they were getting into when they borrowed from him. The numbers racket was an unimportant nuisance that gave little people a gleam of hope. Even prostitution was understandable: if there weren't men eager to pay them, there wouldn't be girls available to satisfy their lusts. But, *narcotics* . . .

Vince stared at the ceiling, not wanting to think, yet unable to avoid it. It was easy enough to rationalize when you told yourself you were doing this for a friend, one who had saved your life. But when you looked at it through different eyes, it was something else . . .

Frances got up suddenly and went into the bathroom. She was in there a long time and when she finally came back into the bedroom she looked crushed.

"Well, Mr. Maggione, you are very definitely not a father."

"Oh? That's a relief."

"For *you*— Yes, *that* way it's a relief for me, too. But I'll not be my best for the balance of today. Or tomorrow— Why are you looking at me like that? Are you still mad?"

"No, I'm not still mad. How was I looking at you?"

"I don't know. Different. The way you look at me when you have something on your mind. And you're afraid to bring it up because you haven't figured how to get around me."

"I guess you're the expert on Vince Maggione."

"I'm the only expert we have around here. What's on your mind?"

"I— Damned if I'll tell you!"

"Mad, mad— Maybe you don't have to. Maybe I know."

"Okay, since you know so much. What?"

"You want to buy a car."

"What in hell gave you *that* idea?"

"Don't deny you've been wanting to. And you told me you spent practically all yesterday afternoon with Bennie. *And* Uncle Joe."

"Damn it— What's wrong with buying a car?"

"Nothing, if we can afford it. And if it won't damage your leg to drive it."

"Listen, my leg is coming along okay!"

"And I want to keep it that way, too. If you feel we can afford it, and if you'll ask the doctor when you go there Wednesday, and if he says it's all right for you to drive a car, then I won't object to your buying one."

"Well— Okay, then."

"You'll ask the doctor?"

"For Christ's sake, *yes!*"

"Of course, I think your first thoughts and plans should be about returning to St. John's. A car won't make that much difference. In fact, it might make things easier for you in getting to and from school. But, as I told you last night, if you want to go into business instead, if you *really* want to, I won't stand in your way. As long as you go in by yourself, and not with someone else, like Charley Bennett—"

"I thought we weren't going to mention him again!"

"I—I'm sorry, Vince. I didn't mean to, honestly. It just slipped out—"

After she got back into bed, it was a minute or two before he realized she was weeping, and it took him that much longer to get over his anger and put his arms around her. After a while she became quiet and he began thinking again, *What in Christ's name am I going to do?*

eleven

The house directly across the street from the Maggiones was occupied by Aurelio Montalbano, who worked in a liquor store on Liberty Avenue and walked home for lunch. Mr. Montalbano had lived in his house longer than the Maggiones had lived in theirs and he remembered many things about the area, including the days of Prohibition. Thus when he arrived home, at five minutes past noon on Monday, he saw the black Lincoln Continental, with two men in the front seat and one man in the rear, standing with its motor running in front of the Maggione house. He had not recognized the two in front, but he knew the man in the back seat well enough even though he hadn't seen him on this street since Crazy Mother Maggione was taken away. He wondered what *this* visit meant; he wondered, but he didn't want to know badly enough to investigate further.

Mrs. Montalbano, however, had different ideas. She was in the living room, peering around the edge of the drawn window shade. His first impulse, which he nearly choked on, was to shout at her; his next, which he controlled, was to smack her across the rear and drag her away from the window. His final impulse, which he obeyed, was to wait. In two minutes, she let go of the shade and came away from the window. She was looking pleased with herself. She knew Aurelio expected her to say something so she said, "Vince got into the car and they drove off."

Tony Angelo himself seated them at a secluded table and laid a fresh cloth for them. Then he personally inspected the water tumblers and immediately caused them to be removed along with the everyday utensils; in a moment, they were replaced with crystal goblets and polished silver. With the same obsequious speed, menus and wine lists appeared and, while Vince wasn't feeling the least bit hungry, he agreed to his Uncle Vincent's order of filet mignon for both of them. Uncle Vincent, who did not believe in drinking in the middle of the day, snatched the wine list from Vince's hands and scowlingly returned it, together with his own, to Tony Angelo. He didn't consult Vince, either, about a choice of salad and vegetables. When you dined with Uncle Vincent, you ate what he ordered for you.

One of the men had remained in the car. The other, who had preceded them for a look around before motioning them in, was seated at the bar where he could watch both the front door and the entrances to kitchen and rest rooms without taking his eyes from the bar mirror. His order was a glass of water and the bartender served it with as much unction as if it had been champagne.

Uncle Vincent observed Vince's reaction and his mouth twisted in a smile as he said, "I travel first class."

You also travel scared, Vince said to himself. But he nodded politely and said, "So I see."

From then on, until he had consumed the last scrap of his food and finished a second cup of coffee, Uncle Vincent said not one word. While the waiter was removing the remains, Tony Angelo came to Vince's side.

"Something wrong with the filet?"

"Oh no. It was delicious. I just don't eat much in the middle of the day."

"Ah!" Tony Angelo sounded relieved. Then he left.

Uncle Vincent leaned forward, his head cocked a little to the right. There was a quizzical look on his face. "All right, you said you wanted to see me. What's on your mind?"

"I— I need something— For a friend. It's something I can't get, not without help."

"So. Now you need my help. This *friend:* Is it a man friend, or a woman friend?"

"Man. I knew him in the service. He—he saved my life."

"Oh, *that* one! You saw him when we were on the train. It didn't take him long to find you. What is this 'something' you need for this friend?"

"It's—it's his wife. She's an addict. She has to have heroin. A lot of it. And it's breaking him up to keep her supplied."

Uncle Vincent drew back as if Vince had suddenly displayed a knife or a pistol. His head turned and he glanced agitatedly around the restaurant, at the other diners and at the bar patrons. When one of the waiters started toward him, he stopped the man short with a curt shake of his head. His glance jumped to the body-guard who was sitting up straight, half turning while watching him in the bar mirror. Then he looked at the table and everything on it as if hunting a hidden microphone. And then he directed his hot, angry eyes to Vince and said:

"You goddamned stupid son of a bitch!"

"What?"

"You heard me— I should have your goddamned head busted for this!"

"Listen, I didn't—"

"It couldn't be a loan. Oh, no. It couldn't be a job, or maybe speak to somebody to get something cleared up. No. It has to be *this*. And *you* have to say it in *words!*"

"Okay, forget it. Thanks for the lunch—"

"Sit down, you. And listen to me. This is a word you *never* say to me. You understand? Even if you need it for yourself and you are dying! You hear me?"

"Okay. I'm sorry I mentioned it. I don't—"

"You're sorry! It's a good thing they know me in this place. You know how many people would like to hang that on me? You got any idea how many there are, just waiting for the chance? What the hell made you think— Wait a minute. *Who put you up to this?"*

"Nobody put me up to it. It was my idea. I thought I could help my friend."

"Friend! Jesus, Mary and Joseph— You stay sitting where you are until I have left this place. You can walk home. And don't worry about the check. I'll pay it."

Vince sat where he was while his uncle got up, took a crisp twenty from his wallet and dropped it on the table. Then, without a backward glance, his uncle stalked from the restaurant with his bodyguard behind him.

Vince had been back in his house for an hour when the telephone rang. Fearing that it might be Charley Bennett, he slowed his steps to the hall and then stood in front of the telephone for a time. But the ringing persisted and at last, hesitantly, he answered:

"Hello?"

"Mr. Maggione?" The voice was one he had never before heard.

"Yes."

"Mr. Vince Maggione?"

"*Yes!*"

"Take it easy, buddy— I understand you're in the market to make a purchase—for a friend?"

"I— Oh! Who—"

"We don't mention who. And we don't get specific. You understand what I mean?"

"I think so. What's your proposition?"

"That depends. How much do you want to buy?"

"An ounce."

"An ounce, pure?"

"Yes."

"Now, we assume you know what you're talking about. How much do you expect to pay?"

"Six hundred."

"Six? You've got to be kidding! It's worth ten bills. A grand."

"Not to me it isn't."

"You got another source? Why bother me?"

"I didn't bother you. *You* called *me.*"

"Take it easy, buddy— Only six hundred? I'll have to see what I can do. When are you home?"

"Every day this week but Wednesday."

"This week! Anywhere near that price, I'll need more time. What about next week?"

"As far as I know, I'll be home in the mornings."

"If you could do better it would take less time."

"Better? Oh—no."

"Six is the best you can do? How about splitting it down the middle? Eight?"

"No."

A long pause. Then, "You'll maybe hear from me, next week. Thursday."

Vince replaced the telephone. He felt slightly ill. For no reason at all he remembered Bishop Loughlin High School study hall and the "Ms"—*Maggione, Vincent; Mastretta, Louise; McNulty, Frances*— That was the tight little group they had sat in, and Frances told him how many blushes she'd wasted thinking he was looking at *her* until she realized what he was looking at was something inside himself. Louise— Well, all the boys looked at Louise— It hadn't taken Uncle Vincent long to set things in motion; just about an hour. The hypocritical son of a bitch. Vincent Spotafore . . .

Vince felt slightly ill. And, for the first time, he was afraid.

At ten o'clock the next morning, Charley Bennett phoned. Vince had been up long enough to have nearly finished reading the *Times*.

"You really think you can get it?" asked Charley.

"I'm afraid so."

"Jesus, Vince, I'm sorry about this, I really am. I know I shouldn't've asked you to do it. Maybe you'd better forget it."

"It's too late now. He said I would *maybe* hear from him, next week, Thursday— He'll call me, all right. You should've heard his voice— And we'll get it at our price, just as Noble said we would."

"Well— When he calls you, remember Noble or I take it from there. We'll have the money ready and we'll arrange the pick-up. You'll be out of it—" Charley inhaled quickly and his voice took on a different note. "You haven't asked me anything about Blanche, and God knows I don't want to burden you with it. But, since you are doing this for me, you have a right to know if you're just getting a monkey on your back; if, six months from now, when this supply runs out, will I be around again— It isn't going to be like that. I'm only buying some time for myself, Vince. I've *got* to get some rest and back on my feet again so I can think straight— Six months from now, if she hasn't either kicked the habit or died, I'll have her committed. I mean it."

"Why don't you do it now?"

"Vince, as God is my judge, I can't. I haven't got the strength— Right now, I'm beat. If I can cut back to just one job for six months, I can make it— Do you see that, Vince?"

"I—think I do, yes."

"I'm grateful to you, Vince. And I'm sorry I got you into it— I don't have a telephone, but you can reach me or leave a message at the paper. And in any event, I'll call you a week from Friday."

On Wednesday, Vince completed the last of his weekly visits with the psychiatrist at the VA Hospital. The visit was routine, as the rest of them had been; the half dozen in the group and the less than ten minutes for individual interview reflected the hospital's current state of understaff. Vince's ten minutes were important, however, because he had promised Frances he would not buy a car until the doctor gave him permission. He came away from the interview with a conditional approval: in exchange for the privilege of owning and driving an automobile, which could cause him to forego walking to the point that his leg would atrophy, he was to play a game. He was to construct a chart, a piece of cardboard with lines and squares. In a row down the left side, he was to put all the places he was now walking to; across the top, he was to put the days of the week. Then, each day when he had completed that particular walk, he was to check it off, and when that day's chart was full he was entitled to one ride in his automobile. Vince agreed, and on Friday bought a three-year-old Rambler station wagon from Uncle Joe Maggione. He gave Frances her first ride in it on Saturday. Sunday night they drove to Baldwin and had supper at Carl Hoppl's and when they returned home, Vince put the car in the garage.

He was on his way into the house, through the kitchen, when he remembered the chart and his promise to the doctor. It was too late to do anything about it then. He promised himself that first thing Monday morning, after he'd finished reading the *Times,* he would make the chart and put it up on the wall beside the back door.

Monday morning, Vince put a coat of wax on the Rambler and the chart slipped his mind. He was, however, working on it in earnest after breakfast Tuesday when Frank Mastretta telephoned him, with the news that Uncle Vincent Spotafore had been kidnaped.

part two

twelve

The small green van, with the familiar *New York Telephone Company* on its side panels, the Bell insignia on its cab doors and an extension ladder strapped to the rack on its roof, slowed at the sign that said PRIVATE ROAD—NO THOROUGHFARE. Its directional signal blinked on and, splashing through puddles, the van turned into Juniper Lane. The entrance was discouragingly narrow, and Juniper Lane itself was slightly more than a single car in width, a tarmac road with a high center crown. There had been intermittent heavy rain during the day and water was coursing in the gutters and spilling over on to the grass borders wherever twigs and leaves had collected to form temporary dams. The road slanted up to a crest before dropping off toward the bay; the crest was not visible because of the curve in the road and the trees which arched over it. The trees were heavy with the rain and long, slanting drops were falling from their buds and branches to strike the road and the sloping windshield and roof of the slow-moving van.

The van's driver and its sole visible occupant was wearing a white safety helmet which accented his lean and handsome Negro face. He drove carefully, staying well to the right, and counted utility poles as he went. When he had counted to three he had passed a driveway on his left, a gravel road that curved through tall trees to an unseen house; a neat, gold-on-black sign, HALLER, was attached to a stake at the side of the driveway. The driver counted two more poles, slowed, and the van splashed across the gutter to stop on a grass strip at arm's length from a high, thick hedge of rosethorn.

The driver climbed down from the van and glanced at the watch on his wrist: 6:47. It was nearly dark in the tunnel of trees; overhead, open branches were etched against the fast fading light of day. He moved away from the van and turned to look at the pole which stood naked among the trees. At some recent time, someone had done a thorough pruning job and the pole and the lines it carried were clear.

The white-helmeted driver pulled a raincoat from the seat of the van and put it on. Then he went around to the rear, opened the left door and took out a pair of narrow wooden horses, painted with diagonal black and white stripes and with battery-operated yellow blinker lights attached. He closed the van door and carried the first of the horses to a point about fifty feet in front of the van, where he set it up on the edge of the road and switched on the blinker light. From where he was, in the gathering gloom he could just see brick pillars, set in the hedge and supporting an iron gate, a hundred feet past the curve in the road.

He looked speculatively at the gate a moment. Then he returned to the van, picked up the remaining horse and carried it back another fifty feet toward the Haller driveway. After he had positioned the horse and activated the blinker, he listened briefly to the distant traffic sounds before going back to the van.

Opening the rear door again, he took out an assortment of items including a flashlight with a belt hook, and a telephone handset, which he put on the roof of the van. Over his raincoat, he strapped on a tool belt and hooked the flashlight to it. Then, with swift expertise, he strapped climbing spurs to his legs, hooked an end of a web belt to an eye in the snug-fitting tool belt, slipped a black case over his shoulder, grasped the telephone set in his left hand, closed the van's rear door with his right and walked stiff-leggedly to the pole.

Swinging the web belt around the pole, he caught the free end and fastened it to the remaining eye in the tool belt. Then he dug his spurs in the soft, creosoted wood and, maneuvering the belt, climbed until he had reached the terminal box below the cable.

94

He rested the handset on top of the box before breaking its seal and prying its lid open with a screwdriver. Then, digging his spurs in and leaning back until his full weight was comfortable against the web belt, he glanced at his watch again.

6:59.

He clipped the ends of the handset's wires to the terminals in the box, took the set in his left hand, hooked the receiver-transmitter over his shoulder and with his right hand dialed the seven-digit number which he had committed to memory.

Two rings. Then: "Hello?"

"Good evening. This is your telephone lineman. We've been having trouble due to the heavy rain. Is your service all right?"

"What? Nobody here reported any— Wait a minute!"

A clear, distant voice asked, *You had any trouble with the phone?*

The answer was indistinguishable because whoever it was remembered to cover the transmitter with his hand. After about a minute, a different voice said:

"Hey, I thought you guys were on strike?"

"I'm not. My regular job is supervisor. Party named Haller reported a phone out. That's why I'm missing my supper."

"Haller? They're down the road. We got no trouble."

"Sorry to have bothered you."

He cradled the set and placed it back on top of the terminal box. Then he unclipped the wires and wrapped them around the set. Once more he glanced at his watch; he needed the flashlight now to read the hands: 7:04. Nodding, he opened the black case that hung from his shoulder and drew a length of wire from it. The ends of the wire had attached clips like those on the handset, and he clipped these carefully to the terminals in the box. Then he picked up the handset, and, trailing a growing length of wire from the black case, began to descend the pole. It was quite dark now and he moved with great care, feeling his way. When his feet touched the ground, he let go the breath he had been holding in and, with his free hand, wiped the sweat from his forehead.

"Seven-fifty," Noble S. Wright said softly. "Time for me to go back up the pole."

Eddie Durfee and Charley Bennett, crouched inside the van, nodded at him and at each other. Eddie and Charley were wearing faded coveralls; Eddie's hair was heavily streaked with gray and he was not wearing his dentures, which made him look at least fifty years old. Charley had on a pair of old-fashioned eyeglasses and a brushy mustache that looked real enough, and his right cheek carried a patch of adhesive tape.

Noble had switched on the parking lights of the van and there was just enough glow from the dash light to let them distinguish objects around them.

"Only one car's been by so far," said Eddie. It was a wasted statement since the others were as aware of it as he.

Charley said, "The one we're waiting for is the one out. That should be along in"—he glanced at his wrist watch—"ten minutes."

Noble moved restlessly. "How are our passengers?"

Eddie patted each of two liquor cartons he was sitting between. "I think they're asleep," he said.

Noble squared his safety helmet, looked at his watch and said, "Okay, here I go— Charley, you ready with the jammer?"

"Ready."

"Start it grinding as soon as the car has gone past. When the phone rings, you know what to say."

"I ought to. I've practiced it enough."

Eddie said, "I hope to Christ we're gonna have enough time to do everything we've got to do."

"We'll have enough time. Only thing we've got to watch is that we don't go too fast— Okay. On your toes, you guys!"

Noble slid out of the driver's seat, closed the cab door and walked stiff-leggedly around in front of the van. He had left the parking lights on but the dash light was now off and the interior of the van was totally dark. Whatever brief illumination the headlights of an approaching car would give to the interior of the van would not reveal Eddie and Charley, who would keep their heads down. Noble crossed to the pole and, now that his hands were free, climbed it with the agility of a cat. When he had reached the terminal box, he set himself, unhooked the flashlight and held it ready in his hand. Ahead of him, somewhere beyond the pole, was the house. He could not see it and had never seen it, although he'd sketched a floor plan of it from Vince Maggione's transcribed description and from an exterior picture that had appeared in *Newsday*. A light, steady breeze was blowing in from the bay. If his estimate of the distance was correct, the house should be less than two hundred yards from the pole, on a diagonal to his left. At that distance, and with the breeze, he should be able to easily hear the car with the off-duty members of Spotafore's eight o'clock relief when it left the house.

He settled down to listening and in little more than a minute he heard the barking of a dog, with another joining it almost immediately. *Shut up, you!* came to his ears in a distinct, high-pitched voice and with it the dogs subsided to whining. He heard a car door slam, amazingly near, and an engine start up. There was a crunch of tires on gravel and the sound receded briefly to return even more clearly; then it stopped, with the car apparently waiting at the gate.

Noble smiled. His map of the grounds was about right. He had guessed that the driveway curved toward the bay before coming back to the road.

He leaned back, waiting, and when he heard the car turn into Juniper Lane he switched on the flashlight and held it so his helmeted, raincoated figure would be in silhouette. In half a minute, headlights blazed a path through the tunnel of trees and a car swept by.

When the car was out of sight, Noble switched off the flashlight and swiftly descended the pole.

Inside the van, a telephone rang. Once, twice— Charley Bennett picked it up.

"TV Repair," he said.

"Do you make repair calls at night?" A woman's voice.

"Yes, ma'am. Where you located?"

"On Juniper Lane, in Huntington Bay."

"What seems to be the trouble?"

"My husband and I were watching a program and it was coming in fine. Then, suddenly, all kinds of diagonals and lines started appearing on the screen."

"Uh huh. No picture. Color set?"

"Yes."

"I'd say it's your power pack. You'd better shut off the set or you'll ruin the picture tube."

"It's off. How soon can you come?"

"Well, lemme see— Wait a minute. I think that's my truck, just drove in— Yup. You're in luck. You said Juniper Lane? How far's that from Twenty-five A?"

"A mile and three-eighths, exactly."

"Okay. Be there in fifteen minutes— Name?"

"Spotafore. Vincent Spotafore. It's the only house on the east side, on the right, on Juniper Lane. If you'll tell me the make of your truck and the license number, the gateman will let you in without delay."

"It's a Ford van, black with white side panels. The license number's RV 2407. Your man can't miss it. It's got TV on it in letters a foot high."

"Good. If you'll bring your bill, my husband will pay you when you're finished."

"Okay. I'll be there in fifteen minutes."

Charley Bennett replaced the telephone and Noble S. Wright said, "That was A-okay. Now, we've got work to do."

Eddie Durfee let himself out the back and went to retrieve the barriers and blinker lights. By the time he had returned with them, Noble had shed his spurs, raincoat and helmet, and was busy lashing a collapsed antenna to the roof ladder while Charley was putting the white vinyl side panels in place. The panels, with TV-RADIO REPAIR and an address and phone numbers painted on them, effectively covered the NEW YORK TELEPHONE COMPANY legend and made a startling change in the van's appearance. Eddie stowed the striped horses in the van and then went around to remove the Bell insignias, which were regulation decals mounted on clear plastic and held in place with pressure-sensitive tape. Right behind him came Noble with white, black-lettered panels for the cab doors, and in back of both of them Charley had finished with the side panels and was clipping a new set of license plates over the ones already in place. Then Charley and Eddie together brought out hubcaps imprinted FORD and jammed them into place on the wheels.

Now Noble disconnected the telephone set and attached a small, square black box to the wires trailing down from the terminal box on the pole. With studied care he fastened the box to the side of the pole away from the road and secured it by wrapping several lengths of friction tape around the pole. He didn't have to tell Eddie and Charley; they already knew that this gadget would give a busy signal in either direction from the Spotafore telephone, no matter who dialed in or what number was dialed out.

Then Eddie and Charley, in faded coveralls with TV REPAIR embroidered in washed-out red across the shoulders, moved into the seat, with Charley at the wheel, and Noble, after a last check around, climbed into the rear of the van and closed and locked the door. A brief pop of the flashlight's beam revealed 8:16 on his watch.

"Any time now will be okay," Noble said softly.

Charley touched the starter, bringing the van's engine to life. He eased in the clutch, leaned on the wheel, and the little van wallowed across the ditch and on to the high-crowned road.

Behind the seat, beside Noble, one of the liquor cartons slid along the metal floor and from inside the carton there was a sudden, scratching sound. Noble looked at the carton and said, "Just a little longer, chum, and you'll get all the exercise you want."

thirteen

More than two years ago, Vince had come to this same gate seeking admittance. Was the gateman the same one? Vince decided not. Although he couldn't remember the occasion too clearly, he thought this man was younger. Certainly he was more alert and he had an air of hostility that Vince would have remembered. When Vince stated his name, relationship, and that he had been summoned there by Frank Mastretta, the gatemen took a long time in looking him over. The man stood there as if his eyes were the lenses of a camera and he wanted to photograph every little detail. Then he went to the gate lodge and telephoned. And then, not very graciously, he unlocked the gates to let Vince drive through.

The dogs weren't in sight. As he neared the house, though, he could hear them. Evidently they had been penned up and were protesting in mournful tones. When he neared the flagstone terrace to the house and the circle leading to the parking area he was stopped by a half-dozen large and expensive cars that had been left in the driveway with no regard to order. Blocked, he cut his engine two full car-lengths short of the terrace and left the Rambler there with the key in the ignition.

He negotiated the uneven stone steps and the rough flagstones all the way to the front door of the house to find no one standing either inside or outside. There was an oblong, mother-of-pearl button set in a shiny silver plate in the doorjamb and he pressed it to bring the sound of chimes echoing through the broad entrance hall lying empty beyond the heavy plate-glass door. He pushed the button again and after a moment saw someone emerge from the gloom at the end of the hall. A dark, stocky man wearing a new felt hat and dressed in a new business suit came up to the inside of the door.

"Who're you and waddiya want?" the man asked around a burned-out cigar.

"I'm Vince Maggione. Frank Mastretta sent for me."

The stocky man looked back over his shoulder, hesitated, and turned to inspect Vince again. Then, grunting unintelligibly, he opened the door.

The air in the study was thick and stale with the smoke of cigars and cigarettes. Chairs had been brought in from other rooms and arranged in an irregular square; most of the chairs were occupied. Those occupants who did not belong to the house proper were distinguished by their wearing hats. The hat-wearers looked angry; the others looked merely sullen. Among the sullen ones, Vince recognized Uncle Vincent's two bodyguards. They were in the center of the chair arrangement and, in addition to their sullenness, they looked uncomfortable; the others divided their time between listening to the short, fat, sweating man who was sitting at the desk using the telephone, and eying the two of them.

Nobody showed the slightest interest when Vince came in. He could remember having seen some of them before, somewhere. He was seeking Frank Mastretta and his glance had passed from the man at the telephone to one who was seated a little away from the desk, and was moving on when he suddenly stiffened and his eyes moved back to fix on the man near but not at the desk.

Although Vince had talked to Frank Mastretta on the telephone a little more than an hour ago, it had been nearly three years since he had seen him. Now, in this room, Frank appeared to be a lot more than that many years older. His face was lined and unhealthily flushed, and his eyes were bloodshot. The flush and the bloodshot eyes could have come from lack of sleep and worry over the kidnaping. But that wouldn't have thinned his hair or given him the beginnings of a paunch. He looked up, his lids heavy with tiredness, and his eyes widened briefly when he saw Vince. For a second he seemed undecided to get up or stay where he was. Then, by motions of his hands and eyes, he indicated that whatever he intended to do would be done as soon as the man on the telephone was finished.

"All right, *all right!*" the fat, sweating man was saying. He sat with unmoving rigidity, as if perched on a telephone directory, holding the phone a full inch from his ear. He was nearly bald and the sweat had gathered in globules on his pate; sweat coursed down his forehead, followed a furrow over his left eye and continued down his cheek, but he didn't move.

"Christ no, we haven't called them! You think we're crazy? Listen . . . Listen . . . *Wait a minute!* So you got your ideas. We got our ideas too. And you're talking too much over the telephone . . . What? *No, we're not going to do that, and don't you start anything, either!* . . . All right, that's better . . . You'd better goddamned believe he is! And don't you forget it!"

The fat, sweating man jammed down the phone and said, "Looie, the crazy son of a bitch!"

The man with the dead cigar grunted, "Yah. I suppose he wants to make war— Who's he gonna make it on?"

"You heard what I told him. He talks too much. How did he find out about this?"

"I gave him the word," Frank Mastretta said.

They all looked at him. Over a sudden quiet in the room, Frank said, "Mr. Spotafore felt that, sooner or later, something like this might happen. He took elaborate means to protect himself, to keep it from happening. He also had plans in the event that it did happen— So, it happened. There was a prepared list of people to notify; most of the people on that list are here. At the time Mr. Spotafore made out the list, more than a year ago, Looie wasn't as —troublesome as he has been recently. Mr. Spotafore never changed the list—"

Frank Mastretta paused for a deep breath. When he resumed, his voice was thin: "It was eight o'clock this morning before we could get someone from the telephone company to find out what was wrong with the phone and fix it. I could have gone outside and called you last night, but Mr. Spotafore's instructions in the event of kidnaping were to wait a minimum of twelve hours for a message from him— I also had my hands full last night with Aunt Sophie— Mrs. Spotafore. When I notified Looie, I gave him the code word which all of you know and were given. Looie didn't make any suggestions at the time and he didn't seem upset; he said he'd tell his boys to keep their eyes open. That was nine o'clock this morning. He didn't say he would not be here. His calling back now is his idea. It sounds almost as if he is hoping for a wiretap. I hope to God neither his phone nor ours is tapped."

"The crazy son of a bitch," the sweating man said.

The man with the dead cigar said, "Yah," again. There were nods of agreement, but no one else apparently wanted to make a vocal commitment about Looie's craziness. They didn't appear to want to say anything. They kept their eyes on Frank Mastretta, waiting for him to continue. Then, as it became increasingly evident that Frank had said all he intended to say for the moment, one by one they began leaning back. As if finally aware of the stranger in their midst they began turning their glances on Vince Maggione who was now sitting, with his leg stretched out, a couple of chairs distant from and facing Frank Mastretta.

In a less-strained voice, Frank said, "This is Vince Maggione, Mr. Spotafore's nephew. He has just come back from Vietnam— Well, not *just* back. He's been in hospitals while they were putting his leg together again."

The men in the room looked at him in a different light. He was one of them, and he wasn't. He belonged to them by virtue of blood relationship with the *capo,* closer than any of them, even closer than Frank Mastretta. He was also close to them in another way: he was a veteran, and most of them were veterans. Several had close relatives—a few had sons—who either now were or else had been in Vietnam. In this way or sense, he was one of their own. But in the broader sense, he was not of the Family. He was entitled to wait, somewhere else in the house.

His presence in this room, now officially noted, would have to be explained.

104

fourteen

Frank Mastretta uncrossed and recrossed his legs while he took out a cigarette and struck a match for it. He inhaled deeply, glanced at the fat, sweating man and, through exhaling smoke, said:

"If the phone rings, get the name and number and tell them you'll call back. Everyone here knows *what* has happened but only a couple know *how* it happened. I'm going to tell it straight through from the beginning. Then we'll have lunch. Anybody who has business to take care of or doesn't want to stay for any reason is free to go now."

Nobody moved.

"We've already had the demand," said Frank Mastretta. "It came in the morning mail. Before the banks have closed today we will have gathered the full amount specified and in the proper denominations. From that point on we can only wait for further instructions—"

This must have been news to most of them, for they shot brief, curtailed glances at one another. Vincent Spotafore was a big man; his kidnapers would want a big price. They sat a little straighter. If they expected to hear how much, however, they were disappointed. Frank Mastretta hesitated only the length of time it took his eyes to cover each of them in turn. Then he settled in his chair and said:

"At seven-thirty last night, Mr. Spotafore went into the room at the end of the hall to watch one of his favorite television programs. He was accompanied by Aunt Sophie—Mrs. Spotafore—who took with her some needlepoint, I believe it was a chair seat, she'd been working on for the past month. If you will recall, it rained most of yesterday, the night was cool and raindrops were coming down from the trees so he did not take his customary walk after supper.

"According to her, at shortly after eight o'clock the set began acting badly. The picture jumped and lines appeared on the screen. At first thinking it might be a transmission problem at that station, he changed channels only to get the same jumpy, unclear picture. He then shut the set off and she came in here, using that telephone"—Frank pointed—"to call a TV repair service in Huntington.

"At this time, the telephone was working and Mrs. Spotafore reached—or thought she reached—the TV service man. She told him what the trouble was and he told her his truck would be at the house in fifteen minutes. In order to clear the truck at the gate, she asked for the license number. She wrote it down and I have it here"—he held up a slip of paper—"RV 2407. It is now being checked through the Motor Vehicle Department. However, there isn't the slightest doubt in my mind that the owner of the plates had no connection with the kidnaping and that they were stolen, probably for this specific job.

"The service truck, a black-and-white Ford van, recent model, arrived at the gates at 8:18. It was logged in by Angelo Bellafuocco; acting on instructions from the house, he admitted the van, then closed and locked the gates. Because there had not been the usual wait for questions and telephoning the house, the two German shepherds were a bit slow in getting to the gates. But they did pick up the van and were pacing it by the time it reached the house. Teddy Fell was on the terrace when the van and dogs came past and he watched it, and them, around the circle. The van came back to the terrace where it stopped and the dogs, at Teddy's command, sat while two men got out. Teddy has described them as being white men wearing light tan coveralls. The driver was middle-aged, pot-bellied, medium height, wearing a cloth cap and gold-rimmed spectacles. He had a mustache, a Hitler type, and there was a Band-Aid on his cheek. The other man, the helper, had gray hair, no teeth, and walked as if he had rheumatism; Teddy guessed him to be in his fifties; Mrs. Spotafore thought he was younger than that. He was carrying a rolled-up tool kit and a black cylindrical flashlight.

"These two followed Teddy into the house. As he was closing the door, he noticed the dogs had gotten up to pace around the truck and sniff at it. Teddy was about to speak to the dogs when the driver said, *They must smell my dog. He sleeps in the truck nights. He sure makes the truck stink. But it's better than unloading it every night to keep the goddamned kids from stealing my parts.* This explanation sounded logical and, unfortunately, Teddy did not investigate further—"

Frank Mastretta mashed out his cigarette in an overflowing ashtray on his desk. "Both Teddy and Mrs. Spotafore recall that Mr. Spotafore opened the door to the room to let the repairmen in. He said something about their having made good time. Then Teddy went into the kitchen and got a cup of coffee of which he drank less than half. When he came back into the hall, the sitting-room door was open and he saw that the man with glasses had turned the set so the back was to the door, and had already removed the covering and pulled out the chassis. Teddy said Mr. Spotafore was standing near the repairman, watching what he was doing; Mrs. Spotafore was in her chair, working on her needlepoint. The helper was crossing the room, heading for the door, and the repairman was saying to him, *You'll find one of 'em about a foot inside the rear door— It's in a blue box.*

"Teddy said the helper limped along beside him to the terrace. He acted afraid of the dogs and asked if they would bite. Teddy assured him they wouldn't unless he told them to. Teddy went with him to the truck. The dogs were still pacing around and as soon as they saw the helper they started to growl. The helper acted scared to death, so Teddy made the dogs sit while he went with the helper to the back of the truck. In getting one of the doors open, the helper dropped the flashlight; the dogs were still sitting, but the helper was apparently too frightened to pick up the flashlight, so Teddy bent over to pick it up.

"Then, Teddy said, something went flying out of the back of the

107

truck and over his head. He looked up just as two cats hit the gravel and started scrambling toward the lawn, with the dogs after them. And then all he saw was stars—somebody sapped him, but good—and when he came to he was all taped up, lying behind the bushes in the circle.

"We found the fur from one of the cats on the lawn this morning," said Frank. "The other one must've made it to a tree."

He took out another cigarette. "In the meantime, back in the sitting room—" He held a match flame to the cigarette and inhaled, quickly and deeply. "—they'd heard the dogs. Mrs. Spotafore said the repairman was acting upset. He said, *If those dogs bite Bill, you've got yourself a lawsuit, mister!* Mr. Spotafore assured him that Teddy could control the dogs, that one of them had probably stirred up a squirrel. Then the helper came limping back in, holding two boxes in his hands. *That's it, in the blue box,* the repairman said. *What's in that other box?* The helper replied it was the new silicone polish for the screen. The repairman said, *Oh—glad you thought of it—* He opened the box and took out a bottle and a sponge and said to Mr. Spotafore, *This is the greatest stuff you ever saw. Guaranteed to improve the picture twenty per cent or double your money back— Here, smell it!*

"The repairman saturated the sponge with fluid from the bottle and held it toward Mr. Spotafore's nose. Mrs. Spotafore saw this for just about a second, and it was the last thing she did see. Someone was behind her with his hand over her mouth, pulling her back into the chair. He slapped tape across her mouth and eyes, taped her hands and feet to the chair, passed a rope around her middle and tied the ends behind the chair.

"I'll say this much for her: She's tough. She didn't faint. She didn't lose her head. She remembers hearing the set go back on. The sound was the program following the one they'd been watching when the set quit; she's acquainted with that program and could tell from what was happening that it had been on less than ten minutes. This means that from the time the repair van arrived at the terrace until the men loaded Mr. Spotafore into it and drove off, at the most, twenty to twenty-five minutes elapsed.

"When the truck reached the gates, a transistor radio was playing in the front seat. Angelo opened the gates to let the truck out and the driver leaned from the window and asked him a question. Angelo couldn't hear him over the radio, so he came closer. Then someone who had sneaked out of the rear of the truck while Angelo was opening the gates, stepped up behind and sapped *him*.

"Angelo saw two men in the front seat, just as Mrs. Spotafore saw two men with Mr. Spotafore at the television set, so there were at least three men involved. One of them was hidden in the truck, which explains why the dogs were acting up.

"It was a good fifteen minutes—after nine o'clock—before anybody found out what was going on. Anna came into the sitting room with tea for Mrs. Spotafore and warm milk for Mr. Spotafore and found the situation as I have described it. Angelo had been taped up in the gatehouse and his keys were gone. Not only was *our* lock securing the gate—the so-called repairmen had added *three* of their own, with double lengths of chain. Between crowbars, hacksaws, and trying to shoot those padlocks off, it took another fifteen minutes to get even one of our cars out of the grounds.

"And we couldn't use the telephone. Every damned time we picked it up and dialed, we got a busy signal."

Frank Mastretta had told the story of the kidnaping as if reading from a script. His voice had been distinct, he had paused for breath in the right places, and he had ended one sentence before beginning another. Obviously he had given it a great deal of thought and apparently he had decided to play it with detachment. As a result, he seemed more like a minor agricultural official delivering a crop report than one of the staff reporting that the commanding general had been captured by the Cong. But it was, all in all, an impressive performance; it lacked only two things and Vince wondered how many of the others had noticed.

Frank had very carefully avoided any reference as to where *he* had been while the kidnaping was in progress. And, although he had said that the demand had been received and would be met before the banks closed, he had neglected to mention how much money was involved.

And there was one other detail: just why had he, Vince Maggione, been brought into this?

If Vince expected a deluge of questions, accusations, suggested

109

courses of action, or avowals of loyalty and support, he was disappointed. In addition to himself, there were eleven men in the room. No one said anything. No one looked at anyone else. Each of them, as if by prearrangement, found some point in the walls or ceiling to study, and made a point of studying it.

The telephone rang and the fat man at the desk, sweating less now, answered it by removing the instrument from the cradle, holding it suspended a moment, and replacing it.

Someone in the left corner of the quadrangle said, "Hey, Tony, if that's for me, I'll take it."

"It wasn't for you," said Tony, not bothering to look up.

Vince glanced at Tony again and suddenly recognized him. Sitting sweaty behind a desk he didn't look like much. But standing and dressed in a cutaway coat with striped trousers, a pearl double-breasted vest and a dawn gray ascot tie he had been Anthony LaScola, the man Louise Mastretta had married. Vince tried to catch Tony LaScola's eye, and Tony evaded him. He wondered how in Christ's name a knockout girl like Louise Mastretta ever let herself get married to *him*.

The telephone rang, in a different tone, and in a different voice Frank Mastretta said, "That's the gate. Answer it."

Tony LaScola answered it, saying, "Yes," and then, "I'll see." He put the phone in his lap. "That private dick—he wants to come to the house and make a report."

Frank Mastretta said, "Okay, let him. We're paying for it."

fifteen

There was a noticeable stirring and shifting of chairs, and newly fired tobacco freshly polluted the air in the room. Presently the chimes sounded in the hall and the man in the new suit and new hat, with a new burned-out cigar in his mouth, got up to answer the door. He brought back a man half a head taller than he was and dressed in a sport jacket, razor-edged tan slacks and tan buck shoes. Vince judged him to be about thirty-five and then almost immediately decided he was probably older than that. He had a good head of curly blond hair in need of cutting. His ingenuous face was marked with an inch-long scar along the left jawbone. His eyelashes were as thick as a girl's and his eyes were the color of wet violets. He looked like the kind of a fellow who could get anything he wanted from women. He also gave the impression that picking a fight with him would be highly unprofitable.

His face fixed in an indeterminate smile, he walked with a show of easy confidence to the front of the desk. He was too smart to let his eyes wander around the room. He looked at Frank and nodded, and while he didn't say anything his questioning face asked, *Is it okay for me to talk here? Or do you want to go somewhere more private?*

"Tony and I hired you," Frank said in a loud voice, "but you are accountable to everyone in this room. We're all friends here. We're *family*." There was unconscious irony in his accent of the last word.

"Okay." The blond man nodded again. He took a notebook from his inside pocket, leafed through a couple of pages and, in a businesslike voice, began to read:

"Ten-thirty P.M., answered client's call; eleven P.M., arrived at client's residence—" He paused and to no one in particular said, "You will note that I have not written down names or addresses, just in case—"

Frank cut him off with a handwave. "If we hadn't known you to be discreet, you wouldn't be here. You can cut out this crap ten-thirty P.M. and eleven P.M. and give us what facts you've found out, if any."

The shoulders of the sport jacket lifted in a barely perceptible shrug. "Okay—I went directly from here to the intersecting street, Tilden Road, and wherever there was a light showing I knocked on the door. Whenever I found anybody, I used the story we decided on: that I represented an insurance company and was investigating a burglary that wouldn't be reported in the newspapers because we didn't want the thieves to know it had been discovered. With this line, I had no trouble getting people to talk, and promise to keep their mouths shut.

"I made my first call at eleven-thirty P.M. The time is important because most of the people still up had just come back, from the movies or eating out or whatever, and had taken the babysitter home, so they were of no use. Neither were the three babysitters I managed to track down this morning. I talked to two families who had been watching TV programs and both of them had noticed trouble with their sets, jumpy pictures, diagonal lines, snow, starting at about eight o'clock and lasting maybe ten minutes, but it wasn't bad enough for them to turn off their sets or change channels. Neither of these families had bothered to look out in the street at any time during the evening.

"I stopped at three other houses where poeple had been out for the evening and had just returned and getting ready for bed—Tuesday, today, is a working day and most of the people out there are early-to-bedders. And nobody saw a black-and-white TV repair van either going into or coming out of Juniper Lane, or anywhere on Tilden Road, Neck Road or Bay Drive, at any time during the evening.

112

"I did find a man who had been walking his dogs along Tilden Road to Neck Road and back the full length to Bay Drive, where the traffic light is, and then back on Tilden to his house. It's a mile and three-quarters. I paced it myself this morning, making like I had a pair of dogs on the leash, and allowing for where I figured the dogs might stop and for where they would pull hard, speeding things up, it took me thirty-two minutes.

"This man remembers going out into the street because his dogs were acting up. There was a breeze blowing in from the bay and, while he didn't say so, I have to assume his dogs heard *your* dogs— Dogs can hear sounds that humans can't. I came to this assumption because of the time factor. This man's kids had been watching *Gunsmoke* and when the program was over he made them go upstairs and do their homework. This would have been at eight-thirty P.M. A few minutes after that, the dogs started acting spooky and he took them out. By the time he got outside, *he* could hear dogs barking in the distance although he says he didn't know whose dogs they were.

"As I have said, he was out there for at least half an hour. He walked the length of Tilden and back and did not at any time see the black-and-white TV repair truck either enter or leave Juniper Lane.

"Now, we know the truck arrived at the gates at 8:18, so, unless this man happened to be looking out of the window at that time, he wouldn't have seen it go *in*. But it had come *out* sometime while he was on his walk round-trip between Neck Road and Bay Drive, and he didn't see it. From the corner of Neck and Tilden, you can see the white sign at the entrance of Juniper Lane, so if the truck had come out before he reached Juniper, he would have seen it; if it had come out after he passed Juniper, he would have heard it.

"However, when he was past Juniper, about a hundred yards this side of the traffic light at Bay Drive, he says he saw a New York Telephone Company van coming up Tilden Road from behind him. He wasn't sure if it had come from Juniper Lane; he says it might have come from Neck Road; he wasn't sure. He noticed the van as it passed and saw that the driver was a Negro wearing a white safety helmet. The driver was the only one he could see as

113

the van passed him. The van stopped for a red light at Bay Drive and then, on green signal, made a left toward 25-A.

"Now, your men told me they had seen a telephone truck and a man up a pole, working on the line, when they came out of the house and drove down Juniper Lane at a few minutes past eight o'clock. Also, there had been a call to this house between seven and eight, supposedly from a telephone lineman. In view of the regular telephone repairman's discovery this morning of the device that had been used on your phone line, this is extremely important. It further substantiates the North Shore TV Repair's denial that they had received a call from Mrs. Spotafore last night. Incidentally, they use a recording device which takes down the information and they answer service calls in the order of receipt. There was no recorded call from Mrs. Spotafore.

"After I talked with your men this morning, they having seen a telephone truck on Juniper Road last night, I took Chubby Anselmo with me and he showed me the exact spot where he and the others had seen the truck last night. This was at seven-thirty this morning, before the regular telephone lineman came to restore your service. Chubby and I examined that area of the road, particularly the grass area between the road and the hedge.

"We found clear marks where the van had parked on the grass strip. We also found a number of clear footprints in the soft grass and mud around the tire tracks. By measurements, we definitely established three different sets of footprints. This means that, in addition to the Negro in the white helmet, who was seen, there were two men connected with the presence of the telephone truck on the grass strip, two men who were not at that time seen.

"A few minutes later, on the other side of the road in the grass area near the Haller driveway, we found similar marks which showed that the same truck had stopped there on its way out. I was able to obtain several good casts of tire and shoe prints. I am holding these for the time when we will be in a position to use them for positive identification.

"Now, all this makes it pretty obvious that the people who pulled the kidnaping used a truck, a van, disguised as a telephone repair vehicle; that, through the use of some kind of jamming device, they somehow caused the TV program to be distorted; that

114

they intercepted Mrs. Spotafore's telephone call and, in the interim of the eighteen minutes it took them to appear at the gate, they completely altered the appearance of the van. Then, having accomplished their mission, they reversed the process and in a remarkably few minutes drove out of Juniper Lane in the same way they had entered it—as a phony telephone repair truck."

The investigator took in a deep breath and shifted position. He had been talking in a low monotone, as if under intense pressure, and now suddenly he seemed very tired.

"It shouldn't be necessary for me to tell you," he said in a tired voice, "that this whole job indicates ingenuity and a very high degree of organization. It shows us we are up against a smart and smoothly functioning gang."

He closed his notebook and returned it to his inside pocket. For maybe half a minute, no one spoke. Then Frank Mastretta asked, "That all you have?"

"About all. I checked the Huntington office of the Telephone Company—it's the office handling repairs in this area—and they did *not* have a repair truck anywhere near Juniper Lane last night."

"So. What do you plan to do now?"

"Find out more about that truck. Where it came from. Where it went."

"Don't push it too hard," Frank Mastretta said.

The man in the sport jacket looked at him as if he hadn't heard him correctly.

Frank said, "We want Mr. Spotafore back, alive. If you get too close too soon, you may scare somebody. When people get scared, they're apt to do something foolish— Keep yourself covered. If you feel like you're getting close to something, let me know before you go any further. Is that clear?"

The man in the sport jacket sighed and said, "Okay."

sixteen

When the violet-eyed man in the sport jacket had gone, there was another general shifting around, within limited individual areas, and a minute rearrangement of chairs. The men in the room appeared to be almost undiscernibly gathering themselves into separate groups. More tobacco was fired and somebody got up to empty an overdue ashtray in the fireplace. There still weren't any questions; not out loud, anyhow. But everyone had stopped looking at nothing and their eyes were now focused on Frank Mastretta.

Frank would have had to be either blind or stupid not to notice the hostility produced by the investigator's report. They resented all outsiders; there were plenty of them who still resented *him*. And the investigator had scraped it pretty close; he hadn't had the guts to come right out and say it, but between the lines from start to finish he had been silently screaming *inside job!* It wasn't healthy to let this bunch think such thoughts. His bloodshot eyes became hard and in a hard voice he said:

"Before anyone in here starts to pop off, let me tell you a few things. First, I spent all day yesterday in Jersey City, on business. Harold was with me—"

One of the hatless men inside the quadrangle breathed out as if he had just been reprieved from a firing squad.

"—and we got back here to the house at half-past nine and walked in on this mess. Fortunately, Tony had had presence of mind enough to send Anna to an outside phone to call a doctor; the doctor had just arrived and was taking care of Mrs. Spotafore, Angelo Bellafuoco and Teddy Fell. All of them are upstairs at this moment. Mrs. Spotafore is, or was, sleeping under sedation; Angelo and Teddy are being kept quiet. The doctor is the one who regularly takes care of Mr. Spotafore and he will keep his mouth shut. Luckily, there were no knife or gunshot wounds and he doesn't have to make a police report. Now—"

Frank Mastretta paused while his protruding, bloodshot eyes sought out each of them in turn, including Vince.

"—I've been living with this thing since an hour after it happened. I've had a lot of time to think about it. I know each of you well enough to know what *you* are thinking about it. Let me tell you my conclusions first. Then I will listen to yours— One, as Danzig said, this was a professional job, planned and carried out by a team of professionals used to working together. Two, it was a basic part of the plan to *make it look like an inside job.* You heard what Danzig said, but more important you got what he *didn't* say: the kidnapers had to have intimate knowledge of the inside workings of this place, the dogs, Mr. Spotafore's habits, the time of the changing of the watch, where things are located. Before any of you start accusing anybody, let me tell you this knowledge could have been obtained easily enough by anyone determined enough to go after it. Some of it could have been figured out by anyone in a boat watching the house through binoculars; every night at the same hour, almost the same minute, the TV set goes on in the sitting room and the lighted screen can be seen through glasses from as far away as Lloyd's Neck. Then, this house is a natural object of curiosity. The house is old and at times it has been necessary to call in plumbers, electricians, roofers— These people carry tales. There is information about this house that, with patient piecing together, would indicate the kind of plan of action that was used.

"Now, we can't afford to indulge in guesswork. Most of us can think of a number of people who might have done this job, would be capable of doing it, would be willing to take the risk, would, in fact, be only too ready to take part in an enterprise of this kind— The possibilities are almost endless, including that it may have

118

been ordered done by persons who took no active part, but employed professionals—possibly imported—to do it— However, as I said, if we should start guessing, should start naming names in our minds, it could get us into serious trouble. And I shouldn't have to tell you that, until Mr. Spotafore is back here and able to speak for himself, every man in this organization—whether now in this room or not—*is* in trouble. And you damned well better believe it!"

That got to them. The former stolid silence changed to muttering, and there was a new shifting around. Finally they were definitely in groups and at last one of them, the man with the burned-out cigar, said:

"How much do they want?"

A few glanced at him, but most of them watched Frank Mastretta; it had occurred to them that it was Frank who was in trouble and despite Frank's effort to convince them that *they* were in jeopardy, they were more or less openly skeptical. On his part, Frank withstood their scrutiny with a kind of brusque contempt. With a quick, contemptuous nod he said, "Okay, Tony. It's your turn."

Tony LaScola sat a little straighter on his uneasy perch. His small, effeminate hands reached out to the cluttered desk and picked up two sheets of white paper. Each sheet appeared to be of identical color and size and each had been folded twice horizontally to fit in a business envelope.

Tony said, "I'll tell you what they say. And then I'll pass 'em around so you can see for yourselves. But before I do, I'll tell you: One of the regular guards is a retired City cop; he went to the FBI school and still has his own fingerprint outfit. There were no prints on either the key letter or the demand letter. There were prints on the envelope and he has 'em, although he thinks they're useless. We want these sheets back because, while he has identified the style of type and make of the typewriter, he'll need 'em to check the alignment on typewriters when we really start to go after it. He already has enlarged photographs, but we still want the originals— Okay?"

There were several nods of assent, and Tony continued:

"Okay— The key letter was left on the TV set at the time the

119

boss was snatched. All it says is, *You'll hear from us,* and it's signed, TV. Okay, Frank, you can start that one around— The demand letter came in the mail this morning. The postmark shows it was mailed in Huntington *yesterday noon—*"

Tony made an expressive *What the hell* gesture with eyebrows, shoulders and hands. "Try to figure *that* one. Either they're a bunch of cool sons-of-bitches, or else they're crazy. Taking a chance like that, mailing the demand letter *eight hours before they made the snatch—* Jesus! Well, okay. The demand says, *Put $40,000 in 5's and 10's—no 20's and no marked bills—in a plain, white suit box from Macy's Men's Store. Fasten the box with Scotch tape and tie it with brown cord—three lengths endwise and three lengths crosswise, making one cross in the center. Have it ready within 24 hours. We will call his nephew where to deliver it. If everything is satisfactory, he will be released the same day. If you call the cops or try anything funny, you will not hear from us again.* It's signed, *TV.*"

For a minute, no one said anything. Then the man with the burned-out cigar in his mouth said, "Only forty grand? What the hell!"

He sounded offended.

When you stopped to think of it, Vince told himself, it was kind of an insult at that.

On the surface, the forty-thousand-dollar demand was the one unsure piece of business in the whole affair. To Vincent Spotafore's "Family" forty thousand was chicken feed, representing no more than a week's take in the numbers racket alone. There would have been less surprise if Tony LaScola had said the ransom was a quarter of a million; *that* would have been a reasonable price to redeem the biggest *capo* of them all. But, *forty thousand—* It looked like the mark of a timid amateur, the sort of appraisal and ignorant neophyte might put on a Rembrandt.

But, was that really it? Might the smallness of the amount indicate, rather, a professional contempt? Suppose money had not been the motive? What if each step of the plan had been shrewdly calculated to pile question on question until, their suspicions no

120

longer containable, Vincent Spotafore's men would turn on each other?

It was entirely possible that the kidnapers' real motive was the ultimate destruction of the Spotafore "Family!"

Vince Maggione thought about this, among other things, as he sat there, listening to the talk around him and wondering when, if ever, he would find out just why Frank Mastretta had summoned *him*. The letters had been passed around—he had waved them on to the next man—and were back in Tony's hands. The first babbling flood of conversation had settled into three distinct pools and in the midst of the buzz an elderly woman in a plain black dress, with a starched white apron covering her ample front, opened the door in the fireplace wall and signaled Frank Mastretta.

"Lunch is served," Frank said in a loud voice.

Nobody paid any attention. Whatever they were discussing in individual groups seemed to be along collective lines; they talked for the most part in Italian and in tones too low for Vince to hear even if he had understood the language. Once in a while a name would pop out: he heard *Brooklyn Mike* twice, and *Looie* several times. Then, as the individual groups began signing off, one in the group spoke to someone in the next group. In less than five minutes they had evidently reached agreement and named a spokesman.

Their apparent choice was a short, stocky man with large ears, a long nose and a massive jaw. Under his black felt hat his temples were gray. He had spent the whole time sitting near Uncle Vincent's two bodyguards and he glanced at them before addressing himself to Frank Mastretta.

"Okay to talk now?" he asked in a bullfrog-like voice.

"Sure, Mike."

Mike said, "Okay. We agree. You and Tony handle it. We keep out now. Unless you need us, we wait. We keep Looie quiet. When the boss is back, we find out what he wants us to do. Okay?"

"Right!"

"Okay." Mike turned his glance to Vince Maggione. "Now, we want to know, what is *he* doing here?"

"I'd kind of like to know that myself," said Vince.

Frank Mastretta ignored him. With his eyes steady on Mike, he

121

said, "Vince Maggione is here because he is the one named in the demand as go-between."

"Him? It said *nephew—* Isn't that you?"

"I am *Mrs.* Spotafore's nephew; he is *Mr.* Spotafore's nephew, his closest relative, the son of his sister. There was considerable mention of the family connection in the newspapers both at the time Vince Maggione was wounded in Vietnam and later when he was decorated and discharged from the VA Hospital at Fort Hamilton, Brooklyn. And, without meaning to be nasty about it, Vince is quite easily distinguishable from most other people by the fact that he walks with a definite limp— Oh, there's no question about who the kidnapers meant when they said *his nephew.*"

seventeen

Vince had been ready to leave for a long time, and he would have gone home right after eating his lunch—a roast beef sandwich on rye bread—if Frank Mastretta had let him. Regardless of all his evasiveness, Frank was at least being civil. Patiently and with unassailable logic he had pointed out to Vince that, as the designated intermediary, he could not return to his home to await the kidnapers' call until all necessary preparations had been completed. Frank said they still hadn't gathered all the money. To avoid arousing suspicion, no more than a thousand dollars was being obtained from any one bank; this meant covering forty different banks and having to go as far away as Patchogue, which was time-consuming.

Although he didn't raise a question, Vince was not completely satisfied with this explanation of the delay. The ransom note had been specific that the bills be all fives and tens, and that none of them be marked. It didn't take a great mathematical mind to figure out that $40,000 in those denominations could be assembled in five thousand pieces or less, which was not a sufficient number to prevent their being marked, presumably in a way that would be unnoticed by the kidnapers. Vince couldn't see the Spotafore "Family" parting with all that money without a determined effort to find out who got it. The "Family" would make sure that each piece of the money would be an individual and recognizable death warrant for the unfortunate holder thereof.

123

After he had carefully coached Vince in what to say, Frank did permit him to call Frances. There was no trouble at all in getting through to her at her job in Jamaica. She sounded dissatisfied and upset, which was only natural, and while she was questioning him, Frank, who was listening in, abruptly closed the connection.

At four o'clock, another car arrived in the driveway. It was the first in more than half an hour and it must have been the one Frank and Tony had been waiting for because both of them got up hurriedly and walked out of the study, closing the door behind them. This left Vince and the bodyguard, whose name was Harold, alone in the room.

Vince lifted his right leg, holding it with both hands above the knee, and pulled his right foot even with his left. Very carefully, he stood up.

The bodyguard's eyes flicked at him. "Don't get any ideas," he said in a disparaging voice.

"Am I a prisoner?"

"Not exactly. But you ain't going nowhere, either."

"I see. When do I leave?"

"When they're ready for you to leave."

"Well— Mind if I walk around? My leg is getting stiff."

"I don't mind. Just don't get any ideas."

Vince was out in the hall when Harold evidently made up his mind that he could use some exercise, too. He had reached the door to the sitting room, and the sounds of activity and voices behind it told him this was where Frank Mastretta and Tony LaScola had gone. He heard Aunt Sophie Spotafore's high, rather shrill voice say *You'll find another in my sewing basket* . . .

"It ain't polite to listen at doors," Harold said. "Suppose you take your walk someplace else. You wanta go outside, we go outside."

They went out of the house. The cars had been rearranged and there weren't as many of them as there had been before. Vince's Rambler wagon had been turned around and was now a short way down the drive, headed for the gates.

They walked on the lawn, viewing the bay, for perhaps ten minutes. Then Vince, tiring, said, "Okay. Let's go back in and sit down."

124

In another hour, at half-past five, he was driving back to East New York. On the seat beside him was a Macy's Men's Store suit box, sealed and tied as directed, and in it was forty thousand dollars in five- and ten-dollar bills. Tony La Scola had insisted that Vince see the money before the box was closed. The packages were neatly banded in stacks of $500 each and looked as if they had just come from the banks. The packages didn't quite fill the suit box and wadded-up newspaper had been used to fill the remaining space.

Now, the box was beside Vince. And beside the box was the bodyguard, Harold. Harold's shoulder holster was plainly visible in the opening of his jacket whenever he turned to inspect traffic through the Rambler's rear window. Vince didn't start counting the number of times Harold looked back until they were on the Expressway, but from the time he started counting until he turned into his own driveway, Harold had looked back exactly thirty times.

Frances met him at the back door. She was wearing her apron, she had obviously been holding back supper, and her eyes were red-rimmed as if she'd been crying.

"Thank *good*ness you're here! What—"

Vince moved aside to reveal the bodyguard. "This is— What *is* your name, anyhow?"

The bodyguard removed his hat and said, "Harold."

"Harold what?"

"Just Harold'll do."

"Harold Uldoo, this is my wife, Frances— Harold works for Uncle Vincent Spotafore."

"How do you do," Frances said in a frosty voice.

"Uh— H'lo."

Vince asked, "How much can I tell her?"

"Vince! What's wrong?"

"If I was you, I wouldn't tell her nothing."

"But I've got to tell her something!"

"*Vince!* What is the matter? Are you in trouble?"

"No, I'm—"

"Okay, lady. Mr. Spotafore's been snatched."

125

"*What?*"

"You heard him. Uncle Vincent's been kidnaped."

"B-but w-what has this to do with you? Why are you— *What's in that box?*"

"Forty thousand dollars," said Vince.

"Hey! You shouldn't of told her *that!*"

"*Vince!*"

"All right, so I shouldn't've told her. *You're* the one who told her he was kidnaped— It's the ransom money. And I've been elected the go-between."

"*Vince Maggione, you haven't!*"

"Listen, it wasn't my idea."

"That's right, lady. He didn't want any part of it. He—"

Frances turned on Harold. Her eyes were angry. "You have no right to do this to him," she said, her voice rising. "He has nothing whatever to do with his uncle's affairs. And he can't, he isn't well, he's been in the hospital, for months— His leg is stuck together with pins!"

Harold backed up. "Lady, it wasn't *my* idea!"

"To listen to the pair of you, it doesn't seem to have been anyone's idea. It must have been *somebody's* idea— Whoever it was, let *him* be the go-between. You're *not* using my husband! You can go right back where you came from. And take your box with you!"

"Lady—"

"Shut up, Harold," said Vince. "Look, Frances, it was the kidnapers' idea to use me. They put it in the ransom note. And they didn't leave us any address where we can get in touch with them to make any changes— Can we sit down? I'm getting tired."

So Frances got out of their way and they sat down at the kitchen table with the suit box between them. Frances gave the stove a despairing glance, shut off the burners and removed her apron. Then she walked around the table and leaned against the sink.

"I don't care what anybody says," Frances announced in a firm voice. "I want the whole story. From the beginning."

Vince glanced at Harold, who shrugged his shoulders and averted his eyes. So Vince told her what he knew, beginning with Frank Mastretta's summoning telephone call and ending with the

126

box of money in front of him. When he was finished, Frances said:

"No!"

"No, what?"

"You're not going through with it, I won't let you, I don't care what Frank Mastretta says, or what the kidnapers want— Let Frank do it!"

"He can't," said Harold. He was looking at the ceiling.

"Why can't he?"

"Frances—"

"I'm asking *him!*"

"I know who you're asking. Harold is right. You can't go changing things around to suit yourself. If Frank went in my place, if any change at all was made, the kidnapers might not go through with their end of it. They'd have an excuse. It could mean that Uncle Vincent would be murdered."

"That wouldn't hurt *my* feelings!"

"Frances, you don't mean it."

"Oh, don't I? If you ever needed any proof of what kind of a man your Uncle Vincent is, what kind of people he travels with— Even the kidnapers don't trust his friends! Well, Mr. Harold?"

Harold continued his study of the ceiling.

Frances said, "If they want someone they can trust, we'll get Uncle Joe. He can be the go-between."

Harold brought his eyes down. "Who's Uncle Joe?"

"Joseph Maggione. He's Vince's uncle on his father's side. Everybody around here knows Uncle Joe. And they know he can be trusted."

Harold shook his head. "Lady, if I was you—"

He was interrupted by the soft, insistent ringing of the telephone.

For a brief moment they remained frozen. Then, Vince gathered himself to rise while, across the table from him, Harold was looking around for the telephone while pushing back his chair.

Frances, already on her feet, dashed to the hall.

"Hello? . . . Oh, yes, Uncle Joe . . . Yes, he's here—"

She handed the phone to Vince, who had followed her into the hall, and she said, "Your Uncle J-Joe w-wants t-to t-talk to you—"

Now she *was* crying.

Vince said, "Uncle Joe? . . . Yes . . . Yes, just fine . . . What? . . . Well, uh, yes, I was there— It was about mom . . . No, I didn't see him . . . No . . . *Who told you that?* . . . Listen, have you spoken to anyone about this? . . . You're sure? . . . I'm not saying anything . . . No . . . No! . . . As soon as I can . . . Yes . . . Okay."

He replaced the telephone and looked at himself in the diamond-shaped mirror. "Somebody just called Uncle Joe," he said in a faint, uneven voice. "They as much as told him Uncle Vincent had been kidnaped; they said he was to ask *me*— If he knows who it was that called him, he wouldn't tell me."

Harold shrugged. "It figures," he said.

He sat in his shirtsleeves, hunched forward, at his scarred, almost bare desk, his violet eyes puzzling over the name he had just written down:

Dr. Richard Wentling, Fort Salonga, Northport, N.Y.

Detachedly his left hand pushed the telephone away while his right hand, fingers still holding a pencil, came up and the heel of his hand smoothed back his longish blond hair.

Wentling.

The name was familiar, although not connected with any case he had worked on recently, if ever. He knew that name from somewhere and he tried now to associate it. From the newspapers? Yes. Which newspapers, and when? Some paper, within the past month. Front pages? No. Featured article, with picture? No—

Dr.

He wasn't an M.D. The license plates weren't the right kind. Educator? Minister? Scientist—*Scientist!* Suddenly he remembered: *The Long Islander's* personal columns. *Dr. Richard Wentling, of Brookhaven Laboratories, has returned from*— Where?

At the moment, it didn't matter. If it should prove to be important, it could be checked. You learned a lot by reading the personal columns, especially if you were a private investigator. All you needed was enough time to read the items.

A month ago, he'd had plenty of time . . .

128

He delved into the wide center drawer of his desk, found the directory he wanted and located Wentling's phone number. He pulled the telephone back to him, dialed, and after a moment's waiting said to the woman who answered, "I'd like to speak to Dr. Wentling, please. It's rather important."

After another moment a man's voice came on and he said:

"Dr. Wentling? My name is Danzig. I'm a private investigator. I'm working on a case which involves a theft—I represent the owners and there is the possibility of an insurance claim— The point is, Dr. Wentling, an alert witness noticed and fortunately wrote down the license number of the vehicle involved in the theft. The number was *RV 2407*. According to Motor Vehicle Department records, this number was issued to you."

"Yes! Well, well, what do you know— My unfortunate license plates. So, at last they turn up— They were stolen from me and so reported to the police, and to the agent who handles my insurance!"

"How long ago was this, Dr. Wentling?"

"One month— What day is this, Tuesday? Exactly four weeks ago today!"

"Do you remember *where* they were stolen? It could be very important."

"I shall not be likely to forget! They were stolen from my car when it was parked at JFK International Airport. I had taken the shuttle to Washington in the morning and when I returned in the evening I did not notice their absence until I was stopped by the police— Believe me, it was most embarrassing!"

"Thank you, Doctor. You have been very helpful— Incidentally, no mention of the theft has been made in the newspapers. We don't want the thieves to know it has been discovered. I'm sure I can rely on your discretion in telling as few people as possible."

Over the telephone, Wentling's chuckle was audible. "I have been cleared for far more important secrets than this— By the way, is there any possible liability to me?"

"None at all."

"Good. I hope you catch the thief, or thieves!"

"We will. Thank you, Doctor."

Danzig put the phone down. Four weeks ago. JFK Airport—

Acting on a sudden hunch he reached into another drawer to remove the IBM printout, an inch-thick stack of folded pages made from one continuous sheet with punched holes in either margin. It was the record of new and used commercial vehicles purchased in Suffolk, Nassau and Queens Counties since the first of the year and contained more than two thousand entries.

Before she'd gone for the day, Danzig's girl, Ida, had checked with red crayon all the Ford, Chevrolet and Dodge vans on the list.

Although both Mrs. Spotafore and the gateman had said the kidnap vehicle was a Ford, Ted Key, the doorman, hadn't noticed what make it was. Mrs. Spotafore had not *seen* the van; she'd been told by the supposed TV repairman and she had passed the information along to the gateman. The bogus repairman had also described the van as *black* and white; if the van was, as Danzig firmly believed, the same one that had been disguised as a telephone truck, instead of being black the dark portion of the body would actually have been green.

Anyone smart enough to plant spurious information as to color would scarcely stop at make, especially when in conditions of darkness and to the uninitiated, Ford, Chevrolet and Dodge vans were quite similar in appearance. So Danzig, acting on one of his hunches, had told the girl to check for all three makes.

He'd had another hunch, about the license plates. Thus far, no one at the Spotafore house seemed to have noticed that the kidnap van had been carrying passenger plates, not commercial ones. Danzig's hunch about this—that the TV repair truck wouldn't have gotten far without a 2nd Precinct Suffolk County cop noticing the passenger plates—had led him to thinking that the TV truck hadn't been off Juniper Lane. And that had led him to the probability that the TV truck and the telephone van were one and the same.

It was attention to detail like this that made Danzig one of the best investigators in the business, and if it hadn't been for women problems he would have had little time to read the personal columns.

Four weeks ago, JFK Airport . . .

Danzig rode his hunch and culled from the list the names and

130

addresses of owners in Queens who had bought Ford, Chevrolet and Dodge vans in the last six weeks.

When he was finished, he had written down twenty-four owners. With any kind of luck, he could check them out in two days.

Grinning, he got up from the desk, put on his sport jacket and, with his hand on the light switch, glanced at his watch. In three more minutes, it would be eight o'clock. He might just start checking the list tonight.

eighteen

Since no one could be sure of exactly when the instructions would come, they settled down to the task of getting used to each other and putting up with each other as long as necessary. Frances dried her tears and took up almost where she had left off when Vince arrived. She insisted that they eat something. Harold had two helpings of meat loaf but passed up the salad. Vince ate little of either; he was nervous, out of sorts, and his eyes kept wandering to the telephone which, obdurately, did not ring. He was also a bit angry with Frances for acting as if it was all his fault.

There was rice pudding for dessert, and Harold enjoyed it noisily. After a third cup of coffee, he pushed his chair back and patted his stomach.

"I was married once," said Harold. "It didn't work out."

He didn't pursue it; apparently he wanted them to know he was simply making a statement, not inviting conversation. Frances came to a conclusion Vince had reached several hours earlier: Harold was a little difficult to make out. He looked more a chain store manager than a gangster. His skin was too light for him to be a Sicilian, and how many Italians named *Harold* would you be apt to meet? He had fine, sandy brown hair and a smooth face that could probably go a couple of days without seriously needing a shave. He was neatly dressed in a suit of good quality. He was wearing a large wristwatch with three buttons on the rim and openings in the face that showed both the day and the date. He

133

didn't glance at the watch once and showed no interest in the kitchen clock.

When the dishes were finished and the kitchen was in order, Frances said, "Well, Mr. Harold, since it looks like you'll be staying with us awhile, I'll make up a bed for you in the back room upstairs."

"No, thanks. You got a couch in the living room?"

"We have a couch. It isn't a sofa-bed."

"I'll stay there, near the phone. Not that they want to talk to me, but somebody ought to be down here. Like I said, I don't know how long this'll take. He can go to bed if he wants. Just don't take no sleeping pills."

"I suppose we might as well make ourselves comfortable." Frances led the way to the living room and switched on the floor lamp by the sofa. "Sorry we don't have a TV set." There was an edge of sarcasm in her voice.

"I know some people right now that wish *they* hadn't had one," said Harold. He tried the springs of the sofa before he sat down.

"Would you like something to read?" Frances asked.

Harold grinned. "I doubt you'd have my kinda litercher," he said, and when Frances blushed furiously he scowled. "I mean like a scratch sheet— Why don't you go to bed?"

"Well—"

"You got a phone up there? An extension?"

"No."

"Good. I don't want nobody getting ideas about calling up anybody. Like good old honest Uncle Joe. When we've got the boss back, I don't care who you call up. But until we do get him back, we all keep our mouths shut. Okay?"

Vince couldn't resist. "You should've made that clear before you left the house, you or somebody. It looks to me like one of your boys has already called Uncle Joe."

"Yeah? What makes you think it was one of our boys?"

"Who else knows?"

"The guys that did the snatch. They know."

"What? Why would they call *him?*"

"Why not? It's just as screwy as the rest of it. None of it makes sense— I suppose you think they were smart, snatching the boss

134

because they know we won't call the cops. You want to know something? Before this is over, they'll wish we *had* called the cops. At least, when the cops have you, you get a trial."

Sunlight was filling the room when Vince was wakened by sounds in the bathroom. Startled, he eyed the clock on the bureau. Its hands showed half-past nine. Frances should be at work by now— The bed beside him was still warm.

The bathroom sounds stopped. Then the door squeaked open and Frances came into the room.

"Hey! You see what time it is?"

"Yes. I've already been downstairs. I called M of E and told them I was sick and wouldn't be in today— Don't look at me like that! I am not leaving this house until this business is settled. And that's final."

"Okay— Harold still down there?"

"He's still down there. He's on his second cup of coffee by now."

"He came into the kitchen with you?"

"Yes— Vince, I was wearing my robe!"

"He make any passes?"

"He did not. If he had, I could handle him, and two more like him."

"Hah! Did you see the artillery he's wearing?"

"I saw it. I must say, your Uncle Vincent has some choice types working for him."

"I seem to remember *your* Uncle Vincent used to carry one of those to work, too."

"*My* Uncle Vincent was a policeman. As you very well know!"

"You'd better not say that too loud."

Vince shaved and took a shower. He wanted to think; he'd tried before going to sleep and he'd gotten nothing but a headache. Harold's confidently spoken words, that the kidnapers would wish the cops had been called, gave substance to Vince's belief that the money had somehow been marked. How it could have been done to escape detection until Uncle Vincent was released was probably a secret shared by Frank Mastretta, Tony LaScola and Aunt Sophie Spotafore. There had been a minimum of six to

135

seven hours from the time the first of the money had entered the house until the last of it had gone. In that much time, a lot could have been done. But, what had been done?

The puzzle of the money intrigued Vince. He wanted to go downstairs right now and, under whatever pretext, open the box and examine its contents for the secret markings he was sure were there.

But he didn't have the nerve. In all probability, Harold would say, *Vince, if I was you . . .*

Very likely, Harold had shot people for less.

Harold was about as much company as a piece of furniture. Having made himself a nest on the living-room couch, he didn't stir from it except to have breakfast and lunch, go to the bathroom, smoke cigarettes and drink coffee. He ran out of cigarettes before lunch and Vince sent Frances out to Russo's for them, and for his copy of *The New York Times*. Vince thought that with Frances out of the house, Harold might open up a little; that he might say something about the kidnaping, his work, Uncle Vincent, Frank Mastretta, Tony LaScola, the troublesome Looie, Brooklyn Mike, anything. Harold didn't. He kept his mouth shut and his eyes distant. He didn't talk. He didn't read. He wasn't even interested in the *Times*.

The phone rang once while Frances was out and before Vince could reach it, Harold was on it.

"H'lo . . . Yes . . . No . . . Okay."

That was his total conversation and when Vince looked questioningly at him, Harold merely shrugged and said, "Frank wanted to know if we heard anything yet."

The phone rang again, a minute after noon. Frances had just come in with Harold's cigarettes and before either Vince or Harold could get to the telephone, Frances had it.

"Hello? . . . Yes, this is Frances . . . Oh, Marge! I didn't recognize your voice . . . Yes, I'm feeling better; it was just a little upset . . . No, I'll be back tomorrow . . . Well, I'm sorry you have to go back on the extra list, but it *is* my job . . . Thanks for calling; 'By— *I beg your pardon!*"

Harold, who had shed his coat and was walking around with

his hardware showing, was unembarrassedly standing with his ear to the back of the telephone receiver in Frances' hand. When she hung up, he smiled vaguely and went back to his couch.

At three o'clock, a girl stopped by. She was selling chances on a basket of cheer; it was a benefit for the Sodality. The chances were twenty-five cents each, five for a dollar. Frances bought five and printed her name on the stubs. The girl went away.

At four, the telephone rang again. This time Harold, who had been in the kitchen pouring himself a cup of coffee, got to it first.

"H'lo . . . Who? . . . Justa minute—"

He covered the mouthpiece with his hand. Vince had followed him into the hall, and he looked at Vince's reflection in the diamond-shaped mirror.

"I think this is it," said Harold.

Frances had heard the ringing upstairs. She was halfway down the stairs and she stopped where she was.

Vince took the phone. "Yes?"

"Are . . . you . . . Vince . . . Mag . . . gione?"

Although he understood what was being said, he wasn't sure he was listening to a voice. Not a human voice; it was more a collection of sounds, as if someone had made marks on a sound track and constructed a voice from them. It reminded him of a sound he'd heard while in the hospital. There was a fellow whose larynx had been removed and he'd learned to talk again by pressing an amplifying tube against the muscle of his throat.

"Yes, this is Vince Maggione."

"I . . . am . . . Tee . . . Vee. . . . You . . . have . . . the . . . mon . . . ey?"

"Yes."

"Lis . . . ten . . . care . . . ful . . . ly. . . . Leave . . . your . . . house . . . in . . . five . . . min . . . utes. . . . Take . . . the . . . bus . . . to . . . Penn . . . syl . . . va . . . nia . . . and At . . . lan . . . tic. . . . Walk . . . to . . . Bush . . . wick. . . . Turn . . . left . . . three . . . blocks . . . to . . . ward . . . Brook . . . lyn. . . . Tel . . . e . . . phone . . . booth . . . on . . . the cor . . . ner . . . to . . . gas . . . sta . . . tion. . . . You . . . know . . . where?"

"Yes—the gas station, three blocks west on Bushwick."

137

"You . . . en . . . ter . . . the . . . booth. . . . Phone . . . will . . . ring. . . . You . . . get . . . your . . . in . . . struc . . . tions . . . then. . . . Have . . . the . . . mon . . . ey . . . with . . . you . . . and . . . go . . . a . . . lone. . . . Start . . . in . . . three . . . min . . . utes."

Click. And then, the dial tone.

Vince didn't have to tell Harold. He'd been listening with his ear pressed against the back of the receiver. Harold scowled as he went into the kitchen to get the box.

Frances came the rest of the way down the stairs. "Oh, Vince—"

Avoiding her eyes, he took his jacket from the hall rack and put it on. Then he tucked the box under his arm.

"Vince—please—*be careful*—"

Holding tightly to the box he brushed past her and walked out into the gray afternoon.

nineteen

The day had started bravely, bright and clean-washed, like a fifth-grader going to school. But sometime after lunch the brightness had faded and the cleanness had become hopelessly smudged. And by mid-afternoon a thick, high, all-pervading fog was being pushed in from Jamaica Bay and the Atlantic Ocean by a light southwest breeze. The fog obscured familiar landmarks while the breeze added a dimension of error to sounds. The normal traffic noises of the avenues to the north faded to indistinct rumblings while the whistling echoes of the planes in the stack for JFK, to the south, were shrill and insistently near.

Before Vince reached the corner, he noticed that the automobiles streaming along the avenue had their headlights on. The box threw him off balance and he shifted it from under his right arm to under his left. He had started out with his hands in his pockets, which was no good; he hadn't realized how much he needed the freedom of his arms to help him walk.

Vince hoped the fog would get him past the corner and Bennie's unseen and it would have if both Bennie and his partner hadn't been out front, working on a car. Bennie was filling the car with gas and his partner was examining the windshield-wiper blades, trying to make a sale.

Bennie saw Vince as soon as he was opposite the pump.

"Hey, Vince! Got a new suit?"

"Uh—no."

"Hey, what's your hurry? Stop a minute!"

"I can't right now. I've got to catch the bus."

"I get it. Going to the tailor shop— Been putting on some weight with Fran's cooking, hey?"

"Uh—sure."

Bennie hadn't been watching the pump and suddenly the nozzle cut off and some gasoline slopped out on the car fender and on his trouser leg. "Damn!" he said.

Vince breathed out and moved along, shifting the box again. Not that the box was heavy; it didn't weigh more than a dozen pounds. Twelve pounds of money. If you worked for Vincent Spotafore, you walked into a bank and said, *Give me some money, say about twelve pounds, in fives and tens— What's it come to? What, only forty grand? Make it fifty pounds. I'll write a check . . .*

He passed by Russo's. The awning was down. Mama Russo kept the awning up when the sun was shining and down during fog and rain. The neon tubes on the ceiling helped to project the store out on to the foggy sidewalk. Two people, a man and a woman, were buying something from someone who was concealed by the screen of junk over the counter at the cash register.

Vince reached Liberty Avenue, waited a moment for the WALK signal, and dodged across between right-turning cars just in time to catch the bus.

Bushwick Avenue, full of slow-moving, headlighted cars, was an indication of conditions on the Parkways. The workday pendulum had swung and the rush of Island-bound traffic had begun. People were always mashing into each other on the Parkways, fouling things up even in fair weather, which gave the helicopter-borne newscasters a chance to radio-talk traffic to the avenues and boulevards. But not today; in snow or fog, the grasshoppers were as blind as everyone else.

Vince thought, *They sure picked a great day for it.*

He crossed Pennsylvania Avenue and climbed a fairly steep grade to reach the gas station; it was one he knew, all right. This was where they gave discounts instead of stamps and game coupons, where Fran's father did his business. The telephone booth was at the corner of the station, blocking the way to the ladies' and men's. In any station in East New York, these were always kept locked; even at Bennie's, the key to the comfort station was something you had to fight for.

A man was in the phone booth. The door was open, of necessity, to accommodate his bulk; he was mostly in although partly out and his right hand, which was outside, was gesticulating violently while he argued with whoever it was he had called, or had called him. His argument was loud and profane and at any other time Vince might have been interested in listening. Vince held the box to his stomach and watched the lights moving through the fog. Unseen, an overhead train clattered into hearing, squealed past and rattled on with diminishing sounds.

The bulky man pulled himself out of the phone booth and, walking as if his feet hurt, went over to where his car stood unattended at the pumps, with the gas hose in the tank.

Vince walked to the booth and closed himself in. There wasn't any place to sit down, even if he'd wanted to. The overhead light went on as soon as he closed the door and he looked at his watch: 4:23.

How long had the bulky man held him up? Not more than a minute or two. His dime's worth would have run out in three minutes and if he had been losing the argument he would not have wanted to invest any more.

4:24.

Over at the pumps, the bulky man was now noisily losing an argument for trading stamps. Mad, he was struggling into his car. He started the car with a roar and jack-rabbitted into Bushwick Avenue. The uniformed attendant who had won the argument shrugged and went into the station to get out of the fog.

4:25.

The telephone in the booth rang, and Vince took it down in the middle of the ring.

"Hello?"

"Vin . . . cent . . . Mag . . . gione?"

"Yes."

"You . . . are . . . a . . . lone?"

"Yes."

"You . . . have . . . the . . . mon . . . ey?"

"I told you, I have it—yes!"

"Then . . . go . . . in . . . to . . . the . . . cem . . . e . . . ter . . . y . . . to . . . your . . . bro . . . ther's . . . grave. . . . You . . . will . . . find . . . your . . . fi . . . nal . . . in . . . struc . . . tions . . . in . . . the . . . flow . . . er . . . hold . . . er. . . . Fol . . . low . . . them. . . . Start . . . now."

Click. Dial tone.

The cemetery. Mario's grave . . .

Vince wiped the sweat from his forehead and, holding the box tightly under his left arm, quit the booth.

Danzig was uncomfortably aware of an increasing headache as he drove west on Linden Boulevard, trying to make out street signs in the fog. He'd given up trying to read house numbers; it only added to his headache, and they were invisible anyway. He remembered this section from the days when he'd been a member of the NYPD and had known this as a trouble area, especially for hot cars. He knew the binumeral addressing system well enough to be able to locate, within a block, the number he was seeking, so he watched for street signs.

A Rachel W. Turner had purchased a Dodge van seven weeks ago, and her address on Linden put her west of Pennsylvania Avenue near the intersection of Williams Street. At the moment, Danzig didn't know whether the address would be a private house, a tenement, an industrial building or a vacant lot. Whatever it was, it could not possibly be less productive than the twenty-five other addresses he had investigated since eight o'clock last night. More than an hour ago he had exhausted the first batch and had had to call Ida from a pay phone in a bar, waiting six dimes' worth while she came up with a fresh dozen candidates from the IBM printout.

And if the remaining eleven were as worthless as the first of the dozen—*that* one had been bought by a painting contractor and was sitting, blocking his driveway, with a broken axle—Danzig had blown eighty-five cents.

Traffic lights ahead climbed from a fast yellow to an abrupt red and Danzig jammed on the brakes of his beaten-up Chevy while he cursed the driver in front of him—he could have easily gone

142

through the yellow—and hoped the driver behind him would be able to stop; he was. Danzig was now in the center of three lanes of westbound traffic, mostly heavy trucks, and he watched the flow of cross traffic jouncing by with headlights ineffectual in the fog. He did not have to strain his eyes for street signs to recognize Pennsylvania Avenue.

The light changed and Danzig swore in anger as the driver in front of him stalled his car. Behind, some heavyhanded moron risked a fine by leaning on the horn. Danzig counted slowly to ten and the car ahead started with a roar and lurched across the intersection.

Now Danzig watched his chance, keeping an eye on the rear-vision mirror and working the directional signal for a right turn and, when he was safely past Pennsylvania Avenue, he eased the Chevy into the right lane. Memory jogged him faintly. It had been a long time—it had to be at least five years—since he'd been in this place. He couldn't tell if it had changed. Everything looked alike in the fog.

Linden Boulevard widened suddenly and veered to the left and Danzig found himself groping along alone in the right lane. After about a minute of this the car lights picked out, directly ahead, a stand of tall, dead weeds with an open area beyond, a kind of triangular plaza where several streets came together, dimly opalescent with street lamps glowering at the frustrating fog.

The Chevy bounced over a break in the pavement and its lights showed a black area extending past the weed-grown broken triangle of sidewalk, and Danzig cut hard to the right and pulled into a street that ran on a sharp bias to the northeast. On his left a building loomed, dark and ugly in the fog; the part in the triangle was one-story high and attached to it was a two-story structure. The lower floor looked boarded up, but the upper floor apparently contained an apartment. A light was showing from a window in the wall above the one-story portion; just as Danzig drove past, from the corner of his eye he saw the light go out.

A dozen feet farther, he pulled the Chevy to the curb and cut the lights. He was about to get out when he saw, in his rear-vision mirror, a door open in the boarded-up downstairs of the two-story part of the building. A Negro youth, perhaps seventeen years

143

old, skipped lightly down the steps to the sidewalk. The youth paused, looked up and down the street, and then moved quickly to the single-story portion of the structure.

Danzig hadn't planned it that way, but he had stopped in a pool of fog rendered opaque by the shadow of the building which was blocking the street lights in the triangular intersection. The youth couldn't see Danzig, although Danzig could see him as he stood outlined in the glow from the triangle and from the incident light of Linden Boulevard.

Danzig was about to shout at the youth, to ask him if he knew where Rachel W. Turner lived, when he bent down and opened a garage door by rolling it up. The inside of the garage was dark. Danzig expected the youth to go inside, but he didn't. He stepped back, away from the building, and stood looking up and down the street. Then he motioned with his hands toward the dark interior of the garage.

An engine started up and a pair of headlights came on and a car, an old sedan, rolled out into the street. For a moment, Danzig thought he would be revealed and instinctively he prepared to drop on his side behind the covering barrier of the seat. But while he was thinking about it, the sedan turned right, toward Linden Boulevard. So Danzig held where he was and the sedan stopped with its rear just clear of the wide garage door.

The youth jumped across the sidewalk and grabbed at a length of rope to pull the wide door down, and in that brief moment Danzig's heart nearly stopped.

The powerful beam from the headlights of a big tractor and trailer rig, sweeping around the curve on Linden Boulevard, showed a New York Telephone van standing in the garage.

Danzig froze, watching as the youth closed the door and trotted to the sedan to climb in on the left side.

In the area of the rear window, silhouetted by light coming through the windshield, he saw the heads and shoulders of three people: the youth, on the driver's side; on the right someone—a woman, he decided—and, sitting stiffly in the middle of the rear seat, a man who was wearing a felt hat. Before he could do anything or even think further about it, the sedan moved off, crossed the triangle of pavement and sped west on Linden Boulevard.

Headache forgotten, Danzig waited, counting slowly while he watched the building. When he reached one hundred, he took a flashlight from the glove compartment and stepped out into the street.

The building was silent, and no light showed anywhere. Danzig walked straight to the boarded-up part and turned his flashlight on the door. There had once been plate glass in the door, probably oval shaped, but it was now as securely covered by boards as the windows it was set between. The flashlight's beam picked out a set of hyphenated numbers on the paint-peeled surface of the right doorjamb and, below the numbers, something else: tacked to the wood was a stained and faded business card.

Rachel W. Turner, Dressmaker, the card said.

He'd found the right address.

Danzig moved to the garage part, letting the flash beam play on and around the door. Of segmented and articulated steel sections, it had been a good door, once; with not a crack or chink in it anywhere, it was still good enough to hide whatever was behind it. He tried to open it; it was, as he had suspected it would be, securely locked and he doubted that anything short of a bazooka shell would open it.

He stepped back and his flashlight picked out the board of a sign across the top of the door. There had been lettering on the board once, but the letters had been carefully covered with thick black paint. He would have turned away if the light hadn't caught something faintly discernible on the face of the sign.

Moisture had collected on the surface and the paint-layer-thick raised portion of the lettering was different from the rest.

After experimenting briefly, Danzig found that by holding the flashlight above his head in his left hand and shining it across the sign, he could make out the wording:

Enoch Turner's Taxi Service.

Turner. Enoch Turner. The name rang a faint, distant bell. But, why? And how long ago?

Danzig shook his head.

He turned the beam of light on his watch. Twenty minutes past five. He switched off his light and walked briskly to his car.

twenty

In Woodside, Maspeth, Ridgewood, Glendale, Woodhaven and East New York, the cemeteries are as much facts of life as they are reminders of death. Together they cover a land area greater in size than Manhattan's Central Park. Separately they are marble forests interspersed with high-rise apartment buildings, tenement houses, one- and two-family homes, commercial and industrial complexes and business blocks traversed by streets and arterial highways. It is not by accident that the whole cluster of cemeteries reaches like the spatulate fingers of a giant hand toward the bowl that is Brooklyn: each burial ground was chosen as a nicely calculated carriage ride from the synagogues, churches and funeral parlors that would supply it. Thus that patient and sometimes recalcitrant animal, the horse, was as surely responsible for the location of the cemeteries as it was for the winning of the West.

The cemetery—the one covering the largest land area and most resembling Rome or Jerusalem or the Greek Isles of the Dead—is a collection of sixteen burying grounds clustered around a reservoir and a park. It lies between Myrtle Avenue on the north and a welter of traffic interchanges, including Bushwick Avenue, on the south, and is bisected by the Interboro Parkway. Within the lives of many if not most of its permanent residents, this land had been the open country of farms.

In the graveyards of *the* cemetery, those from every walk of life, religious faith and ethnic background have been laid to rest

147

with geometrically precise segregation. Largest in this group is the Cemetery of the Evergreens, which completely engulfs Most Holy Trinity to the west and nearly overwhelms Mount Judah to the northeast. Slighty less than half of the Evergreens lies in Kings County and the Borough of Brooklyn; the rest is in Queens.

It was here that Vince Maggione, holding tightly to the Macy's Men's Store suit box and dragging his aching leg, came through a miasma of late afternoon fog, hurrying people and impatient, unpredictable, headlighted traffic.

Although he had not visited this place in years—the last time had been the family's visit following a Memorial Day parade—he knew where he was going as if that had been yesterday. The official final resting place of the Maggiones—except Uncle Joe's family—was a plot of eight burial lots, six as yet unfilled. Dominico Maggione had made his second and last real estate investment here, and his gray granite headstone occupied the center of it.

Mario's grave was marked with a matching gray granite block, a small replica of the headstone. Mario had not survived his war and so had no chance for a VFW or Legion medallion. Rose had filled the need by supplying a bronze Army emblem, mounted on a rod; it was fitted with a hole into which a miniature American flag could be inserted and it had a basket of bronze strips for which arrangements of artificial flowers could be obtained.

As Vince limped up the road to Mario's grave, he was thinking that if Charley Bennett hadn't found and saved him, *he* would now be another granite block beside Mario.

As he came nearer, he discovered he wasn't alone in The Evergreens. A little way down to his left, fog or no, a woman and two children were kneeling in prayer. The children looked like gradeschoolers; perhaps this was the anniversary of their father's death and their mother had waited for them to come home from school before bringing them here.

A few yards beyond the woman and children, a man was digging a fresh grave. Although he was facing them, he did not pause in his operation of the machine that was precisely and quietly scooping up the earth and depositing it on a tarpaulin. Beyond him there might have been other people, or none; it was impossible to tell.

148

The artificial flowers honoring Mario's memory were secured in a plastic base of simulated earth that neatly fitted the basket. Vince lifted the arrangement out in one piece.

A folded paper lay in the basket. Spread out, it was half the size of a letter sheet and typed on it was:

Follow road, then path, to right until you reach the wall along Interboro Parkway. Turn left at wall and walk 100 feet to grave of Josiah McKenzie.

With McKenzie headstone at your back, walk straight to the wall and wait there until you hear the sound of a radio.

As soon as you hear the radio, toss the box over the wall.

Your signal that all is okay will be when the radio stops.

You will then return to your home.

His people will be told where to pick him up.

TV.

Vince folded the paper and put it in his pocket. Holding the box in both hands now, he followed the road, then the path until, ahead of him, the wall loomed out of the fog.

Danzig ordered a corned beef on rye to be served with his vodka and water at the bar and, needing change, paid the bartender on the spot. The bartender gave back three quarters, a nickel and two pennies for Danzig's three singles. Danzig still needed a dime, so the bartender changed one of the quarters.

There was a phone booth in the back of the bar and Danzig closed himself into it. He dropped a dime in the slot, dialed *OL 8-1234* and after a ring and a half a woman's voice said:

"Long Island Press."

"Let me have the City Desk."

"Just a moment—"

"City Desk."

"Hal Sappersteen?"

"Uh—yes. *Hal! On four!*"

"Sappersteen."

"Hal? This is Danzig."

"Who?"

"Danzig—Johnny Danzig."

"*Oh*— Long time. How the hell are you? What've you got?"

149

"I don't know. Maybe nothing— I need a look at your microfilm files."

"No problem. When?"

"Half an hour from now okay?"

"Okay. I'd better type out a note. You can pick it up at my desk —I'm halfway down the right side. What's cooking?"

"I'll know more when I've seen your files."

"How far back?"

"Five years, maybe six."

"No problem."

"Thanks, Hal. See you in thirty minutes."

He got back to his place at the bar just as the bartender brought the sandwich. Danzig ate the sandwich hungrily and drank the rest of the vodka and water. In ten minutes he walked out, leaving a quarter tip.

The wall was higher than Vince's head and there were no gravestones near enough, or low enough, that he could stand on to look over it. He couldn't remember what was on the other side of the wall. A strip of grass, he thought; there was a park alongside the highway. He put the box down and rubbed his tired arms and for a minute or so tried to judge, by the sound of the passing cars, how far the Interboro Parkway was from the wall. The traffic noises, the swish of cars and squeal of rubber on wet pavement, drifted through the fog along with the yellowish tinge from the parkway lights . . .

Not a yard from him, on the other side of the wall, a transistor radio began playing rock and roll.

He hadn't heard a car stop.

The music from the radio increased suddenly in volume, a cacophony hardly appropriate for this place.

Vince picked up the box and tossed it over the wall, and the radio noise stopped immediately.

In a moment he heard a new sound, the sudden, sharp exhaust of a cycle. It sounded like a Yamaha, or one of the Italian or Austrian makes; whatever it was, its exhaust increased in volume and then steadily diminished as it sped away.

No wonder the kidnapers hadn't been worried about traffic; a cycle could thread its way through an impasse of stalled automobiles, could even jump a divider strip and head in the opposite direction. In his mind's eye, Vince pictured the cyclist in helmet and jacket, the suit box zippered securely against his chest and stomach under the jacket, leaving his hands free . . .

Vince's eyes were alight and the ache in his leg was forgotten for the moment as he hurried back along the path. When he reached Mario's grave, the woman and the two children had gone and he was afraid the gravedigger had gone, too. Then he heard the crunch of feet on gravel and the gravedigger came trudging through the mist.

Although of more than middle age, the gravedigger was still lean and muscular. His hatless head was covered with a wild thatch of gray hair. He wore coveralls that were threadbare but clean. Only his shoes were muddy.

"Lost?" he asked when he saw Vince.

"No. I was hoping to see you. I wanted to ask a question."

"All right. Ask."

"How can anyone find out where a certain grave is located?"

"Easy. Call the office."

"Is *that* all?"

"That's all. Who are you looking for?"

"*I'm* not looking for anyone. My father and brother, Dominico and Mario Maggione, are buried—there."

"Oh, Maggione. Perpetual care. I know them." He spoke as if they were alive.

"Has anyone been asking questions about them?"

"Not of me. They might've asked the office."

"Have you seen anyone around the plot lately?"

"People around here all the time. You just missed a woman and two kids. But, not Maggione— Come to think, day before yesterday. An old colored lady. She was here again this afternoon. I remember her, going over to look at those plastic flowers— Say, is anything wrong?"

"No— An old colored lady? How old?"

"I'm not much judge of age. And *they're* hard to tell."

"How was she dressed?"

151

"Black coat, brown hat. Neat, I'd say. Yes, neat. She didn't look poor. We get lots of people in here. I can't remember 'em all— We'd better be going or we'll be locked in here."

Enoch Turner.

Danzig slowly turned the crank and, as past pages of the *Long Island Press* flashed on the screen, occasionally saw bits of his life in review. Investigations, informations, seizures and arrests; the good days when a policeman didn't have to be a combination of social worker, lawyer and parliamentarian, when all he had to do was catch a crook and get cuffs on him. Danzig had had a lot of them, some of them tough, which was why he'd been promoted to detective. The small candle Enoch Turner lit was back about that time; he hadn't worked on the case or he would have remembered. But he could remember hearing it discussed, in the squad room. That was in the good days, before he'd met the woman from Forest Hills, the one who'd claimed she was a widow—Enoch Turner hadn't happened after her. If he had, Danzig wouldn't have remembered the name at all . . .

And suddenly, there it was. Not a large headline, but the kind that came days or weeks after the public interest had waned. The story was brief: it said there was nothing new in the Enoch Turner case according to "Big Bob" Schweinberg, detective inspector in charge of homicide in the East New York sector. There was a one-paragraph rehash: Turner, found (date) three blocks from his home on Linden Boulevard, had at first been believed to be a hit-run victim. An autopsy, however, had disclosed that he had died of a massive cerebral hemorrhage after having been severely beaten.

Danzig didn't bother cranking further in search of the original story. He shut off the machine, smiled his thanks at the woman who had let him use it, and went out of the building in search of a pay telephone.

twenty-one

It was after six when Vince got back to the house to find Frances waiting for him in the hall. She had been in the kitchen and when she'd heard his steps, she had run to the door.

"Thank *God*— Are you all right?"

"I'm all right. I *am* tired— Where's Harold?"

"Gone. There was a telephone call for him, then he called a cab, he's been gone about fifteen minutes— Part of the call to him was for you, he said. You're to call Frank Mastretta as soon as you come in, the number's written on that piece of card in the mirror— Vince, you look *awful!*"

"Damn it, I'm *tired!* I've got to sit down, before I call Frank or anybody— Do we have any coffee?"

"Coffee we have. Supper is something else—" She left off her inspection of him, turned quickly and walked into the kitchen.

Wincing each time his right foot hit the floor, Vince followed. When he reached the table, he pulled out a chair and lowered himself into it. Then he stretched his leg out straight, clenching his teeth against the pain.

Frances poured a cup of coffee and brought it to the table before returning to stand by the sink with her back to him and her eyes looking at the darkness outside the window.

Vince took a long swallow of coffee and when he brought the cup down he warmed his hands on it. He glanced at her back.

"I suppose you're mad," he said.

153

"Should I be?" she asked without turning around.

"I don't know. Aren't you interested in hearing what happened?"

"I'm interested that you left this house at four o'clock and that you've been walking and standing, which you shouldn't have been. Certanily not in this dampness. And cold."

"The doctor told me to exercise— All right, I shouldn't have done it. I didn't volunteer for the job. You heard what Harold said."

"What Harold said I couldn't care less. You've gone to a lot of trouble to convince me that your Uncle Vincent wasn't exactly your favorite person. Yet, Monday you had lunch with him, at Angelo's— You could have told me, it would have been easy to say, *Fran, I had lunch today, or yesterday, or last Monday— I had lunch at Angelo's with Uncle Vincent*— But you didn't tell me, I had to hear it from someone else, a stranger. Then, yesterday, you learned your Uncle Vincent was kidnaped. Frank Mastretta—now, there's another person you've spent some time in disenchanting me about—Frank whistled, and you went running, just like his dog— What I'm saying is true, isn't it?"

"Damn it, Fran, I'm not proud that I had lunch with him! I've been trying to forget it— What's the point?"

"I thought I was your wife, I thought husbands and wives were supposed to share. We *did* share, we used to. But something has been happening to you. I don't know what it is, and I don't like it."

"Something's been happening to me, all right. My uncle was kidnaped and the kidnapers named me as the go-between. Or I suppose maybe you think I arranged *that?*"

She was quiet a moment, looking at the darkness outside the window. Then she said, "I don't know. Did you arrange it?"

"For Christ's sake! Where did you get *that* screwy idea?"

"From your friend Harold."

Vince sat in astonished silence.

Now she turned and looked at him. Her face devoid of color and her eyes dull, she said in a listless voice:

"As soon as you'd left the house, he started in on me. About *you,* what did I really know about you, did I know what you do all day, did I know you bought your car and paid for the insurance with cash—"

154

"Of course you know! Out of our savings— Half of it was yours!"

"That isn't what he wanted to know, Vince. He just wanted *me* to know that *he* knew— Then he started turning his questions to your friends: did you have many friends, did I know who your friends were, did I know your *ex-service* friends."

"He— What did you tell him?"

"I told him I'd never met them, and that if you had mentioned their names, I couldn't remember them— He didn't believe me, he laughed in my face. He asked me if any of your ex-service friends lived around here and I said I didn't think so. Then he asked me if I knew which of your ex-service friends was a drug addict, or had a wife who was an addict."

Vince didn't say anything. He felt sick.

"He said you had arranged the lunch date with your uncle because you wanted to buy heroin." She looked straight at him. "Vince, you should have told me."

He stared at the coffee cup. "I should have. I meant to. But I kept putting it off—"

The telephone rang.

Frances said, "That's probably Frank Mastretta. What shall I tell him?"

"I'll tell him," said Vince. He pushed himself up and dragged his leg to the telephone. "Hello?"

"Vince? Frank."

"I just got home. I was about to call you."

"It's just as well you didn't. I'm calling from an outside line, a pay phone. Uh— *He* was picked up in Brooklyn, Prospect Park, a half hour ago. Mike picked him up and is bringing him straight to the house at his own request; they should get there in twenty, twenty-five minutes. Mike said he seemed to be all right, but we'll see what the doctor says— Now, in case he asks, I've got to know everything from your end."

Vince told him, from the first telephone call through the second, the note of instructions at Mario's grave, the wall, the cycle, the Negro woman the gravedigger had seen. When he was quite finished, he thought from the ensuing silence that Frank had left the telephone.

"Hey! You still there?"

"I'm here; I was just thinking— I don't like this, Vince. Not one bit. That business about Mario's grave— Well, I've got to get back to the house. Keep that note. And stand by for a call." And before Vince could ask him any questions, he hung up.

Frances was watching him when he came back into the kitchen. She'd heard all of it and she said, "I guess you know you're in trouble."

"Maybe."

"Vince, you *are!*"

"I'll admit I *would* be in trouble if I'd had anything to do with kidnaping Uncle Vincent. But I didn't have anything at *all* to do with it, not even remotely."

"Not physically, perhaps. But how can you be sure you didn't have something to do with it in some other way?"

"What are you talking about?"

"Your friends, Charley Bennett and Noble Wright. You told *them* about your uncle, didn't you? While they were in this house, drinking beer?"

"What? What makes you think I'd tell them?"

"You may not realize it, but this is something you do. You've told *me* about your uncle; you've told my sister, and her husband, about the *house* your uncle lives in, about the *guards* he has, about the *dogs;* whether you realized it or not, you were bragging. And you told Charley and Noble, didn't you? Isn't it because you made it pretty clear that your uncle is a biggie in the Mafia, isn't that why they set you up to buy heroin from him?"

"They already knew who he was! They knew all about him— Okay, so I told Charley and Noble about my one visit to Uncle Vincent's house! Does that, for Christ's sake, mean they kidnaped him?"

"Not necessarily. But they could have told someone else about that house. Your friend Harold said that the gang knew all there was to know about the house, the dogs, the guards, your uncle's habits, everything— Oh, Vince, don't you realize how it must look to someone like Frank Mastretta? Or Tony LaScola?"

156

twenty-two

"Hello—*hello?* Oh—Emma?"

"Yes."

"Is Bob home?"

"Who is this?"

"Johnny—Johnny Danzig."

"Who? Johnny *Dan*zig? My God—I thought maybe somebody had shot you a long time ago; some *hus*band, maybe— How long is it since you were here to the house? Can it be five years?"

"Something like that. I remember, you had *Hasenpfeffer* and *Kartoffel Klosse*. And you were wearing your new red dress."

"What a memory— You know something? I still got that dress. And it wasn't new *then,* either— Bob's watching the news on TV. I'll get him . . ."

"Johnny?"

"Yes, Bob. How are you?"

"You didn't call me to ask how I am. What's on your mind?"

"You remember anything about Enoch Turner?"

"E-noch Tur-ner— You'll have to clue me, Johnny."

"Turner was a Negro. Five, six years ago he had a taxi business on Linden Boulevard. Your boys picked him up dead; thought it was a hit-run. But the autopsy showed he'd died of a massive cerebral hemorrhage after taking a severe beating."

"Oh! Yeah, now I remember. He *did* take a beating. Looked

like gangster stuff; matter of fact, it was. What do you want with him?"

"Anything. Testimony, witnesses, disposition, anything you can give me."

"Why, Johnny?"

"Because I'm on a case."

"Police case?"

"You know damned well what I've been doing since I was busted from the Department. And you also know damned well I can't tell you any more than that I need the information!"

"Yeah. You weren't such a bad guy, Johnny, if you'd of just kept away from the women— This Turner had a cab business. He was a World War Two vet and had used his GI to buy a couple of cabs and he hired his brother-in-law—what the hell was his name . . . Wright. Willis Wright—and they were doing fairly well, anyway making a living. Then some of their Negro service buddies started drifting in, looking for jobs. I don't know if you remember that war, but along about 1949, 1950 when the GI had run out and they'd spent their bonus money, it was tough for vets to get jobs, especially for Negro vets; there was no Civil Rights and job programs in those days and they were lucky if they could get a job sweeping a floor someplace.

"But, this Turner figured he wasn't doing bad and if he could branch out, buy more cabs and hire guys to drive them, he would do better. So he bought four more cabs, on time payments, and he built a garage alongside his house, mortgaging the house to raise the money.

"He did fair for a while. Then, business dropped off and all his payments caught up to him at once.

"I remember, I talked to the widow. She was a queer one. She even tried to throw me out of the place once, and you know the size of *me*. I couldn't get her to tell me the right time. But, I finally got hold of Turner's brother-in-law, her brother, Willis Wright. I had to go to Harlem to find him; by that time the last of Turner's cabs had been repossessed, the taxi company was out of business, and Wright was out of a job. Period.

"The last thing Wright wanted to talk about was Enoch Turner, so I took him to a beer joint. I remember, his boy insisted on

158

going along with us. The boy was maybe eighteen, nice-looking boy; his name might be in my report, but I don't remember it now. After a couple of drinks, Wright opened up a little. He said his brother-in-law had gotten into financial trouble as soon as he started to expand the business, and it had been going on for close to ten years, he said. Just about the time he'd get one cab paid for another would wear out. Then insurance rates went sky-high. Then his drivers wanted more money— Finally it got so a payment was due every week, and Turner was getting ulcers.

"Then, enter the loan sharks.

"You know how it is, Johnny. In Brooklyn and East New York, they're everywhere; you even fall over 'em on the courthouse steps— To make a long story short, I think it was in '58 or '59, Turner borrowed ten grand.

"According to Wright, Turner paid back the ten the first year, and in the next four years he paid *forty thousand dollars in interest*— You know how they work, Johnny. After the autopsy, we picked up some guys. We never even got as far as the Grand Jury with 'em. Either nobody could identify 'em or else they were scared to— You know how it is, Johnny."

"I know how it is," said Danzig.

"You want records, maybe I can dig 'em up."

"I don't know if I do or not. I'll see what my client says."

"Johnny, I don't know what you want this for, and I don't want to know who your client is. But before I would go up against the mob, I'd want to be damned sure of my money. And my family would be taken care of."

"I guess you've forgotten: I lost my family at about the same time I lost my job."

"Yeah. And for the same reason. I hope you're cured."

"So do I. Thanks, Bob."

"Don't mention it, Johnny."

Danzig put the phone back on its holder. So, Enoch Turner had paid $40,000 in interest on a $10,000 loan that he'd paid back. And when he either refused to or else could not pay any more, the mob had beaten him to death— And, the price to redeem Vincent Spotafore *had been exactly $40,000!*

For a moment, he let his eyes wander over the patrons in the bar. And then, unsmiling, he left phone booth and bar, walking quickly and not looking back.

A cold morning rain was lashing at the bedroom windows when Vince awoke the next morning. Frances was gone; she'd evidently gotten up before the alarm went off. Under the circumstances, it was probably just as well; after last night, she wouldn't be speaking to him this morning.

He shaved and dressed quickly and made himself breakfast. There was a new urgency on him, a feeling that time was running out. Sometime today he would receive a call—a command—from Frank Mastretta, and when it came he wanted to be ready. If he'd ever had any advantage in his cold war with Uncle Vincent, he had lost it. What was worse, despite the confidence he had expressed to Frances, when he faced squarely up to the situation he had to admit that his position was very bad.

There was just a chance . . .

He dialed Suffolk Information for the number of the paper where Charles Bennett said he worked and in due course was talking to the foreman of the composing room.

"What's this for, a credit reference?"

"No. I'm a friend of his. We were in the service together, in Vietnam."

"Okay. Bennett, Charles. Yes, we have him, but he's not on now. He works nine-thirty P.M. to five A.M."

"Can you tell me if he was working Monday night?"

"Monday? Let me look at the card file. Yah, he was. Started here Monday nine-thirty-one P.M., to five-fifteen. He takes his break from one to one-thirty. Anything else you want to know?"

"Do you have his telephone number?"

"He doesn't have a phone. He calls in. If you want to leave a message, I'll see that he gets it."

"Please ask him to call Vince Maggione. He has my number."

"Vince M,a,g,g,i,o,n,e?"

"Right. And thanks."

That would seem to take care of Charley Bennett for Monday night. It wasn't likely that he would have taken part in a kidnaping on Juniper Lane in Huntington Bay some time around half-past

160

eight and reported for his job in Deer Park, a good twelve miles away, only an hour later. It was, of course, possible. But it seemed highly improbable.

Vince's spirits were a bit higher when he took down the phone again and in a few minutes—after a trip to the kitchen for a ball-point pen and paper—he was writing down the names of what turned out to be nine electronics firms listed by the Port Washington Chamber of Commerce.

Systematically, he worked down the list. Eight firms had never heard of Noble S. Wright. The ninth:

"Zen Elec-tron-ics!"

"Do you have a Noble S. Wright working for you?"

"Is he in Planning, Production, Sales or Shipping?"

"Um—I'm not sure. I think he's an electronics engineer."

"That would be Planning, or Production. Wright— We have a Walter F. Wright, in Planning. He's a design engineer."

"No. This is Noble. Noble S. Wright."

"Oh, *Noble!* He's one of the janitors!"

"He's *what?*"

"Oh, dear! Mr. Zen would fire me if he heard that— They're not janitors, they're Maintenance Men and Custodians! Noble was recently promoted from Custodian; he's now a Maintenance Man— He's very bright. Mr. Zen has taken a *personal* interest in him."

"Can you tell me if he was working Monday?"

"Oh, yes. He works days, from nine to five. In fact, he's on now. Would you like to speak to him?"

"I don't want to bother him while he's working. Does he have a home telephone?"

"I'm sorry. I'm not permitted to give that information. But I can get him for you now—"

"Please don't bother. I'll see him—thank you." And in the midst of her insistence that it wouldn't be any trouble at all, he closed the connection.

So, Noble S. Wright *wasn't* an electronics engineer, he was a maintenance man. That is, he was a janitor, first class; not too long ago he'd been a janitor, second class. How much could he make at either job, even with Mr. Zen's *personal* interest?

Vince thought about Noble's tailored suit, his expensive wristwatch and his alligator shoes, and his momentarily high spirits came crashing down.

Now there was something he must do. He had told Charley and Noble about more than Uncle Vincent's home and habits: he'd told them about his dead brother, Mario. And about Uncle Joe Maggione. And on Tuesday, the ransom note had been on Mario's grave, and someone had called Uncle Joe Maggione trying to find out what was being done about the kidnaping . . .

At any other time, Vince would have walked to the corner to ask Uncle Joe, face to face, why his phone call hadn't been followed up by a visit. But now he didn't dare leave the telephone.

He phoned the service station, and Bennie answered. Uncle Joe, Bennie said, was in Hammonton, New Jersey, visiting an old family friend. He'd left right after supper last night and wasn't expected back until late Sunday night.

Vince left the telephone and dragged himself into the kitchen to wait. Like a man lost, he was beginning to be afraid.

twenty-three

Danzig was sitting alone in the booth, facing the door and fingering his second glass of vodka and water, when the door opened and the short, fat man who entered came straight to the booth. For an instant, the scar on Danzig's jaw showed scarlet.

"I was expecting Frank," said Danzig.

Tony LaScola shrugged. "The boss wanted him. The boss only woke up an hour ago, he slept eighteen hours solid. So, Frank told me to take what you got."

Danzig sipped his drink. "There were—uh—arrangements, you know."

"I know. You got a grand in advance against a hundred a day—"

"Plus expenses."

"—plus expenses. You've been working, what, three days? You haven't used up that grand yet!"

"There was to be another thousand when I wrapped it up."

"Huh—you got it wrapped up?"

"Do you have the thousand?"

"For Christ's sake—" Tony reached in his inside pocket, pulled out a fat envelope and contemptuously dropped it on the table.

Danzig smiled and raised his hand to signal the bartender. "What will you have?"

"Scotch and soda," said Tony. "And *you* better have something for me!"

163

"Don't worry. I've got it." Danzig smiled again. He ordered Tony's scotch and soda and another vodka and water for himself. When the drinks were served and the bartender had gone he said:

"I have it all. Names, addresses, the whole bit. Before I *write* my report, I'm going to *tell* you what I have. Then you will have to make a decision."

"A decision?" Some of Tony's scotch dribbled on his chin. He wiped it off with a paper napkin. "Like what? And why me?"

"Because if anything happens to your boss—and it could—you'll probably be the one to take over. Unless he makes a deal with his nephew first."

"What? You're crazy! What kind of a deal? And what could happen to him now?"

"Suppose I told you what this kidnaping is all about?"

"Listen, I'm no private eye. But I'm smart enough to figure they didn't take that chance for a lousy forty grand!"

"Right. The real object was revenge."

"Hell, I already figured that out— What do you mean, *if he makes a deal with his nephew—* Are you talking about Vince Maggione?"

"Yes."

Tony fiddled with his drink while his eyes gathered cunning. "I don't think I understand," he said.

"I think you do. You're pretty good at figuring things out. If, included in the revenge, the idea was to make monkeys out of you and Frank; if this thing was planned so there would be a general housecleaning; if the boss settled his feud with his nephew and called him in to run the legitimate side of the business, where would that put you—and Frank?"

"You're telling me Vince Maggione had a hand in this?"

"I'm telling you that when you hear all I've got, you're going to have to make a decision as to how much of it you want written down in a report."

"I see," said Tony. His voice and eyes were hard.

Danzig said, "It might not be a bad idea if we went to my office. After I've told you what I have, you can tell me how much of it you want typed up."

"We'll go in my car," said Tony. "I'll drop you back here afterward."

Danzig picked up the envelope and put it in his pocket. They went out of the bar, which was on New Street, and Tony drove the three blocks to Danzig's office on New York Avenue. An hour and twenty minutes later, Tony brought Danzig back to the bar and then drove straight to Juniper Lane.

When Frances came home at a quarter to six, she found Vince sitting dejectedly on the second step of the stairs. Although she had no way of knowing, he had been sitting there, off and on, for most of the day, waiting Frank Mastretta's telephone call. The call had not come, and neither had he received a response from Charley Bennett.

The rain had stopped late in the afternoon and Frances' hat, raincoat and umbrella were dry when she stowed them in the hall. She barely spoke to him when she arrived, and while they were eating the dinner she prepared, she did not speak at all. After the kitchen had been cleaned up, she went directly upstairs and in a few minutes, from the sounds, she had gone to bed.

Vince waited, sitting in the living room and reading yesterday's *Times,* until eleven o'clock. Then he dragged himself up the stairs.

Thursday came up a gray, overcast day with a strong southwest breeze blowing and a promise of more rain. Again, Frances had gotten up before the alarm went off and, by the time Vince awoke, she was gone. This war of silence between them wasn't exactly new. The longest it had ever gone was about four or five days when they'd been married maybe six months and Vince had done something which for the life of him he could not remember. The present one would continue until something would happen to end it. Right now, with more pressing things on his mind, he didn't particularly care.

By the time he got to Russo's, the last copy of the *Times* on the stand was creased, smudged and torn; it had been either at the top or the bottom of the bundle when dropped from the truck and he refused to buy it. He walked several more blocks, to a newsstand on Liberty Avenue, found a clean copy and went home with it.

When he reached the house, the phone was ringing; he heard it

165

as he came up the walk. It was still ringing when he let himself in and hurried down the hall to it.

"Yes?"

"Mr. Maggione?"

He didn't recognize the voice right away. "Yes."

"We, uh, discussed a business transaction last week."

Now he remembered. "Yes."

"The deal is all set at your price."

"Well, I don't—"

"You don't *what?* I have gone to some trouble. I hope we're not going to have any unpleasantness!"

"No. What do you want me to do now?"

"That's better— First, have the six hundred, in cash. Nothing larger than a ten. And no counterfeits— In case you didn't know it, there's some damned good counterfeit tens around right now— You do *have* the six hundred?"

"I can have it no later than tomorrow noon."

"That's more like it. You'll hear from me this time tomorrow, Friday. And you'll have the six hundred ready, nothing larger than a ten. And no counterfeit."

At ten minutes past five, Charley Bennett called.

"Vince? The foreman told me you wanted me to call you— He said you called yesterday, too, but he misplaced the note— What's up?"

"They called me. They're ready. I'll need six hundred dollars."

"When?"

"They're going to call me tomorrow morning. Can you be here between nine and nine-thirty?"

"I'll be at your house at nine."

"Another thing. He said nothing larger than a ten."

"What? Jesus, I've got mostly twenties. But, I guess I can get 'em changed— The foreman said you asked particularly if I was working Monday night. Why?"

"Uh—I'll tell you when I see you tomorrow."

"For whatever it means to you, I *was* working!"

Charley sounded a bit huffy as he rang off.

Frances came home looking tired and out of sorts. By the time

166

she had hung up her coat, Vince was barring the way to the kitchen.

"Look, Fran. I'm sorry."

"You said that before."

"Well, I *am,* damn it. I had no right to treat you the way I did night before last."

"That's not what's bothering me."

"What, then?"

"Your not taking me into your confidence. Not telling me."

"But I told you, I won't do that again!"

"Yes, you told me."

"Fran, how long are we going to go on like this?"

"That's up to you. Have you called your Uncle Vincent?"

"Frank was supposed to call *me.* That's the way we left it."

"But Frank hasn't called you."

"No."

"Then I think you should call your Uncle Vincent."

"First you were mad because I called him. And now you're mad because I haven't. I don't understand you."

"Vince, let's get something straight—I'm not *mad!* I am frightened. When you stop to think how this thing looks, all of it, it worries me sick. I can see why Frank hasn't called you, he's probably afraid to have anything to do with you."

"*Him,* afraid of *me?* That's a laugh— Well. If I call him, what will I say?"

"Tell your Uncle Vincent you want to see him, talk to him. Tell him you've been thinking about things and you don't like the way they look, not one bit. And act as if you might be concerned about *him*— For heaven's sake, Vince! Use your head!"

So Vince called, and it was Frank Mastretta who answered the phone. Frank sounded very cool and said Mr. Spotafore wasn't speaking to anyone. Then he seemed to soften a bit and said that if Vince wanted to, he could come out to the house tomorrow at half-past one.

167

twenty-four

". . . five eighty, five ninety, six hundred," said Charley Bennett as he put the last banknote on the pile on the kitchen table. He snapped two rubber bands around the stack and stuffed it into the plain brown envelope he'd pulled out of his shirt the minute he came into the kitchen. "And if there's any counterfeit in there," he said, "it sure as hell fooled me."

Vince took the envelope from him and hefted it. Then he dropped it on the table. He said, "That's a lot of money."

"You're telling me? I had to work like a bastard for it. I'm a month behind in my rent, and I had to borrow from Noble. But I'll be able to get caught up now—" Charley looked up from the envelope. "Why did you ask the foreman if I was working Monday night?"

Vince didn't answer. He got up from the table and angled himself to the stove. "How about a cup of coffee?" he asked.

"Well—okay."

Vince found two cups, filled them and brought them to the table. He reached for the pitcher of cream and the sugar bowl and put them down between the cups. "Help yourself," he said.

Charley poured himself a dollop of cream and heaped in three teaspoons of sugar. He stirred without looking at the cup and, his red-rimmed eyes direct and suspicious, he said, "Vince, I asked you a question."

"So you did."

"Well, what about it?"

"Nothing."

"What do you mean, nothing?" Charley's face was starting to get red. "You must've had some reason for asking if I worked Monday night!"

"It isn't important."

"It was important enough for you to go behind my back and ask!"

"I didn't go behind your back. You weren't there when I called. And you don't have a telephone. At the time, I thought I had to know. So I asked your foreman."

"Christ— Why, at the time, did you think you had to know, damn it!"

"Because Monday night my Uncle Vincent Spotafore was kidnaped."

For perhaps half a minute, Charley Bennett didn't say anything. His eyes seemed to be having trouble focusing on Vince and his red face appeared to be attempting to organize itself into an appropriate expression, and the result came out more annoyance than anything else. Finally he said, "I didn't see anything about it in the papers. Did they get him back?"

"Yes."

"What has his being kidnaped got to do with whether I was working Monday night?"

"I was hoping you would tell *me*."

"What? Are you off your nut? What the hell do you mean?"

"Two weeks ago, right in this room, at this table, I spilled my guts to you and Noble about my Uncle Vincent's house. I told you about the guards, the alarm systems, the dogs, his evening habits, all of it. Ten days later he was kidnaped by someone who had to know as much about him and his house as I did. Or, thanks to me, as much as you did. How does it look to you?"

Charley breathed through his half-open mouth as if he had been running. His face was ugly. "Are you accusing me of kidnaping your uncle?" he asked in a low, ugly voice.

"No."

"Then what in the God damn hell do you think you're doing?"

"I'm thinking you fingered him, you or Noble—or both of you.

170

It's almost as if I had fingered him myself. At first I thought you'd done it unconsciously, that you might have been shooting off your mouth somewhere and the information you had got to the wrong people. But, here this morning you bring this money. Six hundred dollars—that's more money than you've had in one piece since you got out of the service."

"I told you where I got the money! If you don't believe me, I can prove where I got it!"

"It doesn't matter whether I believe you or not, or what you can prove. The only thing that really matters is where you got this money. If you got it, or any part of it, by finding a buyer for information about Vincent Spotafore, you're dead. So is Noble. And —so am I."

Charley pushed his chair back, spilling his coffee. "So, that's what you think! You think I peddled what you told me about your uncle for a lousy six hundred bucks— Thanks, pal!"

"If you did peddle it, I hope you got more than six hundred. The Family paid forty thousand to get him back."

Charley stood up. "I'm damned if I'm going to listen to this shit any longer. You said your mother is crazy? Take a good look in the mirror if you want to see who's crazy—"

He made a grab for the envelope, but Vince got it first.

"Hey—give me that!"

"No."

"God damn it, Vince, I don't want to have to hit you. But I will, if you don't give that back to me—now!"

"If you hit me, it will be the biggest mistake you ever made— In six minutes, at nine-thirty, there'll be a call on that telephone, telling you where to pick up your ounce of pure heroin, where to take this six hundred dollars. If you don't make the pick-up, if you don't have the money, before this day is over you will be dead."

"Who are you trying to kid? You'll be dead, maybe. Not me! They don't know me from Adam!"

"No? I guess you forgot it was your idea that I go to my uncle. What made you think he would sell—or arrange for me to buy— that much heroin without knowing who it was for?"

"You told him about me?"

"I did."

171

"Well, Jesus Christ—" And Charley sat down heavily.

"You see, it isn't quite so simple."

"Jesus—I must've been out of my God damn mind to let Noble talk me into this deal with you— What are you going to do?"

"Wait for the call. Arrange for the pick-up."

"No, I mean about your uncle!"

"I don't know. I'm going to have to see him, that's for sure. Whether it's news to you or not, I was the go-between."

"You're going to have to see him. And I suppose you're going to have to tell him you think Noble and I fingered him."

"He isn't interested in what I think."

"But you're going to tell him?"

"No. It would mean I would have to explain. And then I would get myself involved. And the further it would go, the worse it would get— He's been trying to snare me in his net. I don't intend to give him a chance like that, not if I can help it."

For the first time, Charley seemed to notice the spilled coffee. "Jesus," he said. He got up, took a sponge from the sink and carefully wiped up the mess. Then he returned the sponge to the sink and sat down again.

"Vince," he said in an earnest voice, "I wish to hell I had never asked you about your Mafia uncle. But I did, and you told me, and I suppose that no matter what I do or say, as long as you live you'll suspect that Noble and I had something to do with his kidnaping— That's how it is, isn't it?"

"Yes."

"Suppose I told you I *did* help kidnap him, that the son of a bitch was ripe for it and asking for it and deserved it— Suppose I told you that? What would you do?"

"Nothing."

"What? You wouldn't go to him to save your own neck? To tell him you'd found out that a couple of your ex-Vietnam buddies had planned the whole deal?"

"No."

"Then what in sweet Jesus' name *would* you do?"

"I would warn you to get away, while you can. If you can. You don't seem to understand, Charley. I'm not trying to save my neck. I'm just hoping to God I can save my self."

172

They sat for a while, not talking and not looking at each other. After a few minutes of this, Vince dragged himself to his feet, filled both cups with fresh coffee and sat down to drink his; Charley left his cup untouched.

At ten minutes of ten, the telephone rang. Five minutes later, Charley went out the door with the six hundred dollars in his pocket, and Vince never saw him again.

At half-past eleven there was a fumbling at the front door and for the moment it raised the hackles on Vince's neck. Then he heard the familiar *plop* of mail as it dropped in the hall and the sharp sound of the mail slot snapping closed.

A letter for him, from the VA Hospital; it was probably the new schedule of visits. Two letters for Frances, one of them postmarked *California*. A bank statement. His monthly pension check. The insurance policy for the Rambler wagon. A letter Frances had mailed to her sister, Margaret, in California, returned and marked *Moved—No Forwarding Address*.

What the hell did *that* mean?

He put the envelope with his pension check, unopened, in his pocket and stacked the rest of the mail on the hall seat under the telephone. Then his eyes again sought the kitchen clock:

11:35.

He was due on Juniper Lane in less than two hours and, with traffic the way it was, he should be leaving the house in a very few minutes. His thought about making himself a sandwich was abandoned after a halfhearted search of the refrigerator. There was almost a full cup of coffee remaining in the pot and, after he'd poured it, he decided against drinking it. Then, with the kidnapers' instructions folded alongside the pension check in his pocket, he let himself out the back door.

He was bending down to raise the garage door when a car turned from the street into the driveway.

Annoyed, he straightened and turned around to face the street. The car, low, sleek and wine-colored, cleared the sidewalk and came on into the driveway to stop about thirty feet from him. The driver and only occupant was a woman. An enormous pair of sunglasses obscured her face, a bright scarf covered her hair and, momentarily but effectively, the car's cowling hid the rest of her.

What the hell, he thought. The woman cut the engine and opened the door, showing him a nice pair of legs. And then, when she closed the door and he could see the rest of her, he saw she was wearing the miniest of mini skirts, and her dress had a row of huge buttons down the front.

Her walk was familiar enough, but it wasn't until she had come directly to him and had spoken that he knew who she was.

"Hello, Vince."

"Louise!"

"How are you, Vince?" Her beautifully manicured hand rested on his arm. "I know you didn't expect me, but could we go in for a minute? There's something I must tell you, and I'd rather not have people peeking at us from behind their curtains."

"Well—I haven't much time. I'm due at Uncle Vincent's at half-past one."

Her eyes smiled at him through the sunglasses. "I know," she said in a quiet voice. "That's why I'm here."

twenty-five

Louise LaScola didn't seem to notice the coffee cups, the disarray on the stove, the sponge Charley Bennett had left sitting in a puddle of brown stain on the drainboard of the sink. She stood with her hands at her sides, waiting while he closed the door. He had forgotten how tall she was, and what a beautiful body she had. She took off the sunglasses, leaving a red mark on her nose. She was more reserved than he remembered her.

He attempted heartiness: "Well, Louise, it's been a long time!"

"Yes—of course, I'd heard you were back. You do look well, Vince."

"And so do you— Say, I'm sorry about this kitchen. One of my service friends dropped by— Let's sit in the living room."

"All right."

The space between the table and the stove was narrow and he couldn't avoid brushing against her as he passed by. Her remembered warmth and perfume assailed him and he was unable to check a quick impulsive glance at her face as he passed. Her gray eyes were wide, excited, and already the red mark left by the glasses had disappeared in a flush that spread from the cleavage of her breasts to the roots of her fine, dark hair.

For the briefest instant their eyes met and held. And then he continued his uncertain way through the dining room until he had reached the living-room sofa.

175

"Do sit down," he said, indicating the sofa with a ceremonious gesture. "This old room hasn't changed much, has it?"

"I remember the last time I was here," said Louise, adding, almost as an afterthought, "It's nice that some things don't change."

She'd learned how to sit down gracefully in a mini skirt and she did so. She held her knees together, turning them to the side, and it was then Vince realized she wasn't wearing stockings. He had started to drag one of the chairs near the sofa when she said, "Would you mind sitting beside me? I'd rather you didn't watch my face when I tell you why I'm here."

"Okay." He gave up the chair and sat at the opposite end of the sofa. "What's it all about?"

"Please don't look at me— Thank you. I'll be as brief as I can. Don't go to your uncle's house today, Vince."

"Why not?" Involuntarily his head turned toward her.

"Because—" She hesitated. Clasping her hands together she rested them on her thighs below the ridiculous skirt. Then she looked away. "I overheard Frank and—Tony—talking about your expected visit. I didn't hear it all because they stopped talking as soon as they saw me. But I heard enough, and as soon as I could I got in my car and came straight here."

"What were they talking about?"

"They were talking about you. I heard Frank say, *Vince is coming here at one-thirty. His wife works, so there won't be anyone at his house. And his Uncle Joe is away. That would be the best time*— They had just come into the room and hadn't noticed that I was there, in a corner, reading a magazine. Tony saw me first and he warned Frank with a quick movement of his head— Your Uncle Vincent had told me you were coming. He never misses a chance to tell me about you—" Her head turned toward him and her luminous gray eyes were steady in contemplation.

"The best time," said Vince. "The best time for what?"

"I don't know. Something they were planning to do while no one was in this house."

"I can't imagine what that would be. I know they don't like me. I don't see what they could do to me that hasn't been done already. I'm sure they suspect me of having a hand in Uncle Vincent's kidnaping—my being named the go-between, the ransom letter on Mario's grave— Or maybe you didn't know about it?"

"I knew. Tony got a great deal of satisfaction in telling me about it— You *didn't* have anything to do with it, did you?"

"Certainly not directly, not knowingly. I didn't *plan* to kidnap him. I didn't take any part in it, except to deliver the ransom money. But you know me, Louise. Either I don't talk at all or else I talk entirely too much. And sometimes I talk to the wrong people."

"I never knew you to talk too much—" She gave him a questioning glance. "Or is this something that happened to you as a result of the war? I've always known you to be very careful in what you said—and to whom you said it. But"—her eyes hardened—"I'm under no illusions about either my brother or my husband. You have no idea of what they are capable. That's why I came here to warn you. I don't know what they've planned. Whatever it is, however, depends on you're being away from this house this afternoon."

Vince scowled in thought. "Do you suppose—" he began. Then he shook his head. "No."

"Do I suppose what?"

"Nothing. I had an idea. But it's impossible."

"Vince, believe me, I *know* them. *Nothing* is impossible— What were you thinking?"

"Well— All along I've had a hunch that the ransom money was marked in some secret way. It would have to have been very cleverly done to get by the kidnapers— But it occurred to me that they might break in here and plant some of that marked money."

"Vince! What a fiendish way to turn your uncle against you!"

"That would really clinch it," said Vince. Now he was looking directly at her, savoring her remembered beauty and not caring if his eyes revealed him. "You took some chance, coming to this house. They've probably got spies all around here. Suppose someone has spotted your car? They may have already been told that you're here!"

"It doesn't matter."

He moved nearer and his hand went out, closing over hers. Her

177

hand was hot, burning as if she had a fever. "What happened to us, Louise?" he asked.

Her eyes held steady on his for a moment. Then she looked away, although she did not withdraw her hand. "Don't you know?" she asked in a quiet, distant voice.

"I suppose it was what happened that Columbus Day, when I called to take you to the picnic. We were in your room, and alone in the house, and your zipper got stuck— All right, I shouldn't have done what I did. I wanted to see you, to tell you, but all we did after that was talk a few times on the telephone. You wouldn't go out with me. And the next time I saw you, you were getting married—to Tony LaScola."

"Oh, yes, my zipper," Louise said in a faint voice.

"Why in God's name did you marry *him?*"

"Because he asked me."

"That isn't a reason!"

"Isn't it? After you, I needed someone— Believe me, Vince, I *needed* someone."

"A beautiful girl like you? You could have any fellow you wanted! I was sorry that our—experience—together probably was less than satisfactory to you. I didn't know anything, it was my first time— I figured you were disgusted with me. And I couldn't really blame you."

"You figured that, did you? You aren't very smart, are you?"

"I sure as hell don't know anything about women. What else would have made you sign off on me the way you did?"

"Did it ever occur to you that you might have started something?"

"What? You're not going to tell me, at this late date, that you fell in love with me, so you wouldn't see me again!"

"I was in love with you long before that, Vince. After, for a long time, I hated you. But it didn't last. I could never hate you, not for long, anyway."

"You said, I'd *started something*. What did I start?"

She raised her eyes to meet his. "If you must know, you'd started a baby— *Your* baby."

Astonished and speechless, he stared at her.

"Yes— You didn't call me for more than a week, remember?

178

Maybe the experience wasn't very satisfactory to you. But to me, it was wonderful— Oh, I won't lie to you, you weren't the first. The year before that, before we'd started going steady together, Tony had seduced me— He wasn't fat and ugly then, he was older than I, I was flattered by his attention, and he seduced me. It happened so quickly— I didn't want to see him again. Not that I hated him, I was just ashamed— Then I fell in love, with you, and finally I could think of him as part of growing up and I suppose I was grateful to him— Perhaps if it hadn't been for your Uncle Vincent and my Aunt Sophie and your sisters, all of them scheming to push us together, we might've— But, never mind. I know now where I made my mistake. There was nothing wrong with my zipper, I jammed it purposely. Then, for such a little time, we *were* together. And, for a whole week, oh, how I loved you— I had to fight myself to keep from calling you on the telephone."

"And then"—she drew in a long, uneven breath—"I missed my period. First I thought I'd counted wrong. Then I knew I hadn't, because things started happening to me. And just about then, you started phoning me— It doesn't matter now. We're both married, to someone else. Poetic justice: the girl I didn't even think was in the running got you. And the man who had seduced me, got me—"

"For God's sake, Louise," said Vince. "Why didn't you tell me?"

"Because I didn't want you to feel you *had* to marry me. And when you kept calling me without trying to see me, letting me put you off all the time, I thought perhaps you *knew* I was pregnant and you were afraid I was going to break the news—please, Vince, let me finish—I knew a girl who'd had an abortion, and she arranged one for me. My family didn't notice a thing, although they thought I was getting fat and told me to cut down on the *pasta*. You see, you can stop the baby. But you can't stop the rest of it. My breasts started to fill with milk and my whole body was ready for the baby I wasn't going to have— I went a little crazy, then. Tony noticed, and he *knew* what was wrong with me, what I had done. I suppose you could call it blackmail— Whatever, he asked me to marry him and I accepted. Poetic justice again. He had seduced me, but after he had me legally he told me he'd married me because he wanted to be in your Uncle Vincent's family—that's all."

179

She had been looking at the carpet. Now her eyes, luminous with unshed tears, fumbled for his. "I'm sorry to tell you like this. I didn't mean to. And God knows I'm not looking for sympathy. What happened was my fault. If I hadn't been so greedy—" She sighed.

Vince started to say something and thought better of it. All the time she had been talking, her hand had been beneath his. In the beginning her hand had been relaxed, but at the end it had been clenched in a tight fist. He had listened, at first with dismay, then sympathy, and finally with a kind of rising excitement. Now he made a spasmodic move, to straighten himself, causing her sunglasses to fall off the arm of the sofa and lodge somewhere behind her, on the seat.

Automatically, without thinking, he reached across her to rescue the glasses. The move threw all his weight on his right thigh, causing him so much pain he involuntarily moaned and put his arms around her for support.

She misinterpreted both the sound from his lips and the presence of his arms and, cradling his head in her right arm, she pushed his shoulder with her left hand until he was lying on his side, with his weight off the injured leg and his head against her breasts.

"My baby," she said, beginning to rock him gently. "What have they done to you?"

"Louise—"

Her mouth on his silenced him.

At one o'clock, Louise stirred in his arms and sat up. "Vince—"

"Yes?"

"You must call your uncle."

"I suppose so. What will I tell him?"

"We'll think of something."

"Uh—I'm not so sure he wants me to call him."

"He wouldn't like it if you broke an appointment without *some* word— You don't realize it, but he's very fond of you. And he's terribly proud."

"I'm not fond or proud of him!"

"I know, Vince— There hasn't been much love in his life. He

180

loved his sister, your mother. And I'm sure that in his strange, possessive way he loves you— Call him, Vince. Please?"

"Okay."

He struggled up from the sofa and went to the telephone. After a couple of rings, Ted Key's voice came on and Vince said:

"This is Vince Maggione. I'm supposed to see my uncle in half an hour, but I've been detained— Is he expecting me?"

"He was. But the doctor was here again. The boss caught a cold. He's sleeping now, and I wouldn't want to be the one who wakes him. Could you come out Sunday instead?"

"Uh—yes."

"When he wakes up, I'll tell him you called and we made it for Sunday. If that's okay, I'll let you know."

"All right. Thank you."

Ten minutes later, he and Louise were lying in each other's arms on the living-room rug.

twenty-six

The dryness of his mouth told him he had been sleeping on his back. He hadn't been dreaming, not that he could remember, and he had come straight awake because of a sound that had reached him from the front door.

Someone had been out there, pressed against the door; whoever it was had leaned too close and moved too quickly, and the sound he had heard had been like buttons scraping against wood.

As quickly as he heard it, the sound was gone.

The room was semidark; the hour must have been close on five and reflection from the street lights filtered in around the draperies at the front windows. He pushed himself up from the sofa and moved quickly to the window furthest from the door and, pulling the drapery back frantically, looked out into the street.

He could see no one.

Moving quickly, he crossed into the hall and wrenched open the front door. A blast of freezing air struck him and almost immediately the thermostat in the hall responded and in the basement the oil burner ground on and there was the sound of water circulating in the heating pipes. He stepped outside and saw no one in the street except Aurelio Montalbano, turning into his walk across the way, evidently en route to supper.

He withdrew and closed the door and went through the hall to the kitchen, turning on the ceiling light as he entered. It took a second for his eyes to adjust to the light and then he saw by the clock above the sink that it was five past five. He'd slept nearly three hours. Frances would be coming home soon . . .

Memory engulfed him and his first reaction was to glance down in apprehensive inspection of his clothing. He looked no more mussed than he ordinarily would after a nap on the sofa. The next minute he was in the living room where he turned on all the lights and critically examined the area. It looked all right; Louise had helped him straighten rugs and cushions before she'd left. But there was a faint, telltale trace of her perfume in the air. He returned to the kitchen, located a spray can of air freshener and used it generously on the sofa and the rug. Then he put the spray can back and sat at the kitchen table to still the sudden trembling that had seized him.

It hadn't been a dream, not this time. It had been real and the memory of it was surging strong. *You don't belong to me,* Louise had said as she kissed him good-by, *but I belong to you. I won't bother or embarrass you, I'll probably not call you. But if you ever need me, I'll come to you, or meet you, whenever you want me.* And she'd written her unlisted phone number on a strip of paper torn from the front page of the *Times* and had stuffed it in his shirt pocket.

He had never thought of something like this happening to him, of being involved in an affair, of being unfaithful to Frances. And now that it had happened, when he thought back over each step of it he still could not understand how it had happened. It went against everything about him, all that he had been, all that he had believed; he had thought himself above this sort of behavior— Suddenly he laughed aloud. Less than a month ago he had been incapable of *any* sexual behavior, except in dreams. And now he had both a wife and a mistress— It wasn't funny, and his laughter died.

He loved Frances, now more than ever, with a kind of tenderness and desperation and a new fear that in the past three hours he had destroyed something that could never be replaced. Did he love Louise? He liked her. He was more than fond of her. The harmony he had achieved, in the good days, in bed with Frances paled beside the wild, driving exultation and immeasurable release he had so recently found in Louise's responsive body.

184

And she had come here to warn him . . .

The memory brought him a new kind of excitement. Whoever it had been at the door was probably trying to get in. The would-be intruder would have heard Vince's snoring and, more significantly, when it stopped. The sound of Vince's upward movement from the sofa unquestionably had prompted the listener's flight.

Was the listener still out there somewhere, watching and waiting a chance to get into the house? Suddenly a plan came to him and he got up from the table and took his jacket from the hall rack. He felt quite calm as he moved quickly through the rooms, turning off the lights, and out the front door, which he slammed and tried to be sure it was locked.

He was whistling as he went down the street, walking briskly in the opposite direction from the gas station. In less than four minutes he had cut through a driveway, circled the adjoining houses, gone through a fence and crossed back yards to come quietly up his own driveway, hugging the shadows.

In a deep pocket of shadow he stood off the driveway against the side of the neighbor's enclosed porch. From this point he could watch the front of his own house and, by turning, the area between the house and the garage in the rear.

Minutes dragged by. Occasionally a car moved in the street. Three children, all of them holding to the leash of a mongrel dog, moved past in kinetic silhouette on the opposite side of the street. Aurelio Montalbano, his supper dispatched, came out of his house, framed briefly in an oblong of light, and trudged back for the last two hours of his daily stint.

A car, with only one headlamp functioning, swept past toward the corner.

Someone was running, with scurrying footsteps, from the direction of the gas station; his view of whoever it was was blocked by the enclosed porch. The footsteps paused, then resumed, and as they neared he heard a gasping for breath and a kind of desperate "Mm . . . mm . . . mm . . ." sound like a mute trying to cry out.

He stepped from the shadow of the porch into the driveway to see that it was Frances. She was running again, her eyes fixed on the house, and both hands were holding a large paper market bag in front of her.

185

"*Fran!* What's the matter?"

"Oh—oh, Vince—help—me—"

He came up beside her and took the bag from her. "What is it? What's the matter?"

"At the store . . . just as I was coming out . . . two men. They ran into me, deliberately—" She leaned against him, gasping for breath. Then she said, "They dropped something into the bag!"

"What? Who were they?"

"*I don't know!*"

He put the bag on the sidewalk and turned it on its side. An assortment of groceries spilled out: canned goods, a carton of milk, a loaf of bread, a sealed package of meat . . .

Two glassine envelopes containing some kind of powder.

"There!" cried Frances. "Those envelopes— I saw something flash when— What are they?"

For little more than a second, Vince stared at the envelopes in his hand. Then he said, "Put the groceries back in the bag and go in the house— I'll be right back."

"Where are you going— Vince!"

"Do what I told you. *Quick!*"

And then he was running toward the corner, hop-skipping as fast as his leg would let him. In a hundred feet he stopped beside a six-foot-square storm drain built into the curb and gutter of the street. Surplus water from Bennie's do-it-yourself car wash was running along the gutter and gurgling into the grate of the storm drain. The grate was clear in a Tow-Away zone and its surface was only minimally clogged with leaves and debris.

Vince bent down and dropped both envelopes through the grating. He had straightened and was heading back to the house when a squad car skidded around the corner and came flashing past him.

By the time Vince got to the house, the squad car was standing in the driveway and Frances, white with fear, was letting a uniformed patrolman and a plainclothesman in the front door.

The man in uniform was about Vince's age, probably a service veteran although new to the police force. He stood by the kitchen table, dividing his glance between Frances and the market bag, and he seemed ill at ease. The man in plain clothes had a seamed, tired, middle-aged face and gray showed in the hair his hat didn't cover. For all these signs of age, he had a flat stomach and he looked both tough and ready. He stood with his feet spread, balanced, his left hand resting on his hip and his right carelessly at his side. He stood between the hall door and the door to the dining room and only his eyes moved as he inspected Vince.

"Are you this girl's husband?" His voice sounded tired.

"I am. What's this all about?"

"My name is O'Rourke, Narcotics Squad." His left hand dipped into his side pocket, brought out a pass case and opened it to reveal a shield. "The law requires me to advise you that you have the right to legal counsel, that anything you say may be used in evidence against you, that you should make no statements, sign no papers and in no way commit yourself until you have consulted a lawyer. I am also required to inform you that if you do not have an attorney, the State will furnish one at your request."

"Well, that's just great," said Vince. "Thanks a hell of a lot. Now, since we seem to be on the subject of law, do you happen to have a warrant?"

"I happen to have a warrant, signed by the presiding judge. It names specifically *Vincent Maggione et ux,* that means wife, and this address. I am *not* required by law to show you the warrant. It is sufficient that I have it. Do you have any further questions?"

"You still haven't answered the question I asked you. Why are you here? What is this all about?"

"The fact that I identified myself as being with the narcotics squad ought to suggest something. If you have no further questions, we will proceed with our search—Calderone, you take the upstairs."

"Yes sir," said the young cop. He moved a half-step reluctantly, as if he expected someone to stop him.

Frances' color was returning, pumped into her face by rising anger. Vince said to her. "Call your mother."

O'Rourke glanced at Frances with new interest. "Your mother is a lawyer? Not that it matters. Perhaps you should know: your lawyer, whether it's your mother or who, can not legally interfere with due process of search when a warrant has been issued. A lawyer can only—"

"I know what a lawyer can do!" Vince interrupted in an angry voice. "I also know what Congressman Savoldi and some other people can do. Go right ahead with your search. Have a ball— *Frances, call your mother!*"

Frances gave the man in plain clothes a glance that was about equally divided between defiance and fear. Then she resolutely started around Patrolman Calderone, headed for the hall.

"Just hold it a minute, Mrs. Maggione," O'Rourke said.

Frances stopped.

O'Rourke said, "We're not in a police station, not yet. If we were, I could limit you to one telephone call. We are in your home, legally. We intend to conduct our search, legally. It's up to you, how much time you want to waste in trying to recruit political influence. If you cooperate with us, you'll be rid of us that much quicker. If you have nothing to hide, you have nothing to worry about—" He looked at his watch, comparing it with the kitchen clock. "I'm telling you this because we will not begin our search until you are off the telephone. I assume that, regardless of your married name, Mrs. Maggione, you are Irish and so your mother is Irish, and if your mother is anything like mine, your telephone call might take quite some time—"

The sharp summons of the door knocker hammered through the hall and ended O'Rourke's soliloquy. "See who that is," he instructed the patrolman. "And don't let anyone in."

The young cop moved quickly out of the kitchen. In a minute he was back.

"Bennie D'Agostino," the patrolman said. "Owns the gas station on the corner. Says he's Maggione's cousin."

O'Rourke said, "Tell him to stay out there in case any other relatives want in. Or neighbors. Tell him this is just a routine check— Well, damn it, *go tell him!*"

Patrolman Calderone went to tell him.

Although it seemed longer, in less than an hour by the kitchen clock Calderone and O'Rourke were back at the table where Frances was sitting in stiff silence and Vince was moodily contemplating the cold dregs of a cup of coffee.

"Okay, that's it," said O'Rourke. "This place seems to be clean."

"Disappointed?" Vince's voice was bitter.

"No. I'm sorry if we inconvenienced you. As law-abiding citizens, you should be able to understand and appreciate our position. We have a job to do. We do it the best we can."

"Why did you come here?"

"We had a warrant. We were sent here."

"Why? Who sent you?"

O'Rourke sighed. "Every action like this starts with an *Information*. Sometimes it results when a place has been kept under surveillance and has been found to be frequented by known addicts or pushers. Other times we act on definite, direct information, that is to say, a tip. In either case, the D.A.'s office obtains a warrant—You look like decent kids. For your own sake, I hope to God none of the people you travel around with are users or pushers."

O'Rourke looked at Frances' tired, strained face. Then he shrugged and said, "Okay, Calderone. Let's saddle up."

It took Vince quite a while to get rid of Bennie. His mind wasn't functioning very well and he couldn't come up with anything convincing. His explanation that the whole thing appeared to be a mistake, that the cops had evidently gotten the wrong address, sounded lame even to him. In the midst of it, Frances swept past them and up the stairs. She was still wearing her coat and hat; she hadn't removed them all the while the search was in progress. She didn't speak to Vince or even say hello to Bennie. After a few minutes of standing around, Bennie finally left. Vince was glad Uncle Joe was away. Uncle Joe wouldn't have gone until he'd gotten to the bottom of things.

Vince returned to the kitchen and found that Frances had made him a ham sandwich and poured him a glass of milk. Significantly, only one place was set at the table. He supposed that meant she was going straight to bed. He could hear her, up in the bedroom, opening and closing drawers. He sat at the table and looked at the sandwich. He should have been hungry; he'd had no lunch. He tasted the milk and drank about half of it.

He had picked up the sandwich when Frances came downstairs. He heard her stop briefly in the hall. Then, instead of coming into the kitchen, she entered the living room. O'Rourke had been in there and he must have changed things around in his searching.

189

Vince heard Frances engage in a furious straightening of chairs and thumping of cushions. Then there was an abrupt pause, a moment of silence and complete cessation of activity and Vince thought, *My God, what has she found?*

As abruptly as it had stopped, the activity resumed and continued for about another minute and then Frances returned to the kitchen through the dining room. She was still wearing her coat and hat.

It was as if she had just come from work.

She sat in the chair opposite him. Without looking at him, she said, "I'm not completely stupid, Vince. Dumb, I may be. But stupid, I'm not."

Vince swallowed. "What do you mean?"

"It's very plain. The police have been watching your friend, Charley Bennett. You've been buying heroin for him. You were at your uncle's this afternoon, you weren't home, and the people couldn't deliver your order. So they dropped it in *my* market bag— Those two envelopes. They were heroin, weren't they?"

"I think that's what they were."

"Do you realize what could have happened to me if you hadn't come home when you did? I would be in jail this minute!"

"Fran, it isn't the way it looks. That isn't what happened."

"Don't tell *me* what happened! Two men bumped into me in the market. They dropped something in my bag. You must have been expecting it because the minute I got here you emptied out the bag—and ran to the corner with the envelopes!"

"I know how it looks. But—" His shoulders dropped. How could he tell her?

She stood up. "Vince, I've had it to here! Your friend, Charley Bennett, your Uncle Vincent— Yes, and you! Or maybe you like the way things have been going, with you, with us— Don't you care how I feel? Don't I mean anything to you any more?"

"I care a great deal, Fran— Where are you going?"

She had left the table, walking by him, and now she stood in the hall doorway. "I wonder if you really do care," she said.

"Of course I care! I'm your husband. And you're my wife!"

"Nice of you to remember— You told me to call my mother? *She* called *me* this morning, at work. Jack is in some kind of awful

190

trouble, out in California, and Margaret has wired for money to bring the twins home. I'm going to spend the weekend with mother, maybe I can do something to help her. I certainly don't seem to be able to do anything constructive for you—"

She came back a little way into the room. "Oh, yes. About your father's employment record. I got it a couple of days ago— Wednesday—but I didn't want to give it to you then. The card I copied it on is a new form, it's been changed since his record was closed twenty-seven years ago, but the information is all there. You'll find it on the arm of the sofa, if you're interested."

She turned and walked down the hall. At the foot of the stairs, she picked up her overnight case; she'd packed it and brought it down before going into the living room.

Then she went out the front door.

The employment record was where Frances had put it, and on top of it lay Louise's sunglasses. The glasses had slipped down between the arm and the cushion, and he and Louise had forgotten about them. This was why the activity had stopped so abruptly: Frances had found the glasses. Luckily, she had been too upset about other things to spend much time wondering whose they were.

He brought the employment card into the kitchen and sat studying it with his elbows on the table. Dominico Maggione had started as a track worker at thirty cents an hour— Good God! How had anyone been able to live on *that?* In the nine years he'd held that job he'd been raised—a nickel at a time—until he was getting fifty-five cents. Then he'd been made assistant foreman—a fifteen-cent raise this time—and finally, foreman, at one dollar per hour.

For fifteen years, according to the record, he had been foreman. There were three layoffs when, presumably, he was nothing. And there had been occasional raises. It was carefully noted on his card that he had *not* taken part in union organizational efforts. But when the union had become a fact of life, he had joined.

Two more raises, good ones. And then:

D. Maggione, Deceased, 6/17/41.

191

His birthday.

No reason, no clarifying notes, no location. Nothing.

Vince turned the card over. On the reverse was the heading *Discipline Record* with the sub-headings *Nature of Occurrence, Date of Occurrence, Discipline, Date Imposed* and *File.*

For twenty-four years and nine months, the Discipline Record of Maggione, D. was clear. Then, it began:

> *Intoxicated, sent home— Intoxicated, unable to work, sent home—Disciplined, 10 days layoff without pay due to intox. on job—LT visited his home, found him intox., unfit for duty—*

In the three months before his death, he had been found drunk and unfit for work *sixteen separate times.*

Vince stared at the card a long time. Finally he put it aside and climbed the stairs to drop, fully clothed, on his empty bed.

part three

saturday

At ten o'clock, Eddie Durfee closed the door on the mess in his apartment and went down the unclean stairs to the street. He wasn't going far: a half dozen steps to his right would bring him to the entrance to MOMO'S BAR AND GRILL—LADIES INVITED—NO GENTS IN TEE SHIRTS which was his objective.

The only trouble was the steps took him through crashing bright daylight, and after last night he wasn't up to it.

Not that last night had been so much different from any number of other nights Eddie could remember. Only in some of the details had it been different. Gladys had showed up with one of her part-time regulars, a handicapper from Rochester, New York, who was loaded from winning the daily double at the Big A. Before the night had gotten very old, Gladys had worked Eddie, whom she introduced as her kid cousin, into the slot next to her at the bar and from then on there had been one hell of a lot of free drinks. The regular had won eleven hundred bucks, and even though Eddie had ten times that much in a paper sack under the sink in the apartment upstairs, it hadn't been too long ago he would have considered it important money. Eddie couldn't spend any of *his,* at least not while looking for a job. But, the regular wasn't afraid to spend it and Eddie had gotten good and drunk by the time Gladys decided she was hungry and had Momo call a cab; Eddie had made it upstairs under his own power, and to his own bed.

Momo's was on Old Country Road. The location was handy

and the traffic wasn't so bad after you got used to it. Noble S. Wright had spotted the FLAT TO LET sign, and it was just the kind of a place he was looking for. Not for himself—the last thing he needed was his picture in the papers in a Civil Rights incident— but for Eddie, who, unhoused, was something of a problem. Eddie was supposed to be Charley Bennett's friend, but it had been Noble who had recognized that an anonymous alternate could be very useful to their schemes. It had also been Noble who had invented the "mother" who was mailing Eddie twenty a week, and Momo's flat was only three blocks from a post office.

Eddie would not have exposed his aching head to the glaring sun, but he was expecting a phone call from Charley. If Momo was on duty, Eddie would get the call because Momo would bang on the pipes. But if Harry was on, Harry would say *screw it* and leave the phone off the hook while he went back to tending bar. And last night having been what it was, Momo was probably home sleeping it off; it was a chance Eddie couldn't take.

He got out of the sunlight as if it was a cold shower and pushed his way into the bar. Just as he had guessed, Harry was on. Harry had three Saturday morning regulars, beer drinkers, down at the end of the bar. At the door end were two strangers, dressed for fishing; they had tackle boxes beside them and their casting rods were leaning against the bar. They were lifting shots and toasting their luck when Eddie came by and took a stool at the center of the bar, right opposite the pumps.

Harry was leaning back, wiping a glass and listening to the regulars talk about somebody who had just won a thousand dollars in the state lottery and was trying to keep it a secret from his wife. Harry was about Eddie's height, totally bald, and was probably younger than he looked. He had been having trouble with his teeth, which didn't help his disposition.

Harry knew Eddie Durfee well enough, although not by that name. He gave him a sour glance and, without moving from where he was, asked:

"What the hell do you want?"

"I'll start with a beer. *And* a hard-boiled egg."

"You got the money?"

196

"Have I got money!" Eddie looked offended. "How much is my tab?"

Harry put the glass down and, without turning around, reached back until his skinny fingers closed on a small notebook beside the cash register. He brought the notebook forward, dropped it on the bar and thumbed through pages.

"Okay—Len Larkin. That's you, ain't it?"

"Just a minute." Eddie reached in his pants pocket and pulled out a wallet. Opening the wallet he fanned through a series of hinged, plastic-covered cards until he found, in facing holders, a driver's license and a photo-reduced Army discharge. "Leonard Larkin, it says here— Yup. That must be me."

"Very funny. Nine bucks eighty it says *here*. And Momo says, for Len Larkin ten is the limit. What do you want twenty cents' worth of?"

Eddie dug in the wallet and found a ten-dollar bill. He spread the bill on the bar and said, "I want a beer. And a hard-boiled egg. And if I get any more of this, I'll knock your rotten teeth down your stinking throat."

Harry picked up the bill. "You don't have to get sore," he said.

Eddie was salting his third hard-boiled egg when the phone rang. The phone was in a booth at the end of the bar near the door, and Eddie dropped the salted egg on a paper napkin and slid halfway off the bar stool.

He could have saved himself the trouble. One of the fishermen yelled, "Hey, that's our ride!" and charged into the booth.

In another minute, the fisherman was outside the booth with the phone in his hand. "Anybody here named Larkin?"

Eddie put down the egg he'd just picked up. "That's me!"

"Well, you're the one it's for."

Eddie walked to the booth, past the other fisherman who was worriedly eying two full shot glasses in front of him. "Thanks," he said as he took the phone and folded himself into the booth.

"Len?"

"Yeah—*Stu!*" He hadn't been expecting *this* call. "What's going on?"

"Quite a lot— Who was that, the person who answered?"

"Huh? Oh— A drunken fisherman. He and his buddy have been waiting for a call from their ride."

"I keep forgetting you live over a bar— Lennie?"

"What?"

"Can you talk? Is it safe?"

"Yes."

A long, indrawn breath. Then, "This is what we've been waiting for. It's arriving Monday."

"What time?"

"It's scheduled for ten A.M. It should be ready for pick-up by eleven-thirty. And the rest of it couldn't be better if we'd planned it— Lennie?"

"I'm listening!"

"It's all settled about my part, isn't it? I mean, what I'm to get?"

"Absolutely!"

"You're sure, Lennie? I don't want any last-minute problems."

"I tell you, it's all settled. We share and share alike!"

"When?"

"Like I told you, he said the cash is ready and waiting. We make it Monday, you get yours Monday night, Tuesday the latest. The boys agreed."

A sigh. "This is a big one, Len. The manifest is for a million dollars."

A million! Eddie felt a momentary dizzy sensation. "You'll get yours"—his voice was slightly hoarse—"and we're all set at our end, just waiting the word from you."

"It should net me fifty thousand, right? If you sell at the going price, two hundred, I should get fifty, right?"

"Yes! If we get more, *you* get more. I told you!"

"I'll be happy with fifty," said Stu. He was silent a moment, evidently thinking of what he would do with the money. Then he said, "It's almost too good to be true, Len, but it *is*— TAM bought a new armored truck last week. They traded in the old one, but kept the radio equipment. Well, the radio equipment won't fit in the new truck. So, now they've traded in the radio equipment. But the new set won't be ready until Wednesday or Thursday!"

"Jesus," said Eddie.

"And that's not all! Jake Schlagle, the security director, was

198

taken to the hospital yesterday for an emergency appendectomy. And his assistant, a man named Fred Bossert, has only been on the job *three days!* He was brought in from Burns or one of those agencies and hardly anybody at TAM knows what he looks like; all they know is his name!"

"Je-sus Christ. Fred Bossert— Okay."

"Now, you're to go to the Central Locksmiths, it's on Worth Street just off Church in downtown Manhattan. The keys are ready, so you can go any time. They're in your name, and they're paid for. You'll need both of them to open the truck door."

"Christ, Stu, I don't see how we can miss!"

"It should be all right— Lennie?"

"Now what?"

"When this is all over, when the hue and cry and all has died down, could we take a trip together? Some place where we could swim and sun ourselves on a beach? I have some vacation time coming in July. It should be safe by then, don't you think?"

July? By July, you won't be able to find me with the hounds of hell leading you—I'll be so far away it'll cost you fifty grand just to send me a postcard.

"Why not?" said Eddie.

At nine o'clock, Vince Maggione was up, shaved and dressed, had had breakfast and was walking as rapidly as he could toward Atlantic Avenue. When he went by the gas station, he hoped he wouldn't be seen and for once he wasn't. He came abreast of Russo's and walked by without a glance. The *Times* could wait; right now, his mind was on another newspaper, *The East New York Weekly Record,* and he knew someone would be in the office because he had telephoned before leaving the house.

At one time in his life the *Record* had been important. Forty papers sold and collected for earned him a dollar, and sometimes there were tips. Not large tips, but when you were eleven years old even a nickel was something.

In those days, the *Record* had been printed in its own plant and waiting for copies Wednesday nights had been an event. Now the printing was farmed out and the office was an upstairs room.

199

Vince didn't know who the present owner was, but assumed it was the man whose querulous voice had answered the telephone.

The *Record* had been important to him when he was growing up and it was important to him now. In more than fifty years, it had not missed an issue. If there was any key to his father's death, he should be able to find it in the paper's files.

He pulled himself up the stairs and entered the office. Behind a counter piled with current issues, unopened exchanges and an assortment of wedding announcements and invitation sample books, an old man sat at a cluttered desk and pecked away at a typewriter. With something of a start, Vince recognized him as the man who, fifteen years ago, had fed the cylinder press on which the *Record* was printed.

When he looked up at Vince, however, no memory stirred in his faded eyes.

"I phoned a little while ago."

"Oh? Let's see, you're—"

"I wanted to see the files."

"Oh, yes! Which one did you want?"

"Twenty-seven years ago. June."

"Twenty-seven years," the old man repeated. He pointed vaguely to sagging, laden shelves. "It's there someplace. I have to ask you to be careful—"

The phone on his desk rang and he turned to it.

The files were in bound volumes, one per year, and with surprising ease he located the volume he sought. It was in the middle of a stack and he drew it out carefully and brought it to the counter.

At the desk, the old man alternately clacked on the typewriter and muttered into the telephone. Vince turned the brittle pages, some of them torn. His father had died June 17; when he reached the issue of the 19th, he could hardly contain himself.

And then he was staring in disbelief at a story, headlined in small, square type, at the bottom of page one:

Local Man Killed By Subway Train
Dominico Maggione, 48, of East New York, was killed Monday morning by a westbound Independent subway train just as it was leaving the Liberty Avenue station.

The motorman, Chris Dowd, of Brooklyn, told police he first noticed Maggione sitting on a bench at the end of the platform.

"I thought he was asleep," Dowd said. "Then he got up, ran across the platform and jumped right in front of the train before I could stop."

Maggione, a foreman for the Long Island Rail Road, was pronounced dead on arrival at Brooklyn General Hospital. He is survived by his wife, the former Anna Spotafore; a son, Mario, and four daughters—

He was survived by a wife, four daughters and *two* sons, one of them not yet born. Anna Spotafore Maggione, 47, had been seven months pregnant when her husband discovered that drinking was no release. And for his unborn, unwanted son Vincent, this was the final rejection.

Vince closed the volume and went out of the office. The old man, busy with telephone and typewriter, didn't even look up.

"Whiskey," said Vince.

The white-haired, aproned bartender recognized him. "Yes, sir. What's your choice?"

"It doesn't matter, as long as it isn't scotch."

"Yes, sir. Something on the side?"

"Uh—water's okay."

The bartender reached for bottle and glass and as he turned he signalled with his eye to a waiter standing at the end of the bar. The bartender put a shot glass on the bar, poured whiskey in it, scooped ice in another glass and filled the glass with water.

"There you are, sir."

Vince had his uncashed pension check in his jacket pocket and a solitary five in his wallet. He put the five on the bar. The bartender picked up the five and was fingering it when Angelo came in from the kitchen.

"This is a pleasure," said Angelo, his smile revealing a gold crown. He put his hand on Vince's shoulder. "Your money is no good in here, Mr. Maggione. Anything you want is on the house."

The bartender put the five back on the bar.

Vince said, "If you don't mind, I'd rather pay."

"Not today. Today is special. I am celebrating. If you will do me the honor of joining me— Patsy, I'll have a vermouth and soda."

"What are you celebrating?"

"The good life. The fact that you, my friend, are here. And I am here, *we* are here, to enjoy it—" Angelo lifted his glass and said, "To us!"

Vince drank the whiskey at a gulp, hastily followed it with a swallow of water.

Angelo watched him. "You have troubles?"

"What makes you think so?"

"A man like you does not go into a bar at ten o'clock in the morning unless he has troubles. I am honored that you choose this bar. It is a sign of friendship. When a man has troubles, he needs friends. You have come to the right place."

"Well—I have *some* troubles. Doesn't everyone?"

"True!" Angelo's smile broadened as he waved for another round of drinks. "Everyone looks at Angelo, riding around in his Cadillac, and says, *What problems could he have? Mama mia,* you should hear some of the problems I have!"

Vince's hand strayed to the full glass. "Is my Uncle Vincent one of your problems?" he asked.

Angelo looked shocked. "Your uncle? He is a friend! He has been a family friend for over forty years— To answer your question: No, he is *not* one of my problems."

Vince lifted the glass and poured the raw whiskey down his throat. He shuddered and drank some of the water. Then, in a voice that was almost a whisper, he said, "You've known him all your life. Tell me the truth: What kind of a man is he?"

Angelo nodded. "I think we should sit at a table— Patsy, bring us one more round."

Harry replenished the glasses of the regulars at the end of the bar, poured a shot and drew a beer chaser for the butcher who was on his "coffee" break from the supermarket, refilled the glasses of the married couple who were still arguing about whose fault it was the car had run out of gas yesterday, and generally concentrated on ignoring Momo.

Damn Momo. Someday somebody would walk in here while he was counting the cash and stick a rod in his face. That would be the day, to see Momo part with money without getting anything in return. In Momo's full view, Harry poured himself a generous shot of the best scotch and let the scotch circulate around his bad tooth before he swallowed. He supposed someday he would have to go to the dentist. Thinking about the goddamned dentist was almost as bad as thinking about Momo, and Harry helped himself to another scotch.

Momo was glaring at him and making impatient motions.

"Yeah, boss?" Harry put the glass down hurriedly.

"C'mere, dammit!"

"What's wrong, boss? The cash can't be short?"

"No, the cash ain't short—" Momo moved his broad shoulders until Harry saw, concealed from the patrons in the bar, four folded ten-dollar bills. "Who gave you tens today?"

Momo's voice was menacingly quiet.

"Uh—what's the matter, one of 'em phony?"

"No, one of 'em isn't phony! I asked you, *who gave you tens?*"

Harry looked desperately at the clock—its hands pointed to ten past one—as if it had failed him. "Let's see, uh, I had a couple fishermen in here early. They gave me a ten and drank it up, waiting for their ride—"

"Two fishermen. What did they look like?"

"Big fellows. I know them. They're county cops."

"Okay. That's one. Who else?"

"Uh—that French dame, from the perfume shop. She had a vodka martini with her sandwich— Yeah. She gave me a ten!"

"Keep your voice down. We ain't discussing this with everybody— Okay. That's two. Who else?"

"Christ, lemme think— Oh! Phil Weemus. He paid up his tab. Eight bucks. Then he had a shot and—"

"That's three. There's one more. Who was it?"

Harry's face, muddy with thought, suddenly cleared. "No wonder I couldn't remember *him!* The tenant—Len Larkin. He had six beers and six hard-boiled eggs. I made him pay up his tab, and he paid with a ten."

"Larkin," Momo said. "Is he upstairs now?"

"I don't think so. He got a couple of phone calls. The last one was just before noon. After that one, he went out. But he didn't go upstairs. If he had, I'd've heard him."

Momo nodded. He returned three of the tens to the cash drawer and closed the drawer. The remaining ten he folded and put in his shirt pocket.

The scotch gave Harry courage. "Something wrong with it?"

Momo scowled. "Shut your face and go to work. People been trying to buy a drink for half an hour."

Momo shouldered his way to the open end of the bar, rounded it and walked back past until he reached the telephone booth. The minute he had closed himself into the booth, Harry was at that end of the bar, wiping industriously—and quietly. Harry couldn't hear what number Momo dialed. But, from the sound the coin made, he knew the call cost a quarter.

Angelo said, "Your uncle was a beer runner. He could've made more money with less trouble by handling the hard stuff, but he stuck to beer. He would load a truck with barrels at a brewery on Staten Island or in Jersey and deliver it in Brooklyn at night. Naturally, he had to pay a lot of people off and he took chances with hijackers, and every once in a while he would lose a load of beer, and sometimes a truck. But mostly he was lucky. He managed to stay out of jail and, because he wasn't in the hard liquor racket, the mobs left him pretty much alone.

"He worked hard in those days. I was just a punk kid, working in the kitchen, making salads. But I remember him then. My father used to call him Never Sleep. And he probably wouldn't've eaten, either, if my old man hadn't forced him to sit down with us whenever he came here.

"When Prohibition went out, your uncle was fixed better than most. He'd put his money in real estate—you'd be surprised to know what he owns right around here—and he stayed out of banks and the stock market. The other guys in the rackets went into all kinds of illegal businesses, but your uncle was different: he was a loner. Oh, he had his mob; Brooklyn Mike was one of them, and he's still with him after all these years. But, while the other guys were muscling in on different rackets, your uncle stuck to real estate. And the loan business— Don't get the idea I'm trying to whitewash him. He was, is, hard as hell. If you borrow money from him, you'd better pay back. His vigorish was, is, high, although not as high as some. And if he thought you couldn't—or wouldn't—pay, he wouldn't lend.

"I remember when he took over the Family as *padrone*. He didn't want the job, he wasn't even in the Family then. But the other guys had been in a war, they were killing one another off and getting unpopular with the D.A.'s office. And they were hurting business. So three of the leading *capos* got together and went to your uncle and begged him to take over.

"I remember it because he came to my father. *What do I do?* he asked. *If I go in, I'm a dead man. If I stay out, I'm a dead man— What do I do?*

"My father told him, *You go in. We both know it's a bad business. But you are a good man. They respect you. At least, you can stop the killing.*

"So, your uncle went in, and the killing stopped— All right, he's no saint. His Family isn't clean. But, look at him. He's no gangster, either. He's been married to the same woman for over forty years. He does good things. He just happens to be a good man in a bad business. When he dies, I don't like to think what will happen. The hungry ones are always crowding him, and they would take him if they dared— You see what I mean?"

Vince eyed the remains of an excellent steak and his untouched glass of red wine. "I guess you've told me what kind of a man he is— I never really knew him. We lived in different worlds. I might not have resented him so much if my sister Gloria hadn't always been trying to hard-sell him to me."

Angelo sighed. "This I can understand. I used to go out with your sister Gloria. That was before she met Al."

"You went out with *Gloria?*" Vince asked, astonished.

"That was before you were born—" Angelo sighed again. "You wouldn't believe it now, but in those days Gloria was almost as pretty as your mother was— Vince, I don't know what's bothering you, but I can guess. Your uncle wants you in with him, to oversee the legitimate side of his business, and you don't want to go—

You're a good man, too, like your uncle. You were just born in a different time."

Vince did not abuse Angelo's hospitality by getting drunk, nor did he remain long after lunch. He had brought with him the knowledge that his father had been a suicide, and this had had a profound effect on all his past thinking about Uncle Vincent Spotafore. Angelo's insistence that Uncle Vincent was a *good* man was, of course, Angelo's own evaluation. Certainly, Uncle Vincent had known that Dominico Maggione had jumped in front of a subway train. For that matter, so had Uncle Joe and all the other members of the Maggione family— Why had they lived by the half lie that he had been killed on the railroad? Had they been trying to shield Vince, protect him from the harsh truth, keep him, the youngest, a child all his life?

As if he had crossed a threshold from which there was no turning back, Vince was at last able to see himself in perspective, with no crutches and without illusion. And in the seeing, his Uncle Vincent looked larger, while he, Vince, shrank smaller.

At five o'clock, he tried to telephone Frances at her mother's house. After protracted ringing, there was no answer and he went into the living room to lie on the sofa.

The room and the sofa brought back memories of Louise and, for a time, he resisted; he directed his thoughts to Frances and for spaces of minutes at a time the woman would *be* Frances. Then, at the first touch of intimacy, the woman would become Louise, warm, provocative, beautiful, and he would hear her words:

You don't belong to me. But I belong to you . . .

With the memory of Louise's arms around him and her breasts heavy against his chest and her hair sweet against his cheeks, he dozed off to sleep.

At ten minutes past nine, he was up and at the telephone, trying again to reach Frances. The soft *burr* of futile ringing sounded in his ear for a long time before he gave up.

Then, avoiding his eyes in the hall mirror, he took the scrap of newsprint from his pocket and dialed the number of Louise LaScola.

sunday

Frances and her mother sat in St. Rita's in the pew that the Mc-Nultys had claimed ever since Frances could remember. It was on the left side of the church, near the altar, and thus some distance from the area on the right that Vince and Frances customarily occupied when they attended church as their own family group. Having arrived early, being in the forefront of those awaiting the nine o'clock Mass while the eight o'clockers were still in the final benediction, Frances could not see if Vince was there without turning around, and because she was essentially a shy person, she did not turn around. She realized more than ever that she had never liked sitting in the McNulty pew because of its prominence. And when her father wore his fireman-lieutenant's uniform to the services, which was frequently, she was not proud of him as her mother seemed to be; rather, she was secretly mortified.

Sitting in an advanced pew did have an advantage: at the end of the service it took longer to get out of church so there was more time to see who else was there without being obvious about it. Frances took longer than she had planned in exchanging pleasantries with her mother's friends, so a number of people had gotten out of the church by the time she really started looking. She did not see Vince and felt momentary panic that he might have been sitting toward the rear and thus among the first to leave.

When she finally got outside, she didn't see him either among those departing or with the arriving ten o'clocks. She would have

lingered, but her mother urged her on to where her father was waiting at the wheel of the car.

They were to meet Margaret and the twins at JFK Airport at
noon, and whenever Frank McNulty was going somewhere he
liked to allow plenty of time.

Charley Bennett glanced down at the snug-fitting dark blue
uniform, smoothing the blouse over his protruding stomach and
critically inspecting the sleeves before he looked at himself in the
full-length mirror. Watching him and the image he made were Eddie Durfee, Noble S. Wright and Noble's Aunt Rachel, in whose
bedroom they were gathered. Aunt Rachel was a strong, lean
woman who gave the impression of being older than she was because her hair was prematurely gray. She held a sewing basket on
her lap and it was she, more than the others, who was anxious
about the result of the inspection. They were viewing the tailoring
job she'd done on the uniform, rented from a costume agency,
with objective eyes. Her view was completely subjective: she was
a seamstress, not a tailor, and they, being men, simply could not
understand the difference.

"Turn around, slow," commanded Noble from his vantage position on Aunt Rachel's bed.

Charley turned around slowly.

Noble nodded. "Look okay to you, Eddie?"

Eddie Durfee, who was sitting on the floor with his back against
the bed, yawned and stretched. "Looks like the real article to me,"
he said.

Aunt Rachel stirred and her man-sized hands gripped the sewing basket. "I think maybe that right shoulder—"

"It's okay," said Noble. "Perfect. You look at men. Surprise you
how different their shoulders are, the right from the left— The main
thing is, it fits him. And if you monkey with it any more, the right
side won't fit— Okay, Charley. Now, put on the cap and holster
belt."

From the back of a chair, Charley lifted the regulation holster
belt with its Police .38 pistol, awkward until it was strapped around
his waist, and then hanging easily with just the end of the holster
showing below the bottom of the blouse. Then he picked up the

208

cap with its authentic-looking nickel-plated shield and set it squarely on his head.

"How do I look?" asked Charley, turning this way and that before the mirror.

"Perfect," Noble said in a soft voice.

Eddie Durfee threw up his hands in mock terror. "Jesus, officer! I wasn't doing a damned thing. Honest!"

All of them, even Aunt Rachel, laughed at Eddie. Then she went downstairs to fix them some lunch. Noble got up from the bed, rubbed his elbow and said, "We're as ready as we ever will be. You guys want to hear the tape?"

They said they did, so Noble crossed to an old-fashioned bureau and opened the top drawer. Taking a tape recorder from the drawer he set it on the bureau and pushed the *On* switch.

"Trans-American Metals—"

A woman's voice, as sexy as the utterance of such prosaic words could possibly permit, filled the bedroom. Noble pushed the *Off* switch, waited a moment, and pressed the *On* again.

"Surely . . . One moment, please . . . I'm ringing . . ."

"Hey! Jesus, that's *good!*" said Eddie Durfee.

Noble grinned. "It ought to be. It's their regular operator. I got it over the phone— Now, if those keys Eddie's friend has made for us, if they work, we should be all set."

Charley frowned. "Yeah, those keys— You better have a file in your pocket, just in case. I don't want to end up locked in anything, let alone the vault of an armored truck."

Momo's Bar and Grill had been open for at least an hour and was doing a brisk Sunday-morning business with regulars admitted through the kitchen when, at noon, Momo made it official by rolling up the shades and unlocking the front door. This was Harry's day off, which was just as well; if and when Len Larkin showed up, Momo didn't want Harry around.

Larkin wasn't in the upstairs apartment and hadn't been there all night. He hadn't skipped because his stuff was scattered all over the place and his only suit was hanging in the closet.

Momo considered the possibilities. Larkin could have met someone and gone somewhere as a result of the phone calls Harry had reported. He might have eventually wound up spending the night in Gladys' apartment, in which case he would show up sometime today, hungover and thirsty. Or he might have taken another weekend job driving a truck; if that was it, he might not show up until Monday or Tuesday.

Whatever it was, Larkin would be back; of that much, Momo was sure enough to maintain an outward calm during the day. And as the day dragged on, changed to evening, became night and Larkin did not come in the door or sound off on the stairs, Momo was positive he was off somewhere, driving a truck.

And when the call came at a few minutes before midnight, Momo *said* Larkin was driving a truck, as if someone had told him—although he didn't know the route—and that he would be back late Monday or early Tuesday. And in the moment of telling, Momo believed it as fervently as he hoped the caller would believe it.

monday

The gleaming new armored truck, with TRANS-AMERICAN METALS, INC. discretely gold-leafed on its black panels, detached itself from the southbound traffic of Van Wyck Boulevard and entered the ramp to Conduit Avenue. Although this vehicle was new, the driver was not and he accomplished the transition with the ease of long familiarity. From three to five times a month for several years he had nursed this splendid truck's wheezing predecessor through the Lincoln Tunnel, along the clogged crosstown streets of Manhattan, through the Midtown Tunnel, over the choked lanes of the Expressway, Queens Boulevard and Van Wyck, enjoying the little freedom of prerogative which would end with the locking of the vehicle for the return trip. Now, and for the next half hour, he and his partner would be free for a ham-and-eggs stop at the Pride of Queens diner. When they were loaded and ready to leave the cargo dock at JFK, until they were back in the TAM plant in Jersey, they would be just as much prisoners as if they were in jail.

It was the fifty-first time on this particular run for Scotty Carewe, the driver, and the twenty-something for his partner, Able "Shotgun" Simms of the company security force. It was the first run for the new truck and also the first one in which Scotty didn't have to worry about his two-way radio setting off any premature detonations; there was no radio at the moment. The truck had behaved well enough and Shotgun was not a conversationalist, which left

Scotty free to think about women, including the big, good-looking blonde who would be taking their orders at the diner.

There was an awesome crater between the access road and the diner's parking lot and Scotty negotiated it firmly, aiming at an open parking space and swinging wide to avoid a New York Telephone van that was standing smack in the middle of the No PARKING zone. The van was headed in to a utility pole, and up the pole a lineman had his spurs dug in and his back arched against a wide belt that left his hands free. The lineman was wearing a white safety helmet and a white jacket and Scotty wouldn't have given him a second glance if he hadn't noticed, with surprise, that the man was a Negro. Then he remembered having seen a Negro lineman in a Telephone Company advertisement, and at the time he had thought it was just Public Relations.

Scotty parked the truck, cut the engine and pocketed the keys. Back on the road somewhere, Shotgun had dozed off and the jounce into the parking lot had wakened him; he was now peering through the windshield at the diner.

"Yar-raugh-uh," Shotgun grunted through a yawn as he scratched himself further awake. "Time is it?"

"Ten forty-five, on the button," Scotty replied, sounding smug.

"Um. Made good time." Shotgun lifted his cap with the TAM shield on it and smoothed his graying sandy hair. Then he brushed the sleeves of his gray coveralls, which matched Scotty's even to the *Trans-American Metals* embroidered in blue across the shoulders. He hitched up his holster belt and patted the walnut grip of his pistol.

"Don't forget to lock the cab when we go in," he said.

"You can't forget, with this baby. Once you close 'em, they're locked. And you can't forget the keys, either— You open the door with the key in the ignition and listen what happens—"

Scotty opened the door and under the hood a bell began sounding off like an oversize alarm clock.

"Okay— One thing, don't forget: if your girl friend has a girl friend. But not that Pamela What-was-her-name— Jeeze!"

Scotty grinned. Squaring his cap, he put on his Man-of-Distinction look and said, "I won't forget. Let's go in."

212

The crowd was mostly truck drivers making deliveries or waiting pick-ups although there were some neighborhood types and a sprinkling of passers-through. Scotty spotted a pair of adjoining stools in the section where the blonde worked and he and Shotgun managed to beat out two guys who had just come in from the washroom. The blonde was leaning over the order bay talking to someone in the kitchen. She'd had her hair done a different way and, from the back, Scotty couldn't decide whether he liked it or not.

They adjusted themselves to the stools and Shotgun picked up a menu; the menu was a gesture since he always ordered ham, fried, and one egg, sunnyside, and coffee. Scotty sat with his back straight and both hands on the counter, waiting for the blonde to turn and see him. Her new hairdo didn't look bad from the side: she had a pencil stuck through it, which was kind of cute.

She finished whatever she had been saying and started for the counter. She had a good body and her easy smile showed she knew it. When she saw Scotty, she gave the hairdo a pat.

"Don't forget. Not Pamela," Shotgun said in a low voice.

The blonde stopped opposite Scotty and put her hands on her hips.

"Well, the pride of Jersey!"

"Morning, sweetheart. I had a hard time recognizing you, the way you got your hair. A good thing you spoke first."

"Listen to him— I guess you like it this way?"

"Yep."

"Twenty bucks it costs me and all he can say is *Yep*— Before I forget it, your office wants you to call them."

"Yeah? That receptionist won't let me alone. Wonder what she wants now?"

"Hah! If this was a dame, her voice needs a shave. The name was—Bassett?"

"Bossert," said Shotgun. "He's acting security officer."

This was news to Scotty. "What happened to Schlagle?"

"Had his appendix out, Thursday. Bossert's filling in."

"What the hell do you suppose he wants?"

"Probably the plane's stacked up. Or they had to change to a different cargo dock. You're the driver. You have to call him."

213

The blonde said, "I'll bet he's heard about me and wants to be introduced."

"Him? He looks more like Pamela's type," said Shotgun.

"Trans-American Metals," the sexy female voice said.

Scotty scowled. Of all the phony dames. She ought to have her voice laundered and starched to go with the rest of her. "Let me talk to Mr. Bossert, in Security," he said.

"Surely . . . one moment, please . . . I'm . . . ringing . . ."

Then, "Security—Bossert."

"Mr. Bossert, I'm Scott Carewe, driver number ten. Simms and I are at the diner— You left word for me to call?"

"Oh, yes, Carewe! Unfortunately, with no radio— We had to reach you before you got to the airport. We've had a tip from the New York City Police Department. There may be an attempt to hijack the shipment."

"Yeah? Holy cow!"

"There's probably nothing to it, but we can't take chances. We've agreed to allow the city police to supply you an armed escort."

"You mean like a convoy?"

"Not exactly. You'll be followed *from* the airport by an unmarked police car. You'll be accompanied *to* the cargo dock by a patrolman, name Nevins, badge number one four zero seven, and a detective, name, Harrington. They will join you there at the diner. Since it has been some time since I talked to the headquarters— they called right after you'd left here—they should be along any minute now. The patrolman will be in uniform and the detective will be in plain clothes. As a formality, you are to require them to identify themselves. Now, you have their names?"

"Nevins is the cop. Harrington is the detective."

"Right. They'll outline their plan to you. Of course, you as the representative of the company are in charge and Harrington has been instructed to deal directly with you. Needless to say, Carewe, this is not to be discussed with anyone in the diner. We don't want to take any unnecessary risk."

"Yes, sir. I can keep my mouth shut."

"Tell your partner, so he'll know what to expect— If the city police arrive before you've finished your breakfast, it won't hurt them to wait. I'll see you when you get back here."

"Yes, sir. Am I to make the usual security call?"

"Uh— What call is that?"

"Schlagle always has me make a phone call from the dock as soon as I'm loaded and ready to go."

"Schlagle— Oh, *that* call! Yes, by all means. When you make it, however, be sure it's exactly the same as always. Don't mention anything about the city police or hijacking or anything else. The inspector said there's good reason to suspect that a lot of this stuff is coming from inside the airport, from the employees, and we don't want to tip them off. You understand?"

"Yes, sir, Mr. Bossert."

Scotty got back to the counter just as the blonde was bringing his ham and eggs. He was so preoccupied he forgot to ask her about a date, and when she went to wait on someone else he told Shotgun in a low aside to expect an escort.

The patrolman came into the diner first. Behind him was a flat, lathy man who looked more like a used car salesman than a detective. He was wearing a snap-brimmed felt hat on his undistinguished brown hair. Once he was inside, he hung back, letting his eyes wander over the people at the counter.

The patrolman had a fair start on a bay window and he pushed it forward as he passed and inspected the people on the stools. While he was still three stools away, Scotty could read the 1407 on his shield.

"Who owns this *Trans-American Metals* truck out here?" the patrolman asked in a loud cop's voice.

"I don't own it," said Scotty. "But I sure as hell drive it."

That got a laugh from the customers and a straight, hard glance from the patrolman. Then the nothing-looking man in the felt hat pushed by him.

"Your name Carewe?" he asked, looking Scotty over.

"Yep."

The man matched Scotty's and Shotgun's caps and coveralls, pulled at his right ear and said, "Okay, Nevins. Tell the driver to go on back."

The patrolman made a little ducking movement of his head and turned around, steering his baby bay window out the way he had come in.

The lathy, nothing-looking man let go of his ear long enough to take a pass case from his breast pocket and open the case to reveal a badge.

"I'm Detective Harrington," he said. "Maybe you ought to call your office."

"I already have," said Scotty.

"Then we might as well go."

Behind the counter, the blonde was standing with her head cocked on one side and her hands on her hips. "I knew they would catch up to you, sooner or later," she said.

There was no delay at the cargo building. Scotty produced papers calling for a shipment of twenty-two 60-pound cartons—total weight 1320 pounds—of palladium, and an air freight official checked the Customs receipt and confidential numbers on the way bill. There had been a recent theft by someone who had driven a stolen truck and presented forged papers, and this was remarked on by the official who, fortunately, had not been involved in the fraud. Scotty and Shotgun both remembered reading about it in the newspapers and during the shuffling, signing and exchange of papers it was a conversation piece. Then the shipment was loaded in the vault of the truck under the watchful eye of Patrolman Nevins while two airport security officers, one of whom knew Shotgun, stood by with the TAM guard and admired the new truck; at the same time, Scotty Carewe and Detective Harrington were at the pay telephone in the rear of the cargo bay. Scotty made his security call first and was in the booth only a minute. Harrington took slightly longer, doing quite a lot of dialing; when he got back to the truck, Scotty was already behind the wheel and Patrolman Nevins and Shotgun were in the vault.

"All okay?" asked the airport security officer with the sergeant's stripes.

Scotty eyed Harrington. "If you have to pee, this is your last chance. When he closes that door back there, we're locked in until we get to Jersey."

216

"Nevins and I are okay," said Harrington. He settled himself in the seat and pulled his pistol from his shoulder holster. He flicked his wrist, swinging the cylinder out and rotating it to check the cartridges. Then he snapped the cylinder back in place and returned the pistol to the holster.

The offhand way Harrington checked the pistol gave Scotty a thrill down to his tailbone. Then he squared his cap and gave a thumb-up signal to the security officer which was almost immediately followed by a loud click inside the cab.

"That's it," said Scotty as he pointed to a red light that had appeared on the instrument panel. He checked the cab mirror. In the vault, the overhead light was on and he could see Shotgun explaining to the patrolman how the locking device worked.

Scotty started the engine and pulled out of the cargo dock. "Bossert said you'd tell me about your plans," he said. "Any choice which *way you want to go?*"

He had started in a normal voice but ended up by shouting because a descending plane passed over the cargo building and the hood of the truck so close it seemed they could touch it.

Harrington turned from watching the plane. "We're to take the 150th Street exit. Our following car will pick us up as soon as we reach Lefferts Boulevard."

"Oh! I know that way—I guess your people figured the hijackers would pick us up on Van Wyck and trail us to Jersey. There's one stretch over there that would be a dandy place for it."

"Maybe that's it— Say, what the hell is palladium?"

"It's a precious metal, comes from Russia. TAM buys it from a broker in Holland, where it's shipped from. The broker clears it through Customs and supplies us with the papers."

"Yeah? Sounds like it's valuable— I hope this stuff about hijacking is a lot of hooey."

Scotty breathed out, a long breath. "Me too, buddy."

They left the airport by 150th Street and when they had reached Lefferts Boulevard, Scotty said, "See anything of your car?"

"It just pulled out. He'll catch up— Follow Lefferts to Linden Boulevard."

"Linden? Okay. I think I know where we're going."

They reached Linden. But, instead of turning right as he expected, Scotty heard Harrington tell him to cross over and go around the block so they would be heading west on Linden.

"West?" Scotty looked surprised.

"West. And when we reach Pennsylvania Avenue, we turn south."

"Hey, I get it. We'll go on Flatlands Avenue through Brooklyn to the bridge."

"You're beginning to get the picture," said Harrington.

Scotty drove across Linden and around the block and got into the westbound traffic. When he had a chance, he looked in the outside rear-vision mirror and tried to pick out which of the following cars might be the police escort.

Harrington read his mind. "They're supposed to stay five cars back," he said.

Scotty made the left turn into Pennsylvania Avenue, but when he began seeking the right lane so he could swing into Flatlands, Harrington pulled the pistol from his shoulder holster and stuck the muzzle of it in Scotty's side.

"I'll tell you when to turn," Harrington said. "And don't touch anything with your hands or feet. Just keep driving with both hands on the wheel."

Frank Mastretta didn't like to drink before noon, at least not in a public place. He was much more in awe of Vincent Spotafore than Tony LaScola seemed to be, and he didn't want anyone carrying tales back to the mansion on Juniper Lane. But it didn't appear to bother Tony who, at eleven o'clock, was on his second scotch and soda. And if the man they were waiting for didn't show up pretty soon, Tony would be on his third. Frank was impressed by the way his brother-in-law had been acting since the kidnaping. While the old man was away, Tony had handled things with amazing sureness. And now that the old man was back, Tony was still handling things, although presumably under the old man's orders. It was hard to figure the old man: either his "going away" had suddenly made him senile, or else he was playing it very cool. He had all the information Tony had brought back from Danzig. He knew the names of two of the three kidnapers and their connection with his nephew, Vince Maggione. And he knew who the owner of the kidnap vehicle was. Yet, not one single move had been made toward retribution. True, Vincent Spotafore had come out of his experience with a nasty cold. But that hadn't stopped him from seeing his nephew yesterday and remaining closeted with him for more than an hour. It was also true that Vince hadn't looked too happy when he left the house. But the old man had been strutting like a rooster.

It didn't make sense.

Frank shifted uneasily on his side of the booth and glanced nervously at Tony's diminishing scotch and soda.

"What the hell do you suppose is keeping him?" asked Frank.

"How the hell should I know?" responded Tony. "He said he'd meet us here. He's probably been held up by a phone call or something— You sure you didn't hear anything the boss said to Vince yesterday?"

"Not a damned word. They were in the study, with the doors locked. I even went around under the window, but it was closed."

"Well— We'll just have to wait and see."

"You *did* give him Danzig's full report?"

"All of it, including Vince's relationship with the two guys, and that they spent three to four hours with him at his house the week before the—before the boss went away."

Frank stirred uneasily. "I wish to hell I knew—"

"Hold it. Here he is."

Danzig suddenly appeared at Frank Mastretta's left. His blond head was bare although he was bundled in a topcoat that looked new. He carefully removed the topcoat and hung it on one of the hooks in the rack behind the booth. Then he picked up a chair from a table opposite the booth and swung it around and sat at the end of the booth table.

Danzig nodded gravely to both of them before addressing himself to Tony. "I have a report," he said. "It took me a while to type it up; Ida's down with the flu and I had to type it myself. That's why I'm late."

Tony said, "You can give me the typed report when we leave. Now, suppose you tell us what you've got."

Danzig cast a quick, cornerwise glance at Frank Mastretta. He said, slowly, "It might be the wisest thing to—"

"Suppose you let me be the judge of that," said Tony. "It's Frank's money as well as mine that's paying you. So he's entitled to hear what you've got."

Danzig gave Tony a long, searching look. For a moment the scar on his jaw showed brilliant red.

"If it's about my sister and Vince Maggione," said Frank in a tired voice, "I already know the first part of it. The woman across the street told my mother, and my mother told me. That's one of the reasons why Tony and I hired you to keep a tail on Vince until we tell you to stop."

Noble S. Wright took a last worried look at the rear springs before he climbed into the driver's seat. Behind, and backed up to the overloaded little van, was the Trans-American armored truck. The keys had worked like a charm and the truck's vault was now empty of all except two subdued and taped-up TAM employees. Both the armored truck and the van were hidden from Pennsylvania Avenue by a pair of sagging tractorless trailers, and Charley and Eddie had now finished covering the truck itself with some rusted corrugated sheets they'd found.

The Honda cycle which had been carried in the van was resting on its stand, behind the trailers, with a pair of helmets slung over the handlebar. Just as soon as Charley changed from his policeman's tunic and Eddie shed his suit coat—and both of them had put on leather jackets and the helmets—they would be on their way back to Aunt Rachel's on Linden Boulevard.

Project One was now in its final stage, and Noble's worry about the van's springs dissolved in his satisfaction over the smoothness with which the operation had gone. It had been carefully planned and smartly executed; the almost incredible combination of TAM's truck radio problems and the regular security officer's appendicitis had been no more than breaks in the game and they had been sufficiently organized and alert enough to take full advantage of them. And now nothing remained except to deliver and collect the payoff.

Noble started the van and eased it away. It was lucky this stretch of road was firm. What a hell of a note it would be to founder so close to the finish line! Their figuring had been based on information supplied by Eddie's friend, Stu, for a normal shipment of 660 pounds; it hadn't been until Saturday they'd known it would be twice that much.

But, twice the load meant twice the money. And the money would be ready. When Noble had passed the final information to the dried-up little guy in the shabby office in Brooklyn, the guy hadn't batted an eye. Noble found out about him from connections in Harlem who vouched for his reliability. They had sold him a package of diamonds for fifty thousand and he'd paid them spot cash, taking the money out of the big safe which was in plain sight in the back of his cluttered office. When Noble had suggested it would be simpler to stick up the guy than to go to the trouble of stealing something and selling it to him, his friends had looked at him as if he was crazy. *You stick up a fence, especially that one,* they told him, *and you're out of business for good!*

Noble nursed the van over the rutted road and eyed the traffic going by on Pennsylvania Avenue. One good thing about using a Telephone truck as cover: nobody was ever surprised, where, or when, they saw one. The finishing touch was the safety helmet. He'd even fooled drivers of other Telephone trucks, who would give him thumbs-up when they went by.

Most of the traffic was moving along the avenue's roller-coaster surface at sedate speed. Down at his left, toward the Shore Parkway, he saw a large black sedan halted in the right traffic lane opposite a signboard which said a shopping center would be built on the site. The sedan—an old Chrysler Imperial—was equipped with a long radio antenna fastened to its rear bumper; to Noble's practiced eye this indicated a short-wave radio telephone. He counted five men in the Chrysler. All of them were scanning the wreck-strewn wasteland, which could mean they either had something to do with the real estate sign or else had been attracted by it.

There was a break in the traffic and the Chrysler didn't seem disposed to move, so Noble pulled into Pennsylvania Avenue. The little van groaned with the weight and the right rear spring hit the spring block with a thump. He had no time to worry about it because his hands were suddenly full with trying to steer on the undulating pavement.

221

He tried different speeds, finally settling at 30 miles per hour which seemed to be as much as the van could take, and he hadn't gone far before Charley and Eddie came by him on the Honda. They gave no sign that they knew him. Eddie was driving the Honda, which had been bought in the name of Noble's young cousin and was kept along with the cousin's window-cleaning truck in the garage at Aunt Rachel's.

The Flatlands Avenue intersection was directly ahead and Noble eased the van into the left lane and set his blinker signal for a left turn. The lane was clear ahead of him but he was four or five car lengths from the corner when the traffic light changed to yellow. His load was too heavy for him to take chances so he applied the brakes. The van stopped readily enough and he used the moment of waiting for a check on the cars behind him. The large, oblong mirror showed a half-dozen vehicles moving up in both lanes. Two cars back in his lane, also signaling for a left turn, was the Chrysler. In his brief glance at the occupants before the car directly behind blocked his view he saw the driver, holding his hands high on the wheel and staring straight ahead, and the man beside him using the radio telephone. Noble wasn't at all sure their interest was real estate. One thing was certain: they didn't look like cops.

The light changed to green and Noble gunned the engine, swinging the van into the westbound lane on Flatlands Avenue. The pavement was better here and he pushed the speed up past 40. Immediately the van began to sway so he lifted his foot and let the speedometer needle drop back to 30. He checked his rear-vision mirror again. The Chrysler was now the next car behind him, with maybe 40 feet separating them.

The man next to the driver was still using the radio telephone.

In addition to buying new heavy duty tires, some of the proceeds from Project Two had been invested in a good radio receiver which Noble had installed in the instrument panel. The set had police and telephone bands and now Noble leaned forward, turned the knob until the indicator showed *Phone* and switched on the set.

It came on in the middle of a flurry of voices and almost at once there was a loud *beep* which lasted for a fraction of a second. After the *beep,* Noble heard part of a word—*lans,* or *lands*—immediately blotted out by another *beep.*

222

Noble glanced worriedly at the set and, after another partial word, *telly,* and another *beep,* he shut it off. It wasn't a bad tube; it wasn't the sound a tube made and it was too regular in occurrence. And it wasn't something wrong with the transistors or diodes; if it had been that there would have been no sound at all.

Noble held the van's speed at 30 and glanced speculatively in the rear-vision mirror. Maybe the Chrysler's radio phone had some kind of jamming attachment making it impossible for anyone other than the base station to receive an ungarbled message. He shifted the indicator to *Standard Broadcast* and switched the set on again.

Out it came: music—*beep*—music—*beep*—music—*beep*—

In a swift agony of fear, Noble shut the set off and looked over his shoulder at the cartons behind him. There were 22 of them; he'd counted while they were being reloaded from the armored truck. And he'd handled every carton—all of them had—in a kind of bucket brigade, with Eddie in the vault, Charley astraddle of truck and van and he, Noble, piling the cartons in the van. Every carton had looked like the others; all of them had felt the same and weighed the same.

But one of them was different.

Somewhere along the line, at the shipping point in Holland, while airborne, while being trucked from plane to cargo dock, or while in the cargo dock—somewhere, someone had slit open a carton and inserted a tiny device, probably with a timer attached.

One of the cartons contained a "homer," an automatic broadcasting device with a range of up to several miles, that was sending out a *beep* a second and was saying, in effect, *Here I am—follow me* . . .

Sweat stood out on Noble's forehead as he shook off the safety helmet and let it fall on the seat beside him. His right foot went down to the floor and the little van surged forward, swaying wildly. When he'd left Pennsylvania Avenue, the road ahead of him had been clear. It wasn't now. Cars and trucks had come from side streets, clogging the lanes, and passing them was a game of broken-field running the overloaded van could hardly hope to win. As he roared through a yellow light at Rockaway Parkway, Noble thought less about who his pursuers might be than he did about how Eddie had wanted to come along with him. If Eddie had been there, he could have dropped one of the cartons in the path of the Chrysler as a delaying tactic. It would have cost ten thousand dollars, but if it had stopped the Chrysler it would have been worth it.

The Chrysler hadn't been quite quick enough to make the light, and hope surged in Noble's pounding heart. The van was doing 50 now and he pulled to the right to pass a heavy, hard-tired, empty truck on the wrong side; he had to cut sharply in front of the truck to avoid overrunning a small sedan in the right lane, and the truck driver gave him an angry horn. For a second the little van went out of control and its left wheels were past the center of the road as Noble crossed Remsen Avenue under a yellow light that had turned red. He saw the white, scared face of a driver who had stopped in the oncoming lane and he fully expected to hear the crunch of metal against metal.

Somehow, by a fraction of an inch, he was clear.

Luck was with him then—not a cop was in sight and the Chrysler was mired in the welter of traffic at least one light behind him. But he had a hunch that such luck couldn't hold, and it didn't. Directly ahead was a school zone, and from the number of kids it must have been the end of the noon recess. Noble cursed, stood on the brakes and brought the van to a squealing halt while a squad of children, convoyed by a uniformed crossing guard, marched raggedly from curb to curb.

He didn't see the Chrysler; his view was blocked by an assortment of vehicles including a cleaner's truck that had pulled out after he'd passed Remsen. But the Chrysler would be back there. It didn't have to see *him*. All it had to do was follow the *beep, beep, beep—*

The last of the children crossed, finally, and Noble gunned the van. For another moment, luck stayed with him and he caught a green at Ralph Avenue. Ahead, he could see Utica, where the light was also green. That wasn't so good: Utica Avenue was so far away the light would change before he could reach it. So he cut to the right, clinging to the steering wheel, and rolled into Avenue I.

He was driving by feel now; there wasn't time to watch ahead and behind and look at the speedometer. He pushed the van as much as he dared; when the front wheels started shimmying and fighting him, he eased off on the accelerator.

224

In the oblong rear-view mirror he caught a flash of the Chrysler turning from Flatlands into Avenue I.

If he'd had any doubts about it before, he had none now. There were five men in the Chrysler, they had radio equipment, they knew about the "homer" because they were following it. That meant they were organized, a member of the gang or gangs that preyed on the flow of freight traffic from JFK Airport; the gangs Eddie Durfee had so knowingly talked about in the other world of Vietnam. The men in the Chrysler could easily belong to the "Family" that had so recently parted with $40,000 to redeem Vincent Spotafore— If they got the van's load of palladium, even at the fence's rate of 20 per cent of retail value, they'd have their money back five times over—

Noble, stopped by a red light at Kings Highway, saw the Chrysler five blocks behind him, similarly halted by a red light and cross traffic. Noble hadn't wanted to see cops before; he would have been happy now to see a whole platoon of them.

The light changed, and in a swift, desperate *gestalt* Noble decided on a plan. He would turn into a side street, park the van and leave it locked and hide somewhere nearby. If the Chrysler stopped by the van, he could at least get away. If the odd chance remained that the men in the Chrysler were not following the van, and drove on past it, he could return and resume his trip to Brooklyn.

He had reached Albany Avenue when this hope was shattered. The Chrysler was suddenly beside him and four of the five men in it were waving at him to pull over and stop; the fifth man, the driver, gunned far enough ahead to force Noble to turn into Albany Avenue before he moved in front of the van.

Noble's desperate eyes, seeking an out in the rear-view mirror, saw another large black sedan, this one a Cadillac, right behind him. It was also radio-telephone equipped and filled with men, and the men looked even less like cops than the ones in the Chrysler did.

Noble tried one last forlorn maneuver. In front of him the Chrysler was applying the brakes, trying to force him to stop, when he abruptly turned the van into Glenwood Avenue. His right front tire scraped the curb, but he had lost the Chrysler; with his front momentarily clear, he pushed the van to reckless speed. Then his mirror told him the Cadillac had made the corner with ease and was mercilessly tailgating him.

And in another block, when he was entering the intersection of Brooklyn Avenue, the Chrysler came roaring up from his right; the driver had gone around the block and was now set to ram him.

Noble spun the wheel hard and skidded to his left into Brooklyn Avenue, and for the space of a block the Chrysler was right beside him, holding him in the left lane as he fought the wheel and kept his foot to the floor.

Side by side the van and the Chrysler shot across Avenue H. And then, suddenly, Brooklyn Avenue narrowed and began ascent to a bridge that had high cement parapets on either side.

Noble had nearly reached the crest of the bridge when his luck finally ran out. Coming from the opposite direction, a huge and cumbersome truck was square in his path.

He jammed on the van's brakes and threw himself sideways and down on the seat just as, with a jolting crash, he hit the truck head-on.

In a last, frantic effort to avoid the crash he had instinctively spun the steering wheel to the right, and it was this move which afforded him at least temporary escape. The impact was all on the left side of the van's front, shattering the windshield and hopelessly jamming the door on the driver's side. But the corner impact wrenched the van's frame, causing the right door to pop open and in a shower of crumpling safety glass Noble shot through the open door just as the tail of the Chrysler flashed by.

He landed on his hands and knees on the rough asphalt, rolled sideways and was on his feet. Behind him, the Cadillac had squealed to a stop and men were pouring out of it; ahead, the bright, angry red of the Chrysler's taillights were at an angle behind the truck.

Noble ran straight to the truck, whose driver was sitting with his eyes round above his open mouth and his hand on his forehead, and climbed to the hood by way of the truck's wide bumper. Then, without even pausing for breath, he put both hands on top of the concrete parapet and vaulted himself over it.

He cleared the parapet with plenty to spare. And then, in a single, all-revealing flash, he saw a railroad track filled with a line of slow-moving freight cars. He was directly over one of the cars which had a ribbed, metal roof and a narrow walkway. He tried to aim himself for the walkway and might have made it if it hadn't been for the wires, one above the other, that he didn't see until he was on them.

The wires caught him in the crotch and spun him around until his outstretched hands hit the metal roof of the freight car. In a brief flash of excruciating pain and a dazzling burst of blue light, like a rocket's flare, the life of Noble S. Wright was spent.

He hung the phone on the hook and, putting the palms of both hands against the golden oak frame, leaned on his hands and shook his head at his reflection in the diamond-shaped mirror. It's no good, he said to himself. If they haven't skipped out by now, it's too late. Noble had neither reported for work today nor called in; if Vince could believe the girl at Zen Electronics, he didn't have a telephone and she wasn't allowed to reveal his address. Charley Bennett didn't have a phone, either, although at five o'clock Sunday night he'd made his customary call to the foreman: Charley had said he was sick and hoped he'd be able to be back at work Monday night. The foreman said he'd given Charley Vince's message and had told him it was urgent; he'd left a message for Noble, too, but thus far both requests had been productive of nothing.

Had they cleared out, both of them?

Vince had some trouble meeting the eyes in his washed-out, reflected face. It was now Monday noon, less than twenty-four hours since the interview with his Uncle Vincent Spotafore; that was only yesterday, although it already seemed as unreal and remote as Vietnam.

Vince had gone to Juniper Lane in response to Louise's urging. He had gone there prepared to keep his lip buttoned about his suspicions concerning Charley Bennett and Noble S. Wright, and in less than ten minutes—the moment the door to Uncle Vincent's study closed—all Vince's ideas, thoughts and decisions had become less than academic; they had been made utterly stupid.

. . . *These were your friends. One of them maybe did save your life, but did you have to pay him back by putting the finger on me? . . . All right, since you like to talk so goddamned much,*

227

*you can tell them I know who they are. And you can tell them I
don't want the money back. But if they try to spend any of it anywhere in my territory, they're dead. And there isn't a thing I can
do to stop it . . . As a favor to you, my sister's son, I've held their
names back, and I'm going to hold them just forty-eight hours
more. After that, if they're not gone— Listen, I don't want them
killed; I don't want anybody killed— All right. Now you can go
home and look at yourself in the mirror. And you can say to yourself, Vince Maggione, you and your big mouth have had it. You
and your goddamned independence are all through— As soon as
it can be arranged, you're going with your uncle to the lawyer to
sign a contract that sends you back to college. The contract will
be for the same terms and conditions as already discussed. And
you can say to yourself, you don't deserve it, Vince Maggione. But
your Uncle Vincent Spotafore is a damned good man, and it's time
you found it out . . .*

Vince sighed and took his eyes from the reflection in the mirror
and took his hands from the golden oak frame. He walked un-
steadily into the living room and sat on the sofa. He'd spent the
night on the sofa to be near the telephone if it rang. But in spite
of the messages he'd left, the phone had yet to ring.

Not even Frances had called.

Now there was only the waiting, and the fear.

Charley Bennett paid off the cab at the visitors' entrance to
Nassau Community Hospital and, as soon as the cab was out of
sight, began the four block walk to the apartment he'd left at five-
thirty in the morning. He was supposed to be in bed, sweating
out the flu. He hadn't been absent from work enough times to
spoil his reputation of being a dependable worker and that was
the way he wanted to keep it. In another month or so, before the
summer set in, he intended to quit the job. But right now it was
important to him to maintain the illusion that, on this Monday,
he was too sick to work. And he didn't want any of his nosey
neighbors to see him walking in the front door when he was supposed to be sick in bed.

The foreman had told him about Vince's call, and had said it
was urgent. He had no intention of returning the call, now or later.

228

Vince had probably figured things out: he'd been close to it Thursday. Well, let him think what he wanted; fear of his *mafiosi* uncle would keep his mouth shut.

A block past the hospital, Charley Bennett turned into the street that would lead him to the service entrance of the apartment building. He wouldn't be running into the super: *he* worked only at both ends of the day, leaving the middle for excursions in search of a property he could buy and manage for himself. Since most of the people in the building worked during the day while Charley worked nights and irregular hours, the super had been happy to give him the key to the service entrance so he could put out his own garbage.

That phase of his life, doing his own chores and alternating between working himself blind and being scared half silly, would soon be over. All the Projects had been successful and the take had been gratifying. When the proceeds from the sale of the palladium were divided, Charley Bennett would have in his hands the best part of $75,000—in cash.

He didn't know what Noble and Eddie would do with theirs, but he knew exactly what he would do with *his*. He would go back to Winfield and buy *The Citizen* from Old Man Potter. He wouldn't go to Potter directly; he would let a broker do the bargaining.

As he neared the apartment building, he thought pleasantly of the look of consternation that would possess Old Man Potter's face when he learned that the buyer of *The Citizen* was Charley Bennett, the boy he'd taught to operate the Linotype machine. And there would be no question about where the money came from. Everyone in Winfield knew that Charley's Aunt Maybelle, who had married a rich man and had moved to Chicago, had recently died; all of them knew Charley Bennett was her favorite nephew and that she would remember him in her will. What they didn't know was that Charley's inheritance, a miserable $300, was already in hand.

He eyed the back of the building as he passed through the service yard. The windows in the rear wall were closed, with most of their shades drawn. At three o'clock, not many of the occupants were at home; in another hour, they would start coming in and by that time he would be in bed.

He let himself in and tiptoed past the super's apartment. No light showed under the door and the radio wasn't playing, which meant the super's wife was out. Ahead, on his left, was the room with the coin-operated laundry machines, one of the few places Blanche visited because he did not encourage her going out of the building. He doubted that she was in there now, although someone was because he heard the rhythmical chugging of a washer. A quick glance in passing showed him a woman, sitting and reading a magazine. She was in curlers and he recognized her as a resident of the fourth floor front.

Covered by the washer noise, he walked quickly up the stairs and through the door into the entrance hall. The lobby doors were glass and he could see through them into the street. The usual cars were parked, and kids were passing by, homeward bound from school. The self-service elevator was right beside him, with its door open, probably waiting for the woman at the washer.

He entered the cubicle, pushed the button for the third floor, and as the doors closed and the elevator began its jerky ascent, he suddenly felt very tired. The elevator stopped at three and just before he got out he pushed the button marked LOBBY, as if he was trying to convince himself that he hadn't just ridden it up from below, or that he hadn't even left the building nearly eight hours ago. His apartment was all the way down at the end of the hall and he forced his tired legs to carry him over the worn carpet. His key was in his hand and he let himself into the gloom of the shade-drawn room and quietly closed the door.

"Hon?" he called softly.

She didn't answer and as soon as his eyes had adjusted to the semidarkness he saw that she was not on the sofa-bed where he usually found her.

He came further into the room and when he had passed by his easy chair, he saw her. She was lying on the floor in front of the bathroom door, which was open. She was in her nightgown and robe. She was lying on her side, with her left arm underneath and her right hand stretched out. Her hair had broken loose from its ribbon and was covering her face.

230

"Hon!"

In two quick strides he was beside her. Kneeling down, he brushed her hair from her face. Her eyes were rolled up in her head, her lips were drawn back over her clenched teeth and there were flecks of dried foam on her lips and chin.

"Jesus Christ," Charley Bennett said. He picked her up in his arms and carried her to the sofa-bed. She was limp, and frighteningly cold. He put her down, lifted her head and pulled the pillow under it. He turned on the floor lamp at the head of the sofa-bed.

Her lips and gums were blue.

In sudden terror he felt her face. It was cold; her whole body was cold. He grabbed at her slack, cold wrist and could find no pulse. He pulled the front of her robe apart, ripping off one of the buttons, and put his ear below her thin left breast.

"Jesus Christ Almighty," said Charley Bennett finally. It was as much of a prayer as he had uttered since childhood. He got to his feet, looking down. And then, seized by memory, he rushed to the tiny kitchenette in the alcove behind the sofa-bed.

He had hidden the pure stuff in a bag in the flour canister. He'd thought it would be safe there. Now he saw flour spilled on the counter and the open canister lying on its side.

In a daze, he walked back, past the sofa-bed and his easy chair, to the bathroom. Her implements: the charred and blackened bottle cap, the burned matches, the needle with its paper tube and eyedropper bulb, all were there. And so was the flour-covered bag of pure heroin.

Instead of the 5 per cent fix she had become accustomed and enslaved to, Blanche had injected pure heroin into her vein.

Charley Bennett walked out of the apartment and down the long hall to the elevator. He pushed the button automatically and only half consciously heard the whine of the motor, the opening and closing of the door and, as one in a dream, rode down. He was out in the street, heading for the drugstore where the telephone was, when the men who had been waiting for him saw him.

They saw him, but he didn't see them. He was in the center of the street when a woman on the sidewalk screamed. He didn't hear her. And the car that hit him, he didn't see at all.

In less than three-quarters of an hour it would be five o'clock, and even if Frances could keep up the pace she had maintained all day she could not possibly finish all the Passenger Redemptions on her desk. The latter part of February and the first half of March there had been an unusual number of late trains and cancellations, and the Redemption Department was so far behind it was pathetic.

In one respect, Frances was glad for the work. It required enough attention to keep her mind occupied with what she was doing instead of what she was going through. Her first full day away from Vince had been a nightmare. She had been so sure he would call. Of course, in fairness to him, no one had been home at her mother's house most of Saturday. Margaret's husband was in bad trouble: he'd cashed a lot of checks in anticipation of his inheritance, which was supposed to have come through on the first of March. Unaccountably and without warning there had been a snag over taxes and the Internal Revenue Department had frozen the estate's bank account. There had been a long and un-satisfactory conference with Jack's mother in the morning, then a stormy, drawn-out luncheon with Frank McNulty who wound up by washing his hands of his daughter's affairs, and a frantic afternoon of trying to scrape together—with the banks closed—three hundred dollars in cash because the telegraph office refused to accept a check. Finally, at half-past four, Frank McNulty had relented, contributing out of his own pocket the sixty dollars that put the Bring-Margaret-and-the-Twins-Home Fund over the top. It had then taken some doing, including a spate of long-distance telephoning, to get the money transferred and reservations con-firmed. This last was accomplished at JFK Airport some time after nine in the evening and they had arrived back at the McNulty resi-dence, completely exhausted, well after ten.

No, Vince would have had to be extremely agile and quite lucky to reach her by telephone on Saturday. But he could have called her any time Sunday. Except for the hour she was in church and the time spent driving to the airport to get Margaret and bring her home, Frances hadn't stirred from the house.

And he could have called today; she had been right at this desk, all the blessed day long . . .

At five minutes before five, Frances covered her typewriter and

232

jammed the unfinished work in the desk drawer. She'd been asked to stay on overtime, but she just wasn't up to it. She wasn't up to going home to Vince, either.

One more night at her mother's, even if it meant sleeping on the divan again, was better than going back to Vince before he called.

It was a quarter past seven when Eddie Durfee walked into Momo's. He and Charley Bennett had separated after leaving the Honda and helmets in Aunt Rachel's garage. Noble's cousin Willie had driven Eddie in an old panel truck to Parsons Boulevard and Jamaica Avenue. Willie was very proud of the truck, which he used in his window-cleaning business; Noble had bought it for him and he was paying back in weekly installments. Willie idolized Noble and he was good to have around because he was an excellent driver, had absolutely no nerves, and kept his mouth shut. Eddie had bought some Army surplus clothing in a store on Jamaica Avenue and had then walked up Parsons to the YMCA where he took a shower and put on his new things, leaving the old ones in a trash can. Then he'd walked back to Jamaica Avenue and spent three hours at a double feature movie which was for adults only. After the movies he had eaten a good dinner before taking a bus to Roosevelt Raceway and then a cab to Momo's.

Momo himself was behind the bar and the place was almost empty, as it usually was on a Monday night. A dame with strawberry blonde hair, artificial eyelashes and a nice figure was sitting by herself at the bar near the door and the telephone booth. She had a half-full highball in front of her and the way she was keeping to herself she was probably waiting for a phone call. At the other end of the bar were two regulars who glanced incuriously at Eddie as he sat on his favorite stool in front of the beer pumps.

Momo had watched him from the time he entered until he sat on the stool. Momo's lumpy face showed surprise.

"I thought maybe you'd skipped."

"What the hell gave you that idea?"

"You. Where you been since Friday?"

"Friday? I was in here Saturday!"

"Okay. Saturday, then. This is Monday night."

Eddie dug in his pants for his wallet, took out a ten and dropped it on the bar. "If you're worried about my stinking chit, here's your dough!"

Momo grunted, "Okay." He picked up the ten, turned and opened the cash drawer. With his broad back blocking Eddie's view he held the ten in his left hand, Hamilton portrait facing him, and with his right thumb and forefinger felt along the edge of the bill. Halfway down, in the scroll work on the right side, he felt three slight projections in a triangular formation. Pricks made with the point of a fine sewing needle, they were invisible to the eye although his fingers found them readily enough. The inspection had taken less than ten seconds. He lifted out the cash tray and dropped the marked bill in the bottom of the register drawer. Then he took the notebook from the side of the register, opened it to the most recent Len Larkin page and ripped out the page.

"Okay?" Momo said as he handed the paper and six dollars and change to Eddie.

Eddie stuffed the money and the page in his shirt pocket. "So you thought I skipped out."

"Today is rent day and usually you're around. But today you weren't. What was I supposed to think?"

"Hey— You didn't rent my place to somebody else?"

"A guy wants it. I'm to call him."

Eddie dug out the wallet again. "It so happens I was working. Maybe Harry told you, I got a call Saturday. I drove a truck, to Washington, D.C. I just got back on the bus a couple hours ago—" He took out two more tens and, as an afterthought, added a five. "There's my rent to next Sunday night. And since you're too goddamned cheap to buy a drink, I'll buy my own. A shot. And a beer chaser."

"Now you're making sense," said Momo. He scooped up the money and turned to the register again. All three bills had the same triangle indentations in the scroll work. Again he dropped the bills in the bottom of the register drawer.

"So, I'm cheap, huh," Momo said. He gave Eddie his change. Then he poured the shot and the beer chaser. "Okay. For every one you buy, I'll buy two. Fair enough?"

"I hear you, but I don't believe you," said Eddie. He tossed off the shot and chased it with the beer. He was shoving the empty glasses across the bar when Momo started down toward the end.

"Hey— Where're you going?"

"Don't worry, I'll be back. I'm going to call that guy and tell him the apartment's still rented."

Eddie used toothpicks to keep track of whose turn it was to buy the drinks. Not that he didn't trust Momo: he did it simply to annoy him. It was a way of getting back at Momo for having the nerve to consider renting *his* apartment to someone else. He would give it up when he was good and ready; in the meantime, nobody was going to push him out.

The toothpicks showed it was Eddie's turn to buy, but after three shots and chasers he was in no immediate need. However, Momo was eying him; maybe he was wondering how long Eddie could remain vertical.

"Give the little lady at the end a refill," said Eddie. "And I'll have the same."

Momo scowled. "She's drinking the best scotch."

"I didn't ask you what she was drinking. I said, give her a refill."

"Okay!"

Momo carried scotch, with soda on the side, to the strawberry blonde. There were no more people in the place than there had been, and Momo's attempt to keep his remarks private was a failure.

"Mr. Larkin's bought you a drink."

"Mr. Larkins?" She cast questioning eyes in his direction, not quite focusing on him. It was a brush off, and it wasn't. She acknowledged his presence and the gift without committing herself to accept either.

"Him." Momo indicated Eddie with his thumb.

Eddie knew better than to overdo it. He gave her a casual glance and returned to a study of his empty glass.

"Oh— I suppose it's— Thank you, Mr. Larkins."

Eddie nodded absently. She wasn't waiting for anybody; she just wasn't ready to go home yet. And, if he played it right, she wouldn't be ready to go until he wanted her to.

Momo came back and gave Eddie his shot and beer chaser and when he'd put the change down, Eddie said, "I bought *two* drinks.

So, that's *four* you owe me." He made with the toothpicks while he enjoyed Momo's scowling face. Then a new customer came in and Momo went over to wait on him.

The newcomer was wearing a hat and his topcoat was turned up around his ears like it might be getting cold outside. Eddie recognized him from somewhere but couldn't place him. He ordered a scotch and water and stood at the bar, blocking Eddie's view of the blonde.

She looked a little like the woman he'd picked up in a bar in Oakland, California, when he'd just gotten back from overseas and was still trying to get used to the idea that he was now Leonard Larkin and that Eddie Durfee was dead. Of course, Eddie Durfee wasn't *dead;* it was Leonard Larkin who was. Eddie hadn't known Larkin from a bunch of beets until, in the attack on Hill 875, the man in front of him had stepped on a mine. The shock had thrown Eddie to the ground and had knocked him out for maybe a minute; when he'd come to, there were chunks of flesh, cloth, helmet, gear and gobs of blood all over him. When he found out he could move his arms and legs and that the flesh and blood weren't his, he was sick as a dog. Being sick wasn't comfortable, but it was assurance that he was alive.

It was about that time he discovered the ID tags in his fist. He didn't remember picking them up; they must have fallen in his hand and his hand had automatically closed on them. He stared stupidly at Leonard Larkin's ID tags for maybe a minute before the idea came to him. Then he jerked off his own tags and tossed them in the middle of the bloody heap and dropped Larkin's tags, with their own severed cord, down inside his own shirt. It was then he discovered that *he* had been hit: some of the metal surrounding Leonard Larkin's exploding body had cut his ammo belt in two and had ripped holes in his blouse. The pocket patch with *DURFEE, E.* on it was hanging by a thread, and he ripped it off and pitched it after the ID tags. And then he found that a lot of the blood soaking through his shirt was his own, and his hands looked like they'd been run through a meat grinder. In the bloody mess of his gear he found a bandage and applied it to a deep gouge in his chest just before he passed out.

He vaguely remembered being carried and put in a chopper and being cleaned up at Long Binh hospital. He didn't own a wallet at that time and they must have burned his bloody combat gear without looking for laundry marks because on the chart he was *Pvt. Larkin, Leonard* with a new serial number. Two weeks later he was in San Francisco and within a month he had been discharged with $780 in back pay and allowances, an Honorable Discharge and a Purple Heart, all issued to Leonard Larkin. He also had some letters from Leonard Larkin's parents and girl friend, postmarked Oneonta, New York. For obvious reasons, other than that his hands were still bandaged, he chose not to answer the letters. And, instead of going back to Oneonta, New York, he moved across the Bay to Oakland, where he met the blonde.

She was older than this girl he'd just bought a drink for, and not as pretty. But she had a body that even now made him groan in memory. There were other things about her—particularly her husband—that made him groan, too, although for a different reason. He'd had her the first night, in the back seat of her car, in front of the house where he'd rented a room. After that, during the daytime, he went to her house. Her husband had been a dentist in San Francisco and would leave for work early; Eddie, hidden behind the hedge, watched him go. Things went on like that for a month. And then one night he and the blonde were having an anniversary drink together in the bar where they'd met, when her husband walked in.

This was the first time Eddie had seen him face-to-face. He was skinny and dried up and a lot older than she was, which answered a lot of questions. And he was queer as a three-dollar bill: he kept putting his hand on Eddie's thigh. When the little man said he was a dentist, Eddie remembered a tooth that needed filling. Right there, the blonde's husband pressed a card and an appointment on him for the next day and said he'd give Eddie a thorough examination and an estimate without charge. The last thing Eddie wanted to do was sit in a dentist's chair, but he was trapped. The next morning, the dentist picked Eddie up at his rooming house and drove him to the office in one of the big buildings downtown. He ushered Eddie past a lot of waiting patients right into a private office where a sexy little brunette dental aide made him comfortable in the chair. Then the blonde's husband put on his white coat

237

and, after washing his hands, explained that the modern method was to have the patient perfectly relaxed. So he adjusted a mask to Eddie's face and in two minutes he was asleep, and when he woke up there wasn't a tooth left in his head.

The two regulars gave up and went home at ten-thirty, and right after they went out, the strawberry blonde left. Eddie had bought her two more drinks which she had accepted in the same vague uncompromising way and without either of them moving any closer to the other. Eddie had just about made up his mind to move toward her—that is, if he could—when she was gone. He wasn't sure for a while that she *was* gone. Things had started jumping in and out of focus and it had been some time since he'd lost count of toothpicks and had lost interest in annoying Momo. The newcomer who had stood at the bar between them, the man Eddie thought he knew from somewhere, had gone out ahead of the regulars and no one had come in since.

Eddie cast an unsteady glance around the empty bar, counted two Momos behind the bar, two bars, and took a deep breath.

"Um—going—to—bed," said Eddie, pushing out the words with conscious effort. He managed to get off the stool without falling, and, using the edge of the bar as a guide, he aimed himself for the door.

Momo stayed where he was behind the bar, watching Eddie and making no move to help him. Eddie got to the end of the bar and waited for the door to settle down into being one door before he stepped out again. He held himself upright, opened the door and pushed himself out into the cold night air.

The door hadn't closed behind him before Momo put out the lights in the bar. Then the door closed and, distantly, Eddie heard the bolt shoot home.

He was at the entrance to the stairs, leaning against the frame with both hands and lifting his rebellious right foot to the threshold, when suddenly he was back in Saigon and two of the Cong were behind him, knifing him in the back and side as they pulled him down. He tried to cry out, to fight back, but his own blood welled in his throat and choked him. And just as the lights of Saigon were going out forever, the Cong ran away and he remem-

238

bered: the newcomer who had stood at the bar between him and the strawberry blonde had been the man who had picked up the flashlight he'd dropped at Vincent Spotafore's house in Juniper Lane.

tuesday

Anthony LaScola was not an habitual early riser, and he did not ordinarily have breakfast in a diner. It suited him that most of his clients did not open their places before noon and were closed either Mondays or Tuesdays to replenish inventory, repair damage, prepare menu and pay bills and otherwise brace themselves for another week. Tony knew the restaurant game: he had gone the whole route from salad maker to assistant chef to buyer and kitchen cashier to banquet manager and front man to, for one unhappy year, owner of his own establishment. He had not been the sole owner; his (silent) partner had been Vincent Spotafore and it had been Spotafore's money which had made Tony's ownership both possible and impossible. He had ended the year owing slightly more in interest than the original amount of the loan. It had remained a frightening problem until Mr. Spotafore had finally consented to take over the restaurant in exchange for a paid-up receipt plus a job for Tony. He had done better on the job than anyone, including himself, had thought he would. He knew everyone in and everything about the restaurant business and he could usually tell just by walking through a place whether it was making money, or could ever make money. In his first year on the job he had brought Mr. Spotafore not one single loser, and he had written some sizable loans. Mr. Spotafore was less grateful than practical; by the time Tony had married Mrs. Spotafore's niece, he was a full-fledged member of the Family and his star was rising fast.

It wasn't devotion to duty that caused Tony LaScola to get up at the unprecedented hour of six-thirty on this Tuesday morning; it was a matter of survival. He had not been at all happy with the way things had been going since Vince Maggione had returned from the wars. Vince was not a member of the Family in a specific sense, although being the boss's closest blood relative made him a latent threat. And he might have continued to be only a threat if it hadn't been for the incredible business of the kidnaping and the crazy turn things had taken since. It had been Tony's decision to lay all the facts before the boss: not only had the kidnapers been his nephew's closest friends, they had unquestionably fashioned their plan on information the nephew had furnished them. *That* should have torn it. But, no. After being closeted with his nephew for the better part of an hour, the boss had turned around and called his lawyer to *draw up a contract.*

Frank hadn't been able to overhear all of it, but he'd heard enough to convince him that, not only had Vince Maggione been completely forgiven—*the boss was putting him on the payroll!*

There was another little matter about Vince Maggione, a personal matter involving Louise. Not that Tony was worried about his wife: she knew which side her bread was buttered on. The fact that she had spent Saturday night and Sunday morning with Vince Maggione in a motel on Jericho Turnpike didn't bother Tony; it amused him, and made him contemptuous of both of them for letting themselves be caught up in a situation that could be used against them. This was the kind of knowledge Tony knew how to use, and he would use it—if there was enough time.

But time had begun to run out.

Not once, since the kidnaping, had the boss taken either Tony or Frank into his confidence. And now, in a diner, for Christ's sake, Tony had to read *The New York Times* to find out what caper Brooklyn Mike had been up to at JFK. More than a million dollars worth of palladium had been hijacked from an armored truck and transferred to a stolen Telephone Company van which, in turn, had been hijacked on Brooklyn Avenue near Avenue H. The driver of the van, identified from his driver's license as Noble S. Wright, 27, had been electrocuted when, in trying to escape, he'd jumped from the Brooklyn Avenue overpass to a moving

242

freight train on the Penn Central's Bay Ridge Branch. Eyewitnesses had seen a dozen men load the cartons of palladium into a panel truck, which had suddenly appeared on the scene . . .

It was small satisfaction to Tony that he was one of four people on the outside who knew the real owner of the "Telephone" van. It would be only a matter of time before the cops would know, too, when they'd finished tracing the serial numbers. They would probably know some time today. And that didn't leave him much time.

He paid for the breakfast and, folding the *Times* under his arm, went outside to the telephone booth near which he'd parked his car. The number Danzig had given him he had committed to memory. It was an East New York number and, after he had dialed and had been answered by the flat, suspicious voice of a woman, in spite of the early morning cold he began to sweat.

He didn't have to tell her who he was; the name he mentioned was enough. He told her where the name's owner would be, and when; how long he could be expected to stay there, and the route he would follow when he left.

He was sweating profusely when he came out of the booth. This was it. In three hours the question of Vincent Spotafore and his nephew would be settled and the only remaining question would be one of succession. And when that came up, he, Tony LaScola, would be firmly in the driver's seat.

Frances made her usual train. She was as tired as if she hadn't slept at all, and the train was so crowded she was forced to stand. It wasn't the first time; she had learned from past experience to catch little cat-naps while standing on her feet. The train ran underground all the way from East New York to Richmond Hill and it was warm and well-lighted, so she alternately dozed and came awake, shielding her eyes from the naked electric bulbs in the car's white ceiling.

The man standing in front of her was reading the *Daily News.* Occasionally he would shift his weight, close the paper in his hands and open it to a fresh page. With no particular interest, Frances noted that he read the paper from back to front, advancing from the sports section and the comics through the features and

243

ads to the news pages. In the process of shifting, he had turned so that his left side was toward her and she could easily see what he was reading. The story was about a hijack at JFK Airport and Frances was on the verge of another cat-nap when a name leaped at her from the page:

Noble S. Wright . . .

Frances gasped, and the man gave her a quick glance.

"You all right, miss?"

"Yes— Please. That article you were reading about the hijacking at JFK—"

"Yeah. A million bucks worth. And in broad daylight!"

"Did—did I see a name, Noble S. Wright?"

The man turned to his paper. "Uh— Yeah. Noble S. Wright, twenty-seven. He was killed trying to get away—"

"Oh, my God," Frances said.

"I guess you know my nephew," said Vincent Spotafore to the white-haired, portly man who was standing behind a large paper-strewn desk in the pleasantly cluttered office.

"I know him." The lawyer nodded with just a touch of formality. He was holding a pair of eyeglasses by one broad bow in a plump pink hand, and as he glanced at Vince the glasses moved in a vague gesture. "I haven't seen you in some years. That was before you went away, wasn't it. Something to do with your sisters, about the house—" He paused briefly and his eyes looked at the glasses in his hand. "Of course, I knew your brother, Mario. I was very fond of Mario. He used to go hunting with my son, the one who was killed in the same war— But, do sit down."

Vincent Spotafore sat in the chair facing the desk and Vince sat in the one beside him. The lawyer put on his glasses and lowered himself into his swivel chair and his pink hands busied themselves with the papers on his desk.

"You've got it drawn up?" asked Vincent Spotafore.

"I have. Before I hand them over—we'll read them together and either of you can ask questions at any time— Before we do that, Mr. Spotafore, I want to be quite sure that I have interpreted your wishes correctly."

"What? I told you what I wanted!"

244

"I am aware of it. I am also aware that this is a very unusual contract."

"What's so unusual about it?"

"You have left yourself no protection. The way this contract is written, if the young man should choose to withdraw *at any time* before its final fulfillment, you have no recourse. That is, if he should abrogate the contract, you could not collect from him, no matter how much of your money he had spent in the meantime. In other words, the way you instructed me to write the contract—and the way it has been written—he does not have to begin repayment of the loans unless and until he has graduated from law school, has passed his bar examinations and has, *in fact,* entered into the practice of law— Do you understand?"

"Certainly. That's exactly the way I wanted it."

"Well—" The lawyer looked uncomfortable. "I must say, Mr. Spotafore, that from your standpoint this is a bad contract. If this instrument had been prepared by someone else and you had brought it to me for my advice, my advice to you would be not to sign it— This does not fit with my concept of you as a practical, hardheaded businessman."

Vincent Spotafore shrugged. "There's a lot about me you don't know. There are some people I wouldn't write a contract with if they had the U. S. Army to back them up. My nephew happens to be different. For one thing, he's honest. For another, he has a very strong sense of obligation. I'll admit that this has sometimes been misdirected. He also talks too much sometimes. But, he has a sense of obligation, and he's honest. If he can make it, he will. If he can't make it, on account of sickness or accident or because he hasn't got what it takes, I don't want him to have a debt hanging over his head. It's as simple as that."

The lawyer blinked his eyes. "All right," he said. Then he got up from his swivel chair and handed Vincent Spotafore and Vince Maggione each a typescript on legal paper and bound in a blue cover. He returned to the chair, picked up a similar typescript from the desk and said, "I will read and each of you may follow the wording. If you have any questions, any at all, don't hesitate to stop me. If a major change is required, we will draft new language and I will have the whole sheet retyped. If the changes are minor, we can make them in ink and append our initials— Are you ready?"

Vincent Spotafore, who had taken his eyeglasses from his pocket and put them on, waved his hand. Vince, already reading the uppermost typed page and conscious of some excitement, said, "Yes."

The lawyer leaned back in his chair and swiveled it a quarter turn. Then he settled down to read. The first portion identified the parties, stated the purpose of the contract, and employed some legal terminology which he carefully explained. The next part covered the amounts to be advanced and the dates during each quarter, named the bank that was to act as trustee and stipulated that Vince should keep the bank informed of his address so the payments could be mailed to him. There was a section devoted to death and taxes and a lot of involved verbiage about avoidance of garnishments and other details which the lawyer also explained.

It wasn't until they had reached page eight that Vince had a question:

"It says here that, beginning in April, I am to enter this law office as a clerk— April is next week!"

"Yes—" The lawyer sighed. "It says you are to *enter*. Like the rest of the contract, there is no penalty if you decide it isn't convenient."

Vincent Spotafore said, "That was my idea. You're going back to college this fall. You're going to study to be a lawyer. You could do a lot worse than be a clerk in this law office—"

The lawyer bowed his head and murmured, "Thank you."

"—and it will probably take you all spring to sell your house. I'm not in favor of you buying another house until you have this one sold. And I think if you're going to be a lawyer, the sooner you start the better. So that's why it's in there."

"I see," said Vince. "Okay."

For the first time, the lawyer smiled. "Shall we get on with it, gentlemen?"

Both Vince and his uncle nodded, and the lawyer resumed reading. There wasn't a whole lot more, and he reached the end without being stopped.

"Well?" Vincent Spotafore asked in an impatient voice.

Vince said, "I can't see anything wrong with it."

246

"Then let's sign it and get it over with. I told Tony Angelo to put a bottle of champagne on ice, and it ought to be good and cold by the time we get there."

The lawyer, who had gathered the copies, stood by his desk and turned halfway around. "Mr. Spotafore—"

Vincent Spotafore interrupted him with a handwave. "We'll sign it and you and one of your clerks can witness it."

"But, I hope you're not planning to leave right away. You promised me we'd go over some of this other business— It's been hanging fire for months!"

"Yes, those old buildings. So, I promised— Tell you what. I'll come back from Angelo's and stay as long as it takes. But right now, I'm going to sign these papers. Then, I'm going to welcome my nephew into the family, in proper style— Okay, Vince. Your name goes here."

Vince signed, and his uncle signed, and the lawyer witnessed both signatures. Then the lawyer opened the door to the outer office and summoned a young man, who was in shirt sleeves, and a female secretary whose shaved eyebrows gave her a startled expression. The young man hurriedly appended his signature to the rest and the secretary, on being assured that both Vince and his uncle knew what they were signing and that they had signed of their own free will, added her signature and stamped all copies with a pocket notarial seal, and the matter was done.

There were some kids playing around the Lincoln and a cop was keeping a hard eye on them and on Harold and the driver. The Lincoln was in a STANDING zone and the engine was running, which probably meant the driver had had to move a few times to keep from getting a ticket. Harold hopped out of the front seat and opened the door to the rear and held it while Uncle Vincent climbed in, followed by Vince. The rear seat was equipped with complete torso harness safety belts, as was the front seat. As soon as he was in, Uncle Vincent went through the contortions of fastening his seat belt harness, which had been adjusted to him, and admonished Vince to follow his example.

"You never know," said Uncle Vincent. "Sometimes you can get hit by somebody when you're pulling away from the curb.

More people are caught dead sitting *on* their seat belts than *in* them."

It was the same lecture he had delivered only an hour before, and practically the same as the one he'd given less than two weeks ago when Vince had ridden in the car for the first time. Having had that much practice, Vince was becoming familiar with the arrangement although he was still slow. Harold stood by, watching with a faintly reproving look.

Vince got the last strap fastened, finally, and Harold hopped back into the front seat, and trussed himself up in no time at all.

The driver turned his head. "We go to Angelo's now, boss?"

"Angelo's. Sure you know the way?" Vincent Spotafore was in rare high humor.

The humor was infectious. "I can ask somebody," the driver said, and Vincent Spotafore, Harold and the driver laughed. The driver glanced in the rear-vision mirror and was easing in the clutch when Harold said, "Hey—hold it a minute!"

The driver looked at him. "What's the matter?"

Harold was watching, through the windshield, someone who was running along the sidewalk toward the car. "Uh— It's your wife," he said, and in the same moment Vince saw Frances.

Frances was holding her coat together with her right hand while she alternated between running and walking. Her face looked strained and terribly tired. When she saw the men in the car she hesitated only fractionally before coming straight to it.

"Roll down the window," Vincent Spotafore said.

Harold rolled his window down, but Frances passed him by and put both hands on the glass beside Vince.

Her voice labored with her breathing: "I've—got—to—see—you."

Vince touched the button and his window rolled down with a tiny sound. Beside him, his uncle leaned as far forward as the seat belt would permit.

"You're just a little late, kid," Vincent Spotafore said. He was smiling.

"Vince—please—can I talk—to you—alone?"

Vince recovered from the shock of seeing her there and shot

248

a quick, embarrassed glance at his uncle. Uncle Vincent seemed to be enjoying himself:

"Go ahead, talk to her. We can wait— Ask her to the party, if she wants to come."

Vince laboriously struggled out of his seat belt. He opened the door and got out, conscious that Harold was grinning at him. He followed Frances across the sidewalk. When she reached the wall of the building, she turned toward him. She was trembling and tears were welling up in her eyes.

Vince said, "How the hell did you know where to find me?"

"I called the house—there was no answer—then I called Uncle Joe. He said you'd just left—with your Uncle Vincent. So I called his house—I made Frank tell me where you were—I was in Jamaica, and I turned around and came straight back—on the bus— Oh, Vince!"

She was weeping.

"Listen— Get hold of yourself! What's this all about?"

"You mean you—don't know—about Charley and Noble?"

"What about Charley and Noble?"

"They're dead— Oh, Vince!"

He felt the color drain from his face. For a moment he stared at her as if he didn't understand. Then he said, "When?"

"Yesterday— Charley was killed in front of his apartment, by a hit-run driver. And they found his wife dead—from an overdose of drugs. And Noble was electrocuted—when he tried to—when he tried to—" She would have fallen if his hands hadn't been holding her so tightly.

Behind Vince, the Lincoln's horn sounded a short, peremptory summons. He was glad his back was to the car so they couldn't see his face. He said, "Pull yourself together! I'll get rid of them somehow. You wait here— *Fran!"*

"I'll be—all right." She took a deep breath and raised her tear-stained face. "Please, Vince, you're hurting me—"

He released her arms, then, and turned. He walked to the car. Harold was grinning like an idiot, but Uncle Vincent had stopped smiling. "I'm not going to sit here while you and your wife argue," he said in an angry voice. "If she doesn't want to come, the hell with her!"

"She— Well, she's upset. But, she'll be okay— Just let me talk to her a few minutes. You fellows go on, and I'll join you. I won't be five minutes— I'll come, with or without her."

"All right. I expect you to be at Angelo's in ten minutes. And if I were you, I would be there!"

Vince nodded, suddenly realizing where Harold had picked up his *If I was you,* and the Lincoln pulled smoothly away from the curb. He was walking back to Frances when he saw the long, black sedan make a left turn into Liberty Avenue, where the Court Building hid it from view.

He had reached Frances and was standing beside her, not looking at her, when the first explosion occurred. It sounded like a shotgun blast and it came from behind the Court Building, in Liberty Avenue, where the Lincoln had just gone. Vince had taken an involuntary sideways step when, closely following the first, the second blast came.

He and Frances were running toward Liberty Avenue when they heard two shattering concussions, so close together they sounded like a single long one. And then, a shrill, piercing scream followed by the sharp report of a pistol.

Incredibly, a cop had seen the whole thing. He had been fifty yards away, across Liberty Avenue and strolling toward Pennsylvania Avenue, when he had spotted two young boys—in broad daylight—stealing the wheel covers from a brand new Buick. The boys hadn't seen the cop, and didn't see him until he had both of them by their collars. The wheel covers went skittering across the pavement as they tried, unsuccessfully, to kick the cop in the shins. He banged their heads together, which cooled them down, and he was straightening them out preparatory to bending them over the hood of the Buick when it happened.

A black Lincoln Continental that had turned into Liberty after traveling south on Pennsylvania slid past him and had gone maybe a hundred feet east of where he was holding the struggling boys when abruptly an old panel truck pulled from the curb, right in the Lincoln's path.

The cop expected to hear a crunch of fenders. But the driver of the Lincoln was good. He brought the big sedan to a smooth

250

stop with his front bumper an inch from the panel truck, which had apparently stalled.

And then there *was* a crunch—two of them—as both rear doors of the panel truck fell outward and down on the Lincoln's hood.

Inside the panel truck, the cop's incredulous eyes saw a Negro woman, kneeling, with a shotgun raised to her shoulder. At point-blank range, she fired the first barrel at the driver's side of the windshield. And then she shifted the shotgun to the right and let go the second barrel.

The cop released both boys and reached for his pistol. One of the boys slid along the side of the Buick and away, but the other one was blocked by a utility pole and he came straight at the cop, with fists flailing, and spun him around. When the cop had righted himself, the Negro woman was gone and in her place a Negro youth was kneeling, throwing something—it looked like a rock—through the shattered windshield of the Lincoln. The cop leveled his pistol across the hood of the Buick just as the youth dropped forward on his face. The cop squeezed off a shot anyway and then a Buick wheel cover banged against the back of his head and the boy who had swung it at him was streaking toward Pennsylvania Avenue.

The cop shook his head and leveled his pistol again, and by that time the interior of the truck was empty. And then, just as the door of the Lincoln opened on the driver's side and a horribly bleeding man fell into the street, the black sedan exploded with two shattering blasts.

In a stopped westbound car, a windshield that a second before had been clear developed a pattern of intricate opaque cracks obscuring the screaming woman at the wheel.

By the time the cop reached the Lincoln, it took him a lot longer to decide there had been only three men in it than to determine that all of them were dead.

Vince and Frances stayed around, at the edge of the crowd, until the ambulance had gone. Frances wasn't used to violence; she'd never seen anyone blown apart, and he didn't want her to see this. But she insisted on staying at his side. She had apparently used up her sense of shock on Charley and Noble; she had never

251

M

met them, but, because they had been his friends, she shared his grief. Her strength of reserve was remarkable. Only once did she show any sign of breaking and that was when the realization hit both of them at once and they looked at each other in fear:

If Frances hadn't come along when she did, he, Vince, would have been in the car.

The police didn't question them. They were looking for eyewitnesses, and there were plenty at hand. The woman and the youth had gotten away, but the police had their descriptions. And they had the panel truck.

Already, in a matter of minutes, it had settled down to routine.

Vince and Frances watched the ambulance go, and then walked back to Pennsylvania Avenue and hailed a cab.

Al and Gloria had been out east until quite late, being entertained by the man—and his wife—in celebration of the agreement of sale for Al's business, so on this morning they had permitted themselves to oversleep.

It was after nine o'clock when a great din of honking woke Al. He slid out of bed and dragged himself to the window.

Up in the sky above the house, in a long line, the geese had begun the last leg of their journey home.

"Gloria—*Gloria!*" cried Al.

Gloria sat up and swung her fat legs from the bed. "What is it?" she asked in some alarm.

"The geese— They're going home!"

"Oh—" Gloria yawned. "The geese." She found her slippers and put them on and went to stand beside Al at the window.